P9-BYQ-464

PRAISE FOR *THE LAST 8*

"*The Walking Dead* meets *Alien* in this expertly plotted debut. Teens will want to follow Clover on her next adventure!"
— Zoraida Córdova, author of the Brooklyn Brujas series

"A fantastic plot following a fierce young woman and an ending that was such a surprise I couldn't stop thinking about it for days."
— Bethany Wiggins, author of *Stung* and *Cured*

"A brilliant exploration of humanity and what it means to be alive when the world around you is dying. Between the aliens, the characters, the apocalypse, and the constant surprises, I couldn't tear myself away from this beautifully crafted, heart-stopping book until the very last page."
— Kaitlin Ward, author of *Where She Fell*

"A sci-fi romp with ample intergalactic twists to keep readers satisfied."
— *Kirkus Reviews*

"A diverse and immersive science fiction… From its dialogue to its action, the story is fluid, maintaining irresistible momentum through to the emotional, unpredictable ending. With its powerful worldbuilding and emotional twists, *The Last 8* is a beautifully fresh take on the idea of an alien apocalypse."
— *Foreword Reviews*

THE LAST 8

LAURA POHL

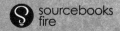

sourcebooks
fire

Copyright © 2019 by Laura Pohl
Cover and internal design © 2020 by Sourcebooks
Cover art © Luke Lucas
Internal design by Ashley Holstrom/Sourcebooks

Sourcebooks and the colophon are registered trademarks of Sourcebooks

All rights reserved. No part of this book may be reproduced in any form or by any electronic or mechanical means including information storage and retrieval systems—except in the case of brief quotations embodied in critical articles or reviews—without permission in writing from its publisher, Sourcebooks.

The characters and events portrayed in this book are fictitious or are used fictitiously. Any similarity to real persons, living or dead, is purely coincidental and not intended by the author.

All brand names and product names used in this book are trademarks, registered trademarks, or trade names of their respective holders. Sourcebooks is not associated with any product or vendor in this book.

Published by Sourcebooks Fire, an imprint of Sourcebooks
P.O. Box 4410, Naperville, Illinois 60567-4410
(630) 961-3900
sourcebooks.com

The Library of Congress has cataloged the hardcover edition as follows:

Names: Pohl, Laura, author.
Title: The last 8 / Laura Pohl.
Other titles: Last eight
Description: Naperville, Illinois : Sourcebooks Fire, [2019] | Summary: After an alien attack devastates the Earth, pilot and future astronaut Clover Martinez bands with seven other teens in a struggle to survive.
Identifiers: LCCN 2018010906 | (hardcover : alk. paper)
Subjects: | CYAC: Extraterrestrial beings--Fiction. | Survival--Fiction. | Friendship--Fiction. | Air pilots--Fiction. | Mexican Americans--Fiction. | Science fiction.
Classification: LCC PZ7.1.P6413 Las 2019 | DDC [Fic]--dc23 LC record available at https://lccn.loc.gov/2018010906

Printed and bound in the United States of America.
SB 10 9 8 7 6 5 4 3 2 1

To Mom.

Live long and prosper.

CONTENT WARNING:

This book contains mention of depression, suicidal thoughts, a suicide attempt, and post-traumatic stress disorder.

PART I

IT'S THE END OF THE WORLD

CHAPTER 1

My abuelo says that there are people who belong to the earth, and others, like us Martinezes, belong to the sky.

High up in the air, there's no doubt that he's right. The airplane cuts the early morning clouds, leaving a white trail over the blue sky. Inside the Beechcraft Musketeer, I can see almost everything—the crops and houses and animals. The cows are no bigger than the dark brown freckles that cover my arms, the houses the size of my thumb. The only sound is the motor, and the blue stretches infinitely.

I flex my fingers and grip the yoke a little harder, keeping my eyes on the horizon.

"Take it in while you can," says Abuelo, who sits by my side, fixing his gaze on the fields that extend for miles to the north. To the south, there are only mountains.

I give him a sideways glance. His skin is medium brown like mine, but his hair has been graying for the last five years. When I was a kid, I never thought he'd look old. He always looked jovial, his smiles long and wide, ready for anything. Now glasses perch on the bridge of his nose, and behind them, his black eyes scan the fields like an eagle. I can hear a tinge of bitterness in his voice, even though he tries to hide it.

"There's still a whole year."

He shrugs slightly. "I know. I didn't say anything."

College is an unspoken subject in our family. MIT used to seem far away. But now there's only one year left until I move across the country to study aerospace engineering. I understand my grandparents' sadness—I'm the only family they have left.

"I thought you were proud," I say, not moving my hands from the controls.

The motor of the plane roars beneath us.

"Of course I'm proud, mija. First engineer in the family." He smiles. "But I'll miss this."

He gestures to the plane. To the two of us. To the tiny world beneath us and the sky that unites us both.

"Abuelo, it's MIT, not Mars." I try not to roll my eyes too hard. "It's a five-hour flight."

"And what plane are you going to take to get there?"

"I can take yours."

This makes him laugh, and he clutches at his stomach

like he always does. He leans back against his seat, calm, even though, technically, I don't have a proper pilot's license yet. But he taught me how to fly when I was five, and I don't think he trusts anyone more than me.

"And when it is Mars, Clover?"

Something catches in my throat.

"I have to get through senior year first," I tell him.

He looks at his watch and swears. "We're late."

I turn the plane around.

I've barely landed the Beechcraft when my abuela comes out the back door, a towel in her hands, shouting from the steps.

"You two are late!"

She's already in her dress, the one she wears to church, black and somber. I run inside the house and take a quick shower. Five minutes later, I'm downstairs and ready to go.

Abuela gives me the once-over. "No makeup?" she asks.

I shake my head.

She sighs dramatically. "How will you look in photos, Clover? In ten years, you'll look back and think, 'Here are all my beautiful classmates, and I was too stubborn to do anything to look nice.'"

"Abuela, it's the science fair. It's not even graduation."

"And? The pictures will still be in the album," she says. "Look at me and your grandfather. We're wearing our best."

It's no use discussing this with Abuela, who thinks every

single school occasion where I have to present something is worthy of putting on her best clothes as if she's about to meet the president himself.

"Fine, I'll do it in the car."

"Carlos!" Abuela shouts, and he comes downstairs just in time, finishing the knot in his tie. "Let's go."

She marches outside like a soldier ready for battle, heading for the truck. I sit in the back seat, Abuelo in the front on the passenger's side. For all the planes we can fly, we don't seem to have a knack for driving cars.

Abuela glares at me in the rearview mirror, unwavering, and I pick up her makeup bag, applying some powder and mascara at her insistence. It takes us almost thirty minutes to reach the school, and by the time I get to the gym, the science fair is already in full swing. I make my way toward my table, where my project is set up. Abuela takes a few photos to keep in her album, and then Abuelo takes her arm, ushering her away to see the other projects. At the next table are Mark Robson and his girlfriend, Emily, with their project on solar energy.

"Martinez," Mark says. "I thought you skipped school activities."

"It wasn't an option this time," I tell him flatly.

He laughs. Mark has a good sense of humor, though we don't talk much. Truth be told, I almost never talk to my classmates outside of school. It's strange being the only Mexican American kid in a small town in Montana, and I never exactly tried to bridge the gap between them and me.

"Are you finally going to tell us what this big mystery project is about?" Emily asks, cocking a blond eyebrow at my table, which is still covered under a linen sheet. "Mr. Kay couldn't shut up about it."

Just as she says his name, the science teacher appears. He smiles gleefully at me.

"You're a bit late, Clover," he says. "But I guess everything is in order?"

I nod. "All ready to go."

He nods to Emily and Mark, who are still curiously staring at me. Then he leans in and whispers, "You know, an admissions recruiter from MIT is here."

"What?" I say, my mouth hanging open. "You're kidding me."

"No," he replies. "I told him over email about your project and how excited you are to apply to MIT in the fall."

My cheeks burn a deep red.

"He's scouting you. So do your best."

"I will," I tell him.

When Mr. Kay walks away to look at the other projects, I force myself to breathe. This is my opportunity to land a good scholarship, the first step in what will eventually take me to NASA and out of here.

Into the sky, just like Abuelo.

Slowly, people trickle by each table. Parents, grandparents, little sisters and cousins, all of them came to see what was happening at the science fair. In a small town like ours, there isn't much to do on a Saturday morning in early April.

My grandparents are the first to officially visit my table, and I demonstrate my project for them, even though they already heard me rehearsing. Abuelo helped me build the model and the motor, and everything works just fine. My presentation becomes almost mechanical as I wait for the MIT recruiter to show up.

Noah comes to my table instead.

"Hey," he says, smiling sheepishly. "How are you doing?"

"I'm fine," I say. "You?"

He nods, pursing his lips. There's an awkward silence between my ex-boyfriend and me. I'm sure he wants to say something, but neither of us find the right words.

Before I can speak again, Ted, one of Noah's football teammates, rams into him.

"We've got it all ready," Ted says with a grin.

"Dude, be quiet," hisses Mark from the next table. "If the teachers find out, we're toast."

Ted grins, careless, and then narrows his eyes at me. "Oh, Clover's not going to snitch, is she?"

Noah looks at me apologetically as Ted throws an arm around him.

"What are you guys up to?" I ask.

"Fireworks," Ted says. "After the fair is over."

I look at all three of them. "You guys are idiots."

"Thanks for your input, Clover, it's always appreciated."

"No problem."

Out of the corner of my eye, I see a stranger approach the table, and the moment between Noah and me is gone. I turn my attention to the newcomer, and I know immediately that he is the recruiter Mr. Kay was talking about—there aren't that many strangers in our town.

"Hi," I say, hoping my voice is bright. "I'm Clover Martinez, and I'm here to guide you through the next phase of human space exploration."

I summarize my project as best as I can, my palms sweaty. My heart beats loudly against my rib cage, but I manage to keep calm and speak clearly. I start with basic information about space exploration, then I move on to talking about viable missions to Mars and Jupiter. I run the test for the motor I've constructed. On a larger scale, it would not only save fuel but also cover longer distances in foreign environments, allowing spacecraft to be lighter in weight and for their missions to last longer.

When I'm done, I look up expectantly.

"Impressive presentation, Miss Martinez," he says, his accent British. "Your teacher tells me you plan to apply to MIT?"

"Yes, sir."

"And after college?"

"Hopefully NASA," I reply. "But I think it's best to take it one step a time."

He smiles at that. "You're right." He takes a card out of his jacket pocket and hands it to me. "I look forward to receiving your application."

"Thank you." I grin from ear to ear as he leaves.

My grandparents approach the table, both of them looking at me.

"How did it go?" Abuela asks.

"I think he liked it."

"He'd be an idiot not to," Abuelo says, hugging me.

The science fair ends a couple of hours later, and I say good-bye to Mr. Kay and thank him for his help. I'm still holding the business card inside my pocket, my fingers trembling over it.

Abuelo helps me pack my things in the truck, and on the trip home, I sit leaning against the window. When I look up, I see something shining in the sky.

At first I think it's one of the fireworks the boys set up, but its path is too straight. Then I realize what I'm seeing.

More than a hundred shooting stars cover the sky. I see them cross it, glimmering silver as their trajectory takes them straight to the ground. It's a beautiful sight, but for some reason, my stomach sinks.

"Meteor shower," Abuela says.

Slowly, Abuelo shakes his head. "See that?" He points to one just above us. "It's slowing down."

That's exactly what it's doing—instead of accelerating and colliding with Earth like a true falling star. It's big, fat, and pear-shaped, and I realize that there's nothing about this thing that resembles a star or a meteor at all. It's a reinforced ball of armor, full of mystery.

The one closest to us crosses the sky, followed by a trail of fire. I gape as it slows down even more and reaches the outskirts of town, too far away for me to get a good look. But I can see smoke rising.

"It's…" I start the sentence but can't bring myself to finish it.

"A ship," Abuelo says, completing my thought.

Not just any ship. A spaceship.

A real one.

CHAPTER 2

When we make it home, Abuelo is the first to get out of the car, moving so fast that no one would believe he's a senior citizen. I follow, close on his heels, and by the time I'm in the house, he already has the TV on and the volume up.

Every channel is showing emergency broadcasts, images of spaceships coming toward Earth.

"The phenomenon has repeated itself all over the planet," the television reporter says. "In the last four hours, we have confirmed sightings of more than one hundred thousand spaceships landing at different points around the world."

One hundred thousand. That's too big a number. And it's surely growing, because no one had the time to count them all if they just landed.

We could be easily looking at a force of five million.

"Government officials ask that all citizens please remain calm while they investigate the situation," the reporter continues. "The president is due to make a statement soon. Please do not try to approach these objects, and it's recommended that everyone stay inside their homes."

Abuelo's expression is indecipherable.

The image on the TV changes, and I'm looking at what appears to be a welcoming committee for the possible aliens. People with signs and party drinks approach a ship, gathering around it. The ship is metallic silver and shaped like a pear. It's closed tight, with no sign of a door, completely impenetrable. It reminds me of an oyster shell.

Abuelo turns the volume down as the reporters repeat themselves and footage is shown from all over the world. Spaceships are landing in Russia and Brazil and France, all over the place, but there's no sign of aliens doing anything.

Yet.

A chill climbs up my spine.

"Qué en el nombre de Dios..." Abuela says as she finally joins us. Then she sees the TV. "Dios mío."

Abuelo moves over to the table and picks up the phone. "I'm going to make some calls. I should probably head over to Malmstrom."

Malmstrom is the closest air base. Abuelo is a retired air force pilot, so his first instinct is to call them.

He calls the number, but no one picks up. He shakes his

head slightly, worry creasing his forehead. He looks at me, just to make sure I'm okay.

I breathe in, breathe out, trying to remember how to function like a normal human being.

Nothing about this feels real.

Abuelo shakes his head. "I'm going to try again. But the best thing would be for me to head over there," he says, his eyes landing on Abuela for a second.

"Carlos," Abuela says, her tone harsh. "You can't fly right now. Those things just came from the *sky*."

Abuelo and I exchange a look. We know it's dangerous, but we understand each other. Our place isn't here—it's up there, with the airplanes.

"Okay." I nod.

Abuela turns to me, her eyebrows creased and her expression heated. "You can't mean that you agree with him going?"

"We have to do something," I tell her.

I don't know how to react. Panic? Fear? I'm not sure I can handle these emotions right now, so I push everything back and focus on what is normal, on what is left.

Yet here we are. More and more pictures and headlines pop up on the TV, but I'm no longer listening.

Abuelo turns to me, knowing that I'm analyzing every piece of information we have. It's the first rule of flying—keep your head level, even when everything is going to hell. And I'm trying. I'm trying hard.

"They'll have information," I say. I shake my head a little, biting my lower lip. "It's a military base. They'll know what to do."

This is what I repeat to myself—the government should know what to do. They'll figure out what is happening. They'll have instructions.

I breathe in. And out.

"No." Abuela shakes her head vehemently. "Carlos, you can't be serious about this."

I meet Abuelo's gaze. His expression is dark, unreadable, but we both know that our best chance of finding out what's really happening is Malmstrom Air Force Base. Besides, it's not like they're going to turn away one of the best pilots in the country.

"Miriam, it's the only way," he says, and his words are final.

The TV is still endlessly playing images of the spaceships crossing the sky, slowing down as they land. Cell phone cameras, Snapchat, and Instagram all contribute to the images on the screen. Who could've imagined that an alien landing would be so well documented?

"Let me talk to him," I whisper to Abuela, and she glares at me, knowing that I'm not going to try to convince him not to go.

She walks out of the room and heads down the hall to the kitchen, her features still stern. I turn to Abuelo, uneasiness settling in my stomach.

"What do you think will happen?" I ask. For once, I want him to lie to me. To pretend that everything we've ever known isn't about to change, that everything is going to be just fine.

But then again, he wouldn't be my abuelo if he did.

"I don't know, mi amor," he says, his voice soft. He reaches out across the table and strokes my hair. "But we'll get answers, I promise you that."

I give him a half-smile as he gets up and unlocks the cabinet in the corner. He grips his Winchester 9422 rifle, the reliable model that we always kept around the house. Abuelo never believed that it would actually bring us safety, but it was good for shooting at the crows when the scarecrow wasn't doing its job. He lays it over his desk and piles up ammunition next to it.

"Take it," he says, looking at me firmly.

"Let me go with you."

He shakes his head immediately. "No, Clover. I'm going there on my own. I'll bring back whatever news I find out."

"You know I can fly better than half those guys at the base," I say, my shoulders tense. "If I go with you—"

"You'll leave your abuela alone on the farm. Is that what you want?"

I'm silent for a beat. "You know I can fly. You know I can fight."

"Clover, you don't have a license. And your abuela would kill me if I put you in danger like that."

"I'm no use down here."

Down here. On the ground. He knows it as much as I do.

I want to do something, to be of help, to get out there. The one thing I don't want to do is sit back and wait for news. I can't take that.

"If something happens, I can help," I argue.

He smiles. "I know you want to. But you're not even seventeen. They won't let you, even if I would." He shakes his head. "No. You stay here and watch over the farm and your abuela. I'll be back with news."

He holds out the Winchester to me. After a moment, I take it.

"Just in case," he says, tapping one of my cheeks. "It won't come to that."

I nod my head, gulping down hard. Whatever happens, I need to be prepared. I can't let myself panic.

"Ready?" he asks.

I nod again. "Ready."

"I'll be back before you miss me," he says, kissing my forehead. "Te amo."

"Yo también."

He smiles one more time before heading down the hall to the kitchen. I take the rifle up to my room, sit down on my bed, and listen to the murmur of conversation downstairs, to Abuela's angry whispers, all in vain. Finally, I hear the porch door bang closed, and a few minutes later, the motor of the Cessna 400 roars to life. I don't bother to get up; I can hear when the plane takes off.

Abuela climbs upstairs and pauses in the doorway.

"At least he didn't take the Beechcraft," she states matter-of-factly.

I almost manage a smile, but my lips are dry and cracked, and it feels like I'm forcing a muscle.

15

She walks into the room and sits next to me on the bed. My room is simple, like the rest of our house. Everything we have goes into my college savings or the planes in the backyard, and we can't afford extra luxuries. The best part of my room has always been the window, where the view stretches out over our own small corn field and the surrounding wheat fields. It ends at the faraway mountains, and where my telescope sits propped in front of it. At night, the city lights blink in the distance, but I can see the Milky Way.

"Your abuelo is impulsive, Clover," she says, pulling my hair away from my shoulders and letting it fall down my back. "Sometimes that's not the best way to deal with things."

"He's right about going there," I respond defensively.

"He would also have been right if he had stayed here."

I meet her eyes, which are a softer shade of brown than mine. My mother has her eyes, based on the few pictures I've seen. She left me on her parents' porch and never bothered to come back.

I bite the inside of my cheek as a strange feeling of breathlessness fills my chest. Nothing feels real anymore. It's like the ground has been taken from beneath my feet, and I'm not sure how to adjust to a place with no gravity.

It feels pointless to ask the question on my mind, but I do anyway. "Do you think something big will happen?"

"It's very likely."

"Good or bad?"

Abuela doesn't answer for a while, but finally, she sighs. "It's not up to us, amor. It's up to them."

Them. Whatever they were. Whatever they came here for.

"And if it's bad?"

Abuela shrugs slightly, her fingers tangling in my hair. "Then we do what we always do." She smiles and pushes her rosary into my hands. The beads are heavy and made of wood. Her fingers always reached for them when she needed comfort. And in a way, that's what I need now. I clutch them tightly, looking up at her.

"What's that?" I ask.

"Survive."

She kisses my brow lightly, and we stare out the window, looking at a horizon that will never be the same again.

CHAPTER 3

For the first few hours, I'm tense, my muscles brimming with adrenaline, waiting to be put into action. But then night falls, and I'm forced to go to sleep, even though I'm restless and shaking in bed.

When I wake up the next day, it's as if everything is normal, except that we can't leave the house. Little by little, Abuela and I settle into a new routine. I check the news on my phone and on television, but even with the president's statement, there isn't much. Everyone is telling us to stay calm while they investigate and to stay inside while everything is sorted out. Abuela cooks and I do the dishes, and we feed the chickens in the morning. We count the items in our pantry, organizing them by type. I help her vacuum the living room, and the afternoon goes by in a daze, with no sign of gleaming silver in the sky.

Every night, we talk to Abuelo through the satellite phone. He tells us what he can, which isn't much. But it's better than nothing. At least they're doing something. They're investigating. But, like us, they're also waiting for something bigger to happen.

Slowly, a whole week trickles by since the spaceships first arrived, and I miss going to school. I wonder if I should email the MIT guy, but I'm sure that they have bigger things to worry about there, too.

That night, when it's time to call Abuelo, I realize that the batteries to the satellite phone are dead.

"Abuela!" I shout from the kitchen. "Where are the batteries?"

"Third drawer!" she yells back. "And don't shout at your elders!"

I ignore the jab, rummaging through the kitchen, but there's no sign of any batteries. I try turning on the phone again, but it's no use. I head to the living room, where Abuela is watching a telenovela. The world is ending, but they still manage to air a telenovela. I guess everyone needs comfort, in one way or another.

"No new batteries," I tell her.

She looks up from the television, frowning. "Are you sure?" she asks. "If I get up and find them, Dios ayúdame—"

"I just looked," I answer. "I could try to get them from town, but…"

I can't go into town during a full lockdown, when everyone is being told to stay in their houses. But if I don't go, we can't talk to Abuelo. We won't have him on call if something happens.

"I could go get them tomorrow," I finish lamely. "It'll be a quick trip."

"I don't like this, Clover."

"I don't like it, either," I answer. "But getting batteries would be good. We can make a list of other supplies that I could try to find."

Slowly, she nods and goes back to the television. She's mulling it over. I'll probably get an answer tomorrow.

It's the middle of the night when a noise at my window wakes me. I jump from my bed, my palms sweaty.

The noise comes again, and I realize it's a rock. I go over to the window, gripping the rifle, and poke my head out, only to find a boy standing in the yard.

Noah smiles when he sees me.

"What are you doing here?" I hiss, shoving the rifle aside. "Abuela will kill you!"

"You aren't answering your phone!" he replies in the same whispered tone. "I wanted to see if you're okay."

"I am. Now leave."

Noah shakes his head. The moon shines on him and his red pickup truck, parked next to the house. He has chocolate in one hand, a six pack of beer in the other. A peace offering.

"Do you have a death wish?" I demand. "We're both dead if Abuela finds you here."

"I just want to talk."

I purse my lips, shaking my head, but then he raises the box of chocolates.

"Fine."

Noah grins. I climb out of the window and onto the roof, wrapping my shirt tighter around me. He climbs onto his truck and manages to pass me the chocolate and the beer before he hauls himself up next to me. The house is silent beneath us, the sky clear and the stars bright above us.

I open the box of chocolates and start eating. Noah opens a beer and looks at me like I'm a problem he can't solve.

"Why didn't you pick up your phone?" he finally asks. "I called like six times."

"The signal keeps going in and out," I tell him. "Abuelo gave us the satellite phone before he went to the air base, but the batteries died."

Noah sits beside me, drinking, but doesn't say anything.

"Why did you come here?" I ask.

He takes another gulp of his beer. Even in the dark, it's easy to see why so many girls think he's one of the hottest guys at school. He has strong arms, blond hair, and gray-blue eyes that remind me of the lake on winter days.

"I wanted to talk to someone who makes sense," he finally says, shaking his head a little. "I've watched the news, but Dad won't stop pretending that nothing's wrong. And then

Mark decided that he was going to throw an alien welcoming party tonight."

I snort, and he grins.

"All I could think of was to call you. And that you'd know exactly what to say in this situation."

"That you have shitty friends?"

Noah laughs, and I touch his arm to remind him not to make too much noise.

"That too." Noah sighs, looking at the crops and the lonely scarecrow near our house. "It's just absurd. I wanted to be with someone who would be reasonable when the rest of the world was going haywire."

"I *was* holding a rifle when you scared the shit out of me with your rock throwing."

He laughs again. "There you go."

I turn back to the box of chocolates, eating another, tasting the sweetness on my tongue.

"Nothing makes sense." I shake my head. "You know that, right? Something bad is going to happen."

"Such an optimist."

"That's why I don't have any friends."

"You don't have any friends because you're an asshole."

I laugh harder than I should. And it's strange, sitting up here with Noah, because he might be the only person in the world, with the exception of my grandparents, who knows me for who I am.

"I always saw past that anyway," he says.

"I thought we weren't going to talk about this."

He glances sideways at me. It's barely been a month since we broke up. It's not that I don't miss him. It's just that I always liked him better as a friend than a boyfriend.

Noah isn't a bad person. But he demanded too much, all the time. The attention, the gestures, the feelings that, for me, weren't really there. In the end, I never had romantic feelings for him. I've never had romantic feelings for anyone.

Noah chews on the inside of his cheek, his gaze lost in the cornfields. We sit together in silence for a while, as I look at the stars. Pegasus is bright above us, and Ursa Major stretches out until I almost can't see it anymore.

"I just…" Noah starts, but he doesn't seem able to find the right words to finish his sentence. I meet his eyes in the semidarkness. "I kind of knew it was coming. I just didn't think it would be so soon."

I turn to him sharply, not wanting to hear anything else. But he's a little too drunk, and it feels a little too much like the end of the world, so I don't stop him.

"It's the reason I fell for you," he says quietly. "We're small here. Everyone goes to college and comes back, gets married, has their kids. It's never bigger than that. But you, Clover, you're *big*. You cut through the skies and talk about going to Mars. And I knew you were going to leave one day to do these big things, and I kind of hoped you'd take me with you."

His confession comes out in a half-drunk drawl, his voice quiet and breaking.

"I should go," he says, putting down his second bottle of beer.

"You're drunk. You can't drive home."

"You think I might crash into one of the aliens?" He laughs a little. "I shouldn't have come here."

"I'm sorry."

He looks at me, and our eyes meet again. "Sorry" is never going to fix the mess our relationship is. In a way, Noah is right—I'll never fit in here. Not because I'm the only Latina in our little town in northern Montana, and not because I've always liked stars more than I like people, but maybe because I've never truly found a place that would welcome me exactly as I am.

"I know," he says.

"Don't mope. You look pathetic."

That gets another laugh from him. "I love you."

I let the words fall into the silence of the stars. I can't lie to him again.

He reaches out and pushes back a strand of my dark hair, looking at me as if there were nothing else in the entire world. He leans in, but I quickly turn away.

He freezes, wincing. "I really should go."

"You're drunk, and there's no way you're driving." I glare at him and get up. The roof tiles are shaky beneath my feet. "Go sleep on the couch."

He looks surprised.

"But I'm talking to Abuela first."

"I'd rather face the aliens," he mutters.

Carefully, we climb down from the roof and into my room. Noah heads downstairs, and I make my way to Abuela's room. She's not asleep. She must have heard us talking.

"Noah is here," I say quietly.

In the darkness, I see her nod. "I thought he would try to talk to you again."

"We're friends, Abuela."

"Not to him," she says, and it's like a stab of pain. "He can sleep on the couch."

"Thank you."

She nods again, and I close the door. This feels like a special kindness from her. Usually, she'd happily chase Noah out the door. I try not to let myself think that it really does feel like the world is ending.

Noah is already on the couch when I go downstairs, his head leaning against a crocheted pillow, his eyes closed. There's just enough moonlight coming through the curtains that I can discern his features.

"I'm sorry," I whisper to him.

"I know." He nods, without opening his eyes. "I'm not sure that makes it better."

Refraining from reaching out for him, I turn and go up to my room.

CHAPTER 4

When I go downstairs the next morning, Abuela is already busy with breakfast.

"Is that your friend's truck?" she inquires as soon as I step into the kitchen.

I hold back a groan. Noah and I dated for a year and a half, but she never called him anything but "your friend," or "your little friend" when she was being especially mean.

"Yes," I answer. "Don't give him a hard time, Abuela."

"You think so little of your grandmother."

I stare at her, waiting.

"Fine," she finally says. "But a boy shouldn't show up at a girl's house in the middle of the night without invitation. It's not right. It was six months before I let your abuelo hold my hand."

"Yes, so I've heard."

"Is that back talk, Clover?"

"No, ma'am." I take my omelet and sit down quickly before she has a chance to say anything else. "He's driving back this morning. I could go with him and get batteries."

"I should come, too."

"If Abuelo calls us on the regular phone, someone needs to be here to pick up," I tell her. "Two hours at the most and I'll be back. Did you get the television working today?"

"The signal is going bad," she says.

My stomach immediately tenses.

"Don't jump to conclusions, mija," she tells me. "You know the signal is always bad on the farm."

"Yeah, I know."

But I'm not convinced.

My fingers fidget with the satellite phone, wanting to push the buttons and make the call to Abuelo. It's been a little more than twenty-four hours since we last spoke, and I'm full of nervous energy.

Just then, Noah's footsteps come stomping down the stairs. He stops in the kitchen.

"I'm so sorry to barge in, Mrs. Martinez," he says shyly, his hands in his pockets.

"No problem," Abuela responds, her voice dripping with disdain. I know she was happy when I broke up with Noah, but she wouldn't say it. I assume that she distrusts all boys because my mother got pregnant at seventeen. Even though I'm nothing like my mother. "Sit and eat something."

Noah gets an omelet and eats very politely, chewing with his mouth closed and his shoulders scrunched up, like he's trying not to take any more space than he needs.

I put my plate in the sink and am about to wash it when Abuela stops me.

"Leave it," she says. "I'll do it. I do everything in this house anyway."

I roll my eyes.

"Don't roll your eyes. You'll get cross-eyed."

Noah raises an eyebrow at me from his chair, and I mouth "bad mood" to him. Not that Abuela is ever in a good mood when Noah is here, which is why it would be best for us to leave as soon as possible.

He hurries with his breakfast while Abuela washes up. I grab my bag and shove the satellite phone inside it, then run upstairs and get the rifle and bullets.

Noah cocks an eyebrow at me when he sees it. "Where do you think we are, the Wild West?"

I glare at him. "Better safe than sorry."

"If people see you walking down the street with a rifle, they're bound to think the worst."

"I think they're going to have more important things to worry about than whether or not I'm carrying a gun," I reply, but Noah keeps staring at me. "Fine. I'll leave it in the back of the truck."

He nods, like I'm crazy for even thinking of something like this. He finishes his plate, thanking Abuela again. I signal with my head for him to wait outside, and he leaves.

"I'll be right back, okay?" I say to Abuela, reassuring myself as much as I am her. "Noah says he has batteries at his house. We'll get the phone working in no time."

She nods once, lost in thought. Then she says, "Ten cuidado, Clover."

"I will."

I hug her and kiss her cheek. She makes the sign of the cross over my forehead, giving me a blessing.

"Vaya con Dios."

"Amen."

I grab my bag and wave goodbye, running outside to Noah's truck so we can make the quick trip into town.

Noah drives with an undeniable air of calmness. With my head against the window, I watch the nearby spaceship, the only one sitting by the side of the road, not twenty minutes away from the farm. I hadn't realized that it was this close. I can see it clearly—its smooth, round surface, with no sign of any doors.

Noah accelerates, leaving the ship behind like it's some strange dream. We make our way in silence, my shoulders tense. There are no other cars on the road. I look at the satellite phone in my hand as if it'll magically spring to life without a battery.

"He'll call soon enough," Noah says, guessing where my thoughts are going. "They're probably really busy over there. I'm sure they've got a plan."

"Was the road empty like this last night?" I ask, frowning.

He shrugs, in true Noah fashion. "I don't know. We took the lockdown seriously for the first few days, but now…"

"It's too empty."

"You think too much."

"One of us has to."

Just then, a car appears, heading straight toward us.

"Do you think this guy's gonna move or…?"

"Watch out!" I shout, and he swerves off the road just in time to avoid the car.

Noah gives me a nasty look. "It's a good thing I'm the one driving."

I don't bother responding, because my attention is immediately drawn ahead of us. The road opens up, and where there should be farms and mountains, all I can see is a huge dust cloud rising up in the air, hovering above town. We don't usually get dust clouds this far north, and never one this big. It clings to the air and the edges of the road, thick and strange.

Noah frowns. "This wasn't here last night," he says.

I tense. He reaches out and puts his hand on my knee. It's meant to relax me, to ground me, but all it does is put me more on edge. In my mind, I see the spaceships crossing the sky, over and over again.

I stay alert as Noah drives forward, slowly entering town. Everything is empty—the cars parked on the street, the houses. Noah checks his watch. It's eight o'clock on a Sunday morning, so most people wouldn't have left their houses yet. But there are usually a few people out and about by now. Silence expands everywhere, and the dust hangs in the still air, with no wind to blow it in another direction. Noah's frown deepens as we approach his house. There's not a person in sight.

He parks in his driveway and turns off the engine.

"We'll be quick," he says, almost as if he's reassuring himself. "I'm sure there are batteries in the kitchen."

I nod. A strange numbness creeps in. Something feels very, very wrong.

He gets out and slams the door. I breathe in once and hold the air in my lungs before stepping out of the truck. I hesitate for a second, then grab the rifle and follow him.

Noah presses the doorbell, like he always does to tell his parents he's home. The house looks empty, and the strange dust clings to my lungs as I breathe. No one comes to the door.

Creasing his forehead, he fishes his keys out of his pocket, but by now he's sweating and trembling, and they fall to the ground.

I pick them up and unlock the door for him. My hands are surprisingly steady, but my whole body is tense.

Noah pushes the door open while I stand on the porch, looking out toward the street. I don't see any movement—not a single curtain flaps in the neighboring houses. A dog barks, but that seems to be the only sound for miles. Scanning the horizon, I see a car with both front doors open, like the passengers just got out and ran.

"Noah?" I call softly, not daring to raise my voice.

But he can't hear me. He runs through the house, his feet stomping on the hardwood floors.

31

"Mom?" he calls out. "Dad? Jacob?"

His yells go unanswered. I can hear him on the second floor, banging open doors. I step inside the house and move toward the TV. White noise buzzes quietly from the set, the image distorted. The hair on the back of my neck stands up.

"*Mom!*" he screams again, as if his voice could tear up half the house. "*Dad!*"

"Noah?" I dare to call out again, louder this time.

He comes downstairs, his shoulders sagging and his eyes welling with tears.

"It's too early," he mumbles. "They wouldn't have left the house yet."

His eyes search mine for an answer, but I don't have one.

"I can't…" His voice cracks and he starts crying. He puts his arms around me for comfort. I try to hug him back, telling myself that he needs me, but my body is stiff. His tears fall easily now, staining the shoulder of my shirt. "Clover, we're—"

"Noah, we have to go," I say, my voice quiet. In control.

He sobs on my shoulder once more, his body shaking. Deep down, he knows the truth. I let go, but he doesn't let go of me. His arms grip me tight, as if I were the only thing that could hold him up.

"Noah," I say again, gently. I stroke his hair, brushing it back from his forehead. "Noah, let's go."

"But they aren't…" he says, stopping midsentence.

I don't want to say the words, either.

There's no time for me to worry or panic. Suddenly, my heart beats normally. My breathing is calm, and I'm in control.

"We need to go." I nudge him toward the door, doing my best not to get angry at his crying. That's not what Noah needs right now. He needs reassurance. "Come on." I nudge him again, and this time, he moves.

He keeps his arms around my shoulders, and together, we reach the threshold, open the door, and step outside. I pick up the rifle on the way out.

I need to find a way to bring him out of this stupor. I hope for something to happen, anything that will snap us out of this disbelief.

And then, of course, it does.

I look up and there they are. Four silhouettes, as tall as door frames. Their lower bodies are like spiders—each one has six legs, sleek and metallic like their spaceships, clinking together on the asphalt. But that's not what staggers me. Four human torsos top the metal structures, and vacant eyes blink from four human heads. *Human.*

I freeze.

And then my body tells me one thing: *run.*

I turn, shoving Noah so hard that his legs start moving again. He stares at the aliens, his jaw dropped, but there's no time to think. They're hunting us.

I start running, and Noah is right behind me. I struggle with the rifle, attempting as I run to load it with the quick precision that Abuelo taught me. I can hear our pursuers' strong, clawed legs clicking behind us and my brain can barely process what's happening—the empty town, the aliens waiting for us. I realize that it must have been Noah's screams that drew them to us. The clanging of metal follows us, a *click-click-click* that tells me they're still on our trail, a sound that pounds into my head.

I go as fast as I can, my muscles burning. All I know is that we have to get as far away as possible. I run toward the edge of town, Noah screaming behind me.

"Just run!" I shout, pulling him forward.

Tears streak his face and his muscles are failing, but he keeps screaming, and I just want to tell him to shut up, shut up, *shut up*!

But he doesn't. He runs, half crying. My eyes are dry. Crying is for later.

Whatever happens, I have to survive.

I turn the corner to take a shortcut to my grandparents' farm, then skid to a stop. A spaceship rises up from the middle of the road, a sleek, silver sphere, closed up tight, with no way to get inside. It's completely blocking my path.

My muscles are sore from running and my lungs feel like they'll explode as I inhale the dust that clings to my skin. Just then, one of the aliens appears, and my eyes widen as I raise the rifle. I breathe in and fire.

The rifle jolts back and the bullet hits the alien. For a second, I can breathe again. But then the alien steps forward, as if the bullet hadn't touched it at all.

I fire another shot, my aim perfect. I watch the bullet hit the alien square in the forehead and ricochet off it.

Gasping, I drop the useless rifle on the ground and grab Noah, turning and running another way home.

And suddenly, just when I think we'll be able to outrun them, Noah trips.

He goes down, crashing hard onto the asphalt. I stop in my tracks and turn around.

Noah lies on the ground, blood spurting from his nose and tears still streaming from his eyes. He whimpers a pathetic little moan. I tell him to get up—or maybe I just imagine saying it. He mouths my name, looking up at me.

I don't move.

I don't get closer.

Everything is a rush of color in my mind, and then they're upon us again, the aliens who are annihilating us from the earth.

Get up, Noah. *Get the hell up.*

And as if Noah means nothing at all, they point a gun at him. I hear a single quiet beep before it goes off. I stand paralyzed as a red laser hits Noah and his whole body explodes in a cloud of smoke. His dust rises, merging with the cloud that we've been breathing since we got into town.

Noah goes up into the cloud of dust, scraped from this world completely. Like he never even existed.

I know what I'm breathing then. The cloud is all the atoms of the town, human skin and blood and bones, coming right into my lungs.

I don't make a sound. My legs are frozen. I can't scream and

I can't move. Panic fills my heart and my brain, but I close my eyes, shutting it out. Noah is gone, and I'm going to be next.

But the aliens don't point their guns at me. They don't approach.

They look straight past me, then turn around. Like I'm completely invisible.

Like they hadn't even seen me.

I turn around and run toward home.

CHAPTER 5

When I finally manage to make it to the farm, it's almost midday. I tear through the fields toward the house, blowing past the scarecrow that wears Abuelo's old clothes. My lungs feel like they could burst, but I'm too worried and high on adrenaline to care.

Stumbling over the front steps, I reach the porch and pause to catch my breath. Then I carefully swing the door open, stepping inside.

The house is empty. Silent.

"Abuela?" I whisper, not daring to speak too loudly.

I creep toward the kitchen, my body tense, my eyes searching in every direction. The kitchen window is open, and the dishes from breakfast rest on the drying rack. The vase that Abuela brought back from our trip to Mexico to visit relatives sits on the table, filled with flowers that she picked this morning. My fingers swipe across the table as I take in the emptiness.

I move on to the living room, but everything is quiet. Dead. I try not to think of that word, but it's impossible. It's been running through my mind since the day began.

"Abuela?" I call out. "Dónde estás?"

I climb the stairs in a rush, but there's only the two empty bedrooms and the bathroom. I run through the whole house, stomping loudly, not caring anymore who hears me. I run outside again, letting the door sway in the breeze, but all I find is more emptiness and silence. I'm the only one on the farm.

I go back inside, my knees shaking. There's no sign of dust and no sign of anything else. I think about Abuela, about whether she'd make enough dust to cling to the room. My stomach heaves, and I run to the bathroom to throw up my breakfast.

Abuela had always tried to prepare me for the fact that she and Abuelo were old and getting older, and that someday I'd come back and they wouldn't be here. But I never expected it to be like this. I always thought I'd have the chance to say goodbye.

I collapse on my bed, on top of the quilt that Abuela sewed for me last year. I feel my lungs pressing together, deflated, and the tears finally come.

My body shakes with sobs I can't suppress. I lie there too long. *Gone, dead, gone, dead.*

Everyone is dead.

My sobs turn my body inside out, and I can't seem to get enough air to fill my lungs. I breathe desperately, my shoulders weak, trying to gather what's left of myself. The image of Noah dissolving into dust flashes through my mind again and again.

My bag sits next to me and I shove it aside, causing the contents to spill out. My wallet falls to the floor, coins flying, and so does the satellite phone. I jump off of the bed, my heart hammering inside my chest. There's still hope.

Abuelo might still be out there. He might be at Malmstrom.

I head back downstairs, wiping my tears away, hoping my knees will stop shaking.

I turn on the TV and flip through the channels, but they're all just white noise. Hands trembling, I approach the TV set and smack it on the side.

One channel comes through, barely.

"The alien attacks—" says a female reporter, her voice cutting in and out. The image is hazy, and all I can distinguish is a dark red suit. "The government has tried…failed once again… significant damage…planet."

I put my ear against the speakers, as if that's going to help me understand her words.

Hazy footage of bombs and aliens appears on the screen. People vaporize as the aliens slowly but surely overcome any kind of attack or attempt to stop them. A plane is shot right out of the sky by a shadow, the spaceship flying too fast for the camera to capture it. In big cities, buildings are being destroyed by our own bombs.

"Viewers…" the reporter continues. "Gather in groups… stay safe."

I turn off the television so I won't have another panic attack. The room is silent again, plunging me into the emptiness that is this house.

Stay safe. What a fucking joke.

I go the desk and rummage through it. In the top drawer lies Abuelo's handgun.

My eyes linger on it.

There is a way out, and it's staring right at me. The aliens might not have gotten me, but there's nothing left for me here.

I shove the thought aside, refusing to think about it. On top of the desk is a picture of the three of us from our trip to Disneyland. Abuela had complained the whole way there, saying that I was spoiled. I was eight years old, wearing a hat with Mickey Mouse ears and a Mulan balloon tied to my wrist so it wouldn't fly away. Beneath the photo, a four-leaf clover is taped to the frame.

Abuelo's lucky charm. I could find four-leaf clovers anywhere. The night that my mother abandoned me on my grandparents' porch, she left a letter and a clover. It's how I'd gotten my name.

There's still a chance that Abuelo's out there. There's still something I can do. I can fight.

I grab the photo, the gun, and Abuela's wooden rosary, and I leave.

The Beechcraft is waiting for me outside.

I put the key in the ignition and the motor roars to life. I can feel the power that flight gives me coursing through my veins. Somehow, even after all of this, I still know that I'm meant to be in the sky.

I hang Abuela's rosary from a knob on the instrument panel for good luck.

Turning the plane around, I head for the fields. I check the gauges on the panel again and again, putting on earmuffs to dull the noise. Pressures, temperature, and fuel all look good.

I accelerate, but the plane is slow at first, like it's reluctant to get off the ground. Just like me. It shakes, but I grab the yoke. It's in my control—just about the only thing that is right now. And slowly, it rises from the ground and up into the air.

I feel a rush as it flies up and up and up, as I leave everything behind. Everything looks so small from up here that it can't matter—when I'm in the sky, nothing else matters.

When I look at the empty seat next to me, my heart breaks. That's Abuelo's seat, but he isn't up here with me. I have no roots anymore.

I fly low for a while, waiting. The Beechcraft is a steady, trustworthy machine, and all the instruments are active as I look around and evaluate the situation. I flip through the radio frequencies, searching for a channel that might hear me. I need to identify my call sign and try to make contact with the base.

"This is Beechcraft November-one-zero-one, flying under the license of Carlos Martinez, United States Air Force pilot number Foxtrot-one-five-four-six."

Silence answers me. I steady the course south toward the base and try again.

"This is Beechcraft November-one-zero-one, trying for Malmstrom."

No answer.

I bite my lower lip, trying not to jump to conclusions.

"This is Beechcraft November-one-zero-one for Malmstrom. Please respond."

Still no answer. My hands are sweaty as I change the channel again and again, trying every frequency.

"This is Beechcraft November-one-zero-one. Is anyone out there?"

Suddenly I hear the sound of a strange engine that I don't recognize. When I look over my shoulder, I see a flash of dark silver iron.

There are two of them behind me—two shining, metallic spaceship hulls. My heart beats fast in my chest as I search the sky for more.

These are different from the others that I've seen up close. They look more like F-15 Eagle fighter jets than landing shells, like they've been designed specifically to hunt in the sky.

I hit the radio again, broadcasting wildly. I still have twenty or thirty minutes to go until I reach the base.

"This is Beechcraft November-one-zero-one, requesting aid," I say. *Please, someone be out there. Anyone.* "I've got two of them on my tail, similar to fighter jets."

I gulp down hard.

That's when I see something glowing in the spaceships behind me.

The first shot doesn't hit me, but the second one does. I flip the plane around, unable to wrap my head around the fact that I'm being chased by alien spaceships. It all sounds mad, like the world has gone to hell in just a couple of minutes. Aliens have invaded my home planet and are exterminating my species like we're nothing. Like we're livestock.

The difference is that livestock are useful. To these aliens, we are nothing but bugs.

They shoot again and all I can think is, *Go to hell, leave me alone, leave me the fuck alone.* A string of Spanish curse words crosses my mind, words that I would catch Abuela saying under her breath when she thought I couldn't hear her.

But the aliens don't go away. They pursue me.

"Mayday, Mayday," I shout into the radio. "Beechcraft November-one-zero-one has been hit. Requesting emergency landing at Malmstrom Air Force Base."

My plane has no defenses. There are no weapons I can use to fight them off. I hear more laser blasts coming toward me, and I spin around madly, avoiding them. If I make it to the base, someone there might hear me. They can take the spaceships down.

I concentrate on this, on getting there, and let the rest of the noise fall away. I can't bear to check the plane's engine, the glaring lights that glow on the instrument panel.

"Mayday, Mayday," I call again, my voice choking, my lungs fighting for air. "Requesting emergency landing at Malmstrom."

My words transmit into emptiness, unheard. The next shot hits the left wing, sending the plane flying out of control. I grab the yoke, but the plane is unbalanced with half of a wing gone. I steady myself, but Abuelo never taught me how to do this. He never prepared me for being attacked.

The shots keep coming, and this time I think that I'm going to die. They're shooting at me fiercely, one blast after another. The fuel tank starts leaking, and I know it's over when the plane catches fire. The motor is failing, and I can't do anything to repair it.

This is nothing like Noah. This will not be a quick, merciful death. They won't stop until they've taken this plane down.

There's no way I can escape this—I'm not going to be able to salvage the last thing that remained of my grandfather. All I can do is go down with it.

The humming behind me stops, and I watch the ships retreat with some relief. It's short-lived, though. I can see the base now, but the plane is out of control and the engine is coming undone in midair.

And where there should be an air base, all I can see is a wrecked and devastated wasteland.

CHAPTER 6

The plane falls full force against the air as it plummets down toward the destruction. I can't control it. My time in the sky is done, and I know—I *know*—I won't be able to get up there again.

The sky slips from my grasp just as I'm trying to reach it.

I crash hard. My head hits the back of my chair and everything darkens, my vision filling with spots. As the plane comes to a stop, I can't feel my legs. My brain throbs from the impact. I just lie there, waiting for death, waiting for anything that will get me out of here. Praying that the aliens have an ounce of pity and just take me, once and for all.

I lie among the rubble, blinking the pain away. Something makes me move. Slowly, I crawl out of my seat. My ribs hurt, my side is smashed, and I can't breathe right. But I'm not giving up now. I collapse to the ground just outside the plane and take in the damage.

The Beechcraft is a complete wreck—the right wing is pierced into the hull, the tail is torn from the main skeleton, and what's left of the motor is engulfed in a cloud of black smoke.

I turn and survey the rest of the ruins around me. I can distinguish a few things through my delirious haze: the landing strip, the hangar where the planes used to be, and what appears to be the roof of the main building.

But that's it. There's wreckage and rubble and chaos everywhere, chunks of broken cement and pieces of exposed wire. This place looks like it's been through hell and back.

When I try to stand, my knees wobble. My ribs are surely broken.

The whole base is devastated—what had once been a huge military complex had been destroyed with ease, like it had simply been blown into the air. We never stood a chance. There is nothing, absolutely nothing, left.

I walk among the debris, limping toward where Malmstrom's main building used to stand. I don't see any bodies, but there's a piece of fabric that might have been part of an American flag. I pick it up, but it falls apart at my touch. The building has collapsed entirely, and the concrete is coming undone in the sun.

Stupid, stupid me. Daring to hope that there'd be anything left. That I could make my way here and find Abuelo, that we could still have a chance to take to the skies together.

I don't belong to the sky anymore.

Hope is the thing that kills me in the end. Because it doesn't take my body, but it takes my soul.

I feel the cold metal of Abuelo's gun. Tears swell in my eyes, and my throat is raw and burning. My knees bend, and all I want to do is scream, scream until there's nothing left in my lungs, until all the dust has cleared away and I can't breathe anymore. Until I can fight the urge to die and find the will to live, because right now I can't do either.

I scream at the top of my lungs.

My shoulders are shaking, my hands trembling in fists. I pick up rocks and throw them away, trying to make the aliens move, trying to shatter them against the metal hulls of the broken airplanes, making a racket.

"Just kill me!"

I want them to, because I can't do it myself. My grandparents and Noah are dead. All I want to do is follow them.

"Cowards!" I shout to the empty space around me. "Show your fucking faces! Isn't it humanity that you want? *Come get me!"*

I kick another stone and topple over the rubble, cutting my lip. I taste iron and blood, and when I turn, I hear it. The sound that haunts me.

The alien approaches the corner of my vision, its metal legs clinking. Its eyes are vacant, its face stretched. It looks around, and I see others join it.

I sob again, and one of them moves forward. My brain screams inside my head, urging me to do something that I can't decipher. Run toward them? Run away from them? Stay and survive? Run and be killed?

I close my eyes, waiting. Waiting for the end to come. *You took everyone from me*, I think. *Take me, too.*

But they don't make a move. If they can hear me, they mistake me for something else, an animal or something not worth their time. The aliens turn away, just like before, like I'm invisible.

On impulse, I raise Abuelo's gun and shoot one of them, straight in the back.

It turns, jumping. Impenetrable skin. But as it scans the area, it doesn't seem to find anything.

The gun in my hand is useless, except for one thing. I put it to my temple, feeling the cold muzzle form a perfect circle against my skin. Put this bullet inside my head. That's all I have to do.

The aliens vanish from sight.

Breathe in. Breathe out.

I have to beat the weaker Clover, the one who wants to crumble. I just have to be stubborn enough to do it. Stubborn enough to know that I can conquer the Clover who just wants to blow her brains out and die, die, *die*.

I lower the gun.

It's just like flying a plane. It's just getting from one place to another, until the day that you run out of gas. It's not a victory, but it's not a defeat, either.

I start walking, one foot in front of the other. Breathing slowly. Destined for nowhere.

Days pass.

The days turn into weeks, and the weeks turn into months. And even though I cross the country, there's no one else to see. No one else is alive.

Earth is empty.

And so am I.

PART II

APOCALYPSE, PLEASE

CHAPTER 7

The car swerves off the road when I blink and crashes full force into the alien spaceship.

The alarm goes off, blasting in my ears. I struggle against the airbag, which has deployed, and try to no avail to stuff it back inside the steering wheel. Sputnik barks.

"Fuck," I say, pushing the door open and stomping my feet onto the asphalt. The spaceship is silent, like everything else on this planet.

I go around the car and the smoke that rises from the motor, billowing into the sky. The front of the car is smashed against the stronger metal of the spaceship in an awkward position, as if embracing it—the spaceship suffered no damage at all, defying all laws of physics. I resist the urge to kick it, mostly because I know that I'll break my toes if I do.

There's no way I'll be able to move the car. I sigh wearily.

Sputnik hops out of the car, wagging her gigantic tail and looking at the spaceship. She sniffs it, quickly losing interest in its chromed metal, and sits on the asphalt by my side.

"Damn this car. Damn this whole planet."

I open the back door and get my bag of supplies, which consists of some stolen clothes and food that I've packed along the way. There's water, too, and I find it hilarious that in the midst of an apocalypse, food and water are the only things in abundance.

I unzip the bag, take out a pack of chips, and open it. I pop one into my mouth, sighing. Sputnik wags her tail, eyeing the chips.

"We'll get you food," I tell her, but she keeps ogling them.

I take out a map and lay it on the trunk of the car, examining a broken road sign to figure out where I am—about ninety miles north of Eldorado, Texas. I should find shelter for the evening, then look for another car tomorrow morning so I can continue this endless road trip. I could get to the border by tomorrow afternoon, if I find a car.

The hot sun toasts me alive, but my one comfort is that if I'm burning out here, so are the aliens. Ever since the invasion, temperatures have gotten weirder. By my count, it's the beginning of October, and it should *definitely* be cooler by now, yet I'm roasting.

Sputnik and I walk, her tongue hanging out of her mouth.

I give her water from time to time to keep her hydrated. Her fur is fluffy in the heat, but she's having a hard time keeping up.

It takes us three hours to reach the next town, which looks like a deserted village now—there's not a single soul in sight. It's like being in a Wild West ghost town. The sun is starting to set, and I want to find a place to sleep soon.

After trying a couple of houses, I find one that's unlocked. It's empty and clean, like the family suddenly decided to go on a trip and left their house open. I throw my bag on the sofa, watching it bounce off of the firm stuffing. Sputnik trots in without a care in the world, sniffing her way around, even stopping to squat and pee in the middle of the floor.

"Gross," I tell her, but she ignores me.

The Bernese mountain dog continues her trek through the rest of the house, nose to the ground, and I follow her.

I go through the cupboards in the kitchen, looking for food. The fridge isn't worth checking—there's no electricity, so it's not working and the food in there is probably all rotten. After all, it's been six months since the aliens came out of their shells and razed the planet.

I find some sealed jars and packages in the cabinets. I pick one up and start chewing on some peanuts that aren't half bad. I have a slight allergic reaction to peanuts, so almost instantly, my skin develops an angry red rash, like I have a bad case of chicken pox. It's not life-threatening for me, but it used to make me feel self-conscious. Now I don't care if my whole face turns into a polka-dot festival, as long as I have food to keep me alive. I find some dog food and give it to Sputnik, although she's never as excited about dog food as she is on the days when we hunt free-range chickens.

I eat more peanuts as I walk through the rest of the house. I go into the bathroom and, miraculously, the water is working. It's cold, but it's better than nothing. I quickly climb out of my filthy clothes.

After showering, I search the bedrooms for clean clothes to wear. Whoever lived here had two young kids, and their clothing is too small. I don't linger in the bedroom with pictures of ponies on the wall. Moving on to the couple's room, I pick up a pair of pants from the woman and a few large T-shirts from the man, along with a nice camo jacket that looks like it was made to fit me. I feel fresher than I have in weeks. My dark hair falls almost to my waist, but I can't bear to cut it.

Before dark, I go downstairs and lock up all the doors and windows, closing the shutters. Sputnik follows me dutifully, her paws heavy on the ground as she, too, seems to check every window. There's no basement in this house, which makes me wish I had been choosier about my accommodations. Paying attention to every single creak the stairs make, I climb upstairs and slide under the bed, taking a pillow with me. I can't sleep in the bed—it feels unprotected. Unsafe.

The space under the bed is confined. Sputnik crawls under, too, her black eyes blinking as she stares at me. Her fur smells like she needs a bath, but it's comforting—the dog is warm and heavy next to me, and she makes me feel safe. I let myself breathe calmly, filling my lungs with air for a long time, then letting go. They don't work half as well as they used to before I crashed the plane. I breathe in, count to eight, breathe out.

The room gets darker and darker as night falls. Some nights are easier, and I can almost fall into a fitful sleep, but other nights I stay awake all night, wondering if one of them is going to barge in and finally take me. I can hear them sometimes, and I wish they'd simply give up and go home.

But they never do. The spaceships remain here, and sometimes, I see shadows crossing the skies.

Tonight, there's no sound outside. My muscles are tense, and I'm hyperaware of my surroundings. Sputnik lays her head on the ground, waiting. She knows, too. There's a pattern—darkness falls, and they come out from wherever they were hiding.

But it's been six months. Six months since moving every day became routine, since I started tucking the gun in the back of my jeans, just in case. Six months since I started pulling it out from time to time, contemplating shooting myself in the head and ending this.

For some reason, I can never bring myself to do it. I've become a new Clover, stuck in an eternal limbo between life and death.

Morning comes, and bright sunlight seeps through the window.

My back is sweaty from sleeping on the ground, but it's a reminder: I'm alive. Sputnik waits. She never leaves before I do. That's the first reason that I let her stay with me, back when I found her roaming around the trash outside a house in Sacramento. She always follows me, hovering around, just like a little satellite. That's why I named her Sputnik.

I roll out from under the bed and notice the curtains flapping, the only movement in the room besides me. I take a careful peek out the window, but there's no sign of life anywhere.

Every morning it's the same thing. When I wake up, I have to come to terms with what happened. Sometimes, like a kid, I pretend that this is just a crazy nightmare conjured directly from a badly scripted Hollywood movie, and that I'll wake up to find everything back to normal. But then I open my eyes, and everything is still here, in the same place as before, and the towns and roads and skies remain empty.

Most days, I pretend that I don't know that I might be the last human on Earth. If I don't acknowledge it, then I don't have to take responsibility for it. Besides, not even Hollywood would cast a teenage Latina girl with survivor guilt and a ridiculously large dog who likes to run in circles as the heroes.

"Stay," I tell Sputnik, and she sits down. She always waits as I run the perimeter of the house, checking that everything is okay. The aliens can't see me, but they can see her, which makes her a liability. They never bother with animals, though.

I straighten my clothes and very carefully go downstairs. The stairs creak a little, and I hold my breath, calming myself.

The front door is locked, just as I left it last night. I breathe a sigh of relief, then turn toward the kitchen.

And freeze.

It's right there, behind the counter, in the middle of the ceramic floor. Its form rises from the kitchen tiles, huddled on six insect-like legs that crawl and click as it slides from side to side, looking for something. But that's not the worst part.

Its upper half looks so completely human that it's a shock to see another human face after so long.

But it's not human, I remind myself. The alien clinks over the tile floor like a middle-aged, suburban mom out of some TV sitcom. Its face is older than others I've seen, like someone in their early forties, with sleek brown hair the same color as mine. My stomach churns, but I keep holding my breath. I can't let myself collapse.

It clinks toward the door, stopping right in front of me.

I don't breathe.

I don't move.

I don't make a sound.

The alien doesn't turn. It stands facing me, with its weirdly human face and insect-like legs, as if waiting to hear something. But whatever it's waiting for, it doesn't come. It clinks back on its legs, retreating toward the kitchen, and goes out the back door. The wood swings as it exits, and I stand there and watch it in the sunlight, moving fast with its wickedly sharp legs.

The door swings again and I collapse onto the floor, tears running down my face while my whole body shivers. My heart beats again and my lungs fill with air.

It doesn't return for me. It hasn't seen me.

They never, ever see me.

CHAPTER 8

The muzzle of the gun feels familiar against my temple.

Escape is just one quick squeeze away.

Just one.

I look at the gun and it stares back at me, and I can almost hear it whisper "coward" in my ear. I'm just not sure if I'm a coward for not pulling the trigger or because I'm thinking about doing it in the first place. Sputnik comes down, cocking her head sideways, her ears perked. As she approaches, my trembling hands get a little steadier. She licks my nose, and I let go of the gun, at least for now.

I've survived 178 days. I just have to survive one more.

I stroke Sputnik's fur, taking a deep breath. It's time to leave again.

I pick up a few more pieces of clothing and other items that I might use. The one good thing about the aliens being so damn efficient is that there was almost no time for people to pillage. It's like everyone on the planet had a sudden urge to move away and left everything they owned behind.

The car in the garage is a blue SUV with a full tank of gas, and it starts right up. It's also an automatic, thank God.

I get out onto the road and start maneuvering around abandoned cars. The map is laid out on the seat next to me, pointing me toward more wasteland. I drive around the nearby spaceships. They don't usually bother with moving cars.

I've been driving for more than two hours when I start to feel sleepy from the monotony of the road. Sputnik likes the back seat and, with how many cars I've crashed, she's figured out that it's the safest place for her to sit. Here and there I see the silver shells of spaceships, the only things noticeable among the scrubby green landscape. I don't want to stop—because there's no point stopping until I find a town—so I look around for some CDs that might help me stay awake.

There's nothing good in the car. That's one of the worst things about the end of the world—no music. All the good bands are probably dead. I still carry my iPhone with me, but more out of nostalgia than usefulness. There's no electricity anymore, unless I manage to find a solar-powered house. Those things really keep going.

I click the button for the radio and it turns on. I try to slide in a CD, but the port is jammed. I curse, trying again to get it in, but to no avail. The radio is playing, but I know there's only going to be white noise. White noise for miles and miles.

I throw the CD on the passenger seat and reach to turn the radio off, but I accidentally change the station.

And a song comes on.

It's "Earth Angel." I recognize it from *Back to the Future*, one of my favorite movies. I decide that I must be dead. This can't be happening. There are no more radio stations. And if there were, they wouldn't be playing a random fifties doo-wop song like this. I have definitely died. I crashed the car and died, finally.

But the song doesn't stop and the car doesn't crash and I'm not dead. The song keeps on playing and I keep on seeing stunted trees rushing past as I drive down the empty interstate.

After the song ends, a voice comes on.

"This is the Apocalypse Radio Station, where we celebrate the end of the world every day and now," a girl's voice says. Her New York accent is painfully clear. "If you're out there, you are not alone. Come find us."

There's a pause.

"Unless you're one of the aliens. Then, please, don't come. But if you are entirely and one hundred percent human, you know where to find me. Come to the place where *they* used to be kept. This is Brooklyn Spencer, and you're listening to the Apocalypse Radio Station. Songs to keep you entertained after the world ends."

Another song starts playing.

I'm not alone.

For a minute, I can't believe it. The world ended six months ago, and this is too wild. But even so, I'm not alone.

Fuck.

I crash the SUV.

CHAPTER 9

It doesn't take a genius to figure out Brooklyn's message—I solve it in two minutes. I pick up another car that has plenty of gas and get on a different highway. All I need to do is cross Texas and go through New Mexico, then Arizona, then Nevada.

The fact that it could be a trap doesn't scare me. I just don't care anymore. The risk is worth it. I've been dead inside for months, so if they're going to kill me now, by setting a sick trap like this, it won't make any difference.

Besides, if there really are more of us…then there's still a chance. A chance that we can find a solution together. A chance that we can fight back.

A chance that there's still a reason to stay alive.

Even Sputnik senses my sudden change of mood. I put a

seat belt on her, and she sits with her head stretched out of the window, feeling the wind.

The landscape slowly starts changing, with desert plains becoming more visible the farther west I go. I've never visited this part of the country before. When the gas light comes on and the car is running on fumes, I stop and find another car with a full tank. I change cars three more times, then stop to sleep. I'm not going to risk traveling by night, but I can barely force my eyes to close. Not because of the aliens this time, but because I might meet someone like me. A survivor.

I find myself always tuning in to the Apocalypse Radio Station. Whoever Brooklyn is, she has good taste in music, ranging from sixties songs to movie soundtracks to eighties hard rock, and an awful lot of musicals. Not to mention that she has a bit of dark humor to go along with it. And after every few songs, she repeats the message that I heard the two days before.

I wish I could travel faster, but I'm not going to risk a plane. Not after what happened last time. So I just slam on the accelerator, watching everything fly by in a rush of speed.

I think about Brooklyn's message again. She's obviously in a place where she can connect to some kind of electricity, enough to power a radio station. And she feels safe enough that she thinks it's a good idea to broadcast messages to others— although I haven't figured out yet how she's doing it. She's in a secure place with access to food. It has to be a base or compound of some kind.

The other part of the message is clear: "that place where

they used to be kept." There's only one *they* she could mean. We don't know their species or where they came from or even what they are. We weren't given a chance to name our destruction. It was just *they*, us versus them, whoever they are.

There were hundreds of theories about aliens in many places around the world, but if Brooklyn is in the United States, then there's only one place that fits the description. A place that's a legend of its own.

It takes almost twenty hours of driving down I-40 to get there. Every song that plays on the radio is an incentive for me to drive faster. To drive like my life depends on it, because it probably does.

I know this place is in the middle of the desert, somewhere no one would really look for it, so I take yet another car, since I wouldn't be able to cover much ground on foot. I keep crossing the desert, going one hundred miles an hour. Finally, on the third day, I find it.

I can see some kind of warehouse in the distance, its walls stark and sober. Three different barbed-wire fences protect it. Security towers—empty now—rise up every few miles, but I don't bother stopping.

As I approach the gates, I don't spot any breaches in the surrounding fences that I could go through. Barely reading the Restricted Area sign, I floor it and drive the car straight through the gates.

No one shoots at me or tries to stop me. I drive toward the main building and, in the distance, I think I see a figure. But I can't see it properly and I can hardly believe that there would be anyone out here. Suddenly, my heart stops as I realize that I'm driving straight toward a person.

I slam on the brakes, but somehow the car doesn't stop, and I scream as the person jumps out of the way and the car crashes into the side of the building, the engine crushing against it. I'm wearing my seat belt, but I still jerk forward, and my head bangs against the steering wheel. Sputnik barks. She's been through more car wrecks than any dog in history. I stay there, my head throbbing, tasting blood in my mouth.

But I don't care. Because right outside the car, I can hear voices. Human voices.

"Bloody hell," says a guy. "She went straight for it. This girl can't drive at all."

"Shut up, Flint," another voice says. "Let's see if she's alive."

"If she's dead, I'm not burying her," the guy replies.

The car door opens and I look up at three faces gaping at me. Yes, I am alive, and so are they, and I don't know which of us is more surprised. They stand there, blinking, as if they've seen a ghost.

"Hi," I try to say, but I don't even know if the word comes out of my mouth. I can't feel anything, except for my head, which hurts so much that I just want to close my eyes.

I see a Black guy standing on the far right, looking concerned. He's wearing a Star Wars T-shirt. On the far left is a girl with russet-brown skin and straight dark hair, holding the biggest gun I've ever seen.

Right in the middle stands a girl with spiky black hair and a nose piercing.

"Hey," she says, and I recognize Brooklyn's voice from the radio station. I can't help but smile. "Welcome to Area 51. Home to the Last Teenagers on Earth."

CHAPTER 10

When I open my eyes, it takes me a few seconds to remember where I am. I jump up, my head spinning.

"Sit down," says an authoritative voice. "You're going to reopen the wound I just stitched."

I blink, slowly lying back down on what appears to be a bed of some sort. I turn my head and see a girl wearing a white lab coat and a surgical mask, her dark hair tied into a bun with a couple of pencils to hold it in place. Her dark-brown skin is in opposition to the whiteness of the coat and the sterile room around us. When I blink again, I realize that I'm in some kind of lab, filled with beeping equipment.

I realize that the lab is beyond a glass wall in front of me. I'm sitting inside a room with nothing but a bed and a closed door. Then again, it's not a room.

I'm sitting inside a cell.

"You're going to be fine," the girl says as she approaches me and flashes a light in my eyes. "No concussion or anything."

"You a doctor?" I ask, eyeing her suspiciously.

"We improvise," she answers, shrugging.

"Where's Sputnik?" I ask, looking around. A dog that big would make a racket, but she's nowhere to be seen. "Is she okay?"

"The dog is fine," the girl assures me. "We had to take her out of the room. She was making too much noise."

I sit up, more carefully this time, and take in the space. They've searched me—my gun and the rest of my possessions sit on the other side of the glass. It looks like a giant warehouse, with equipment and tables taking up most of the work area, and strange machines that I have no idea how to work, not to mention what they do.

But it's all beyond the glass.

"Oh, she's awake!" Another person appears, stopping in front of the glass. I recognize Brooklyn. She wears too much eyeliner, a surprising feat at the end of the world, and her light brown skin is muted by the lab lights. By her side is Sputnik.

Sputnik runs toward the glass, smashing her head against it. When she can't get through, she starts whining, destroying everything around her as she circles the cell, trying to find a way to get to me.

"Brooklyn!" the girl shouts. "I told you to keep the dog outside."

"It wouldn't listen," Brooklyn complains, half-amused by the mess Sputnik is making.

"Sputnik," I order. "Sit."

She sits down, but her whining is deep.

The girl nods and walks out of the cell, leaving me locked inside. She stops next to Brooklyn, taking off her mask, and gives me a kind smile.

Brooklyn puts an arm around the girl, who immediately slides it off and glares at her. "She needs rest. She hit her head pretty hard when she crashed that car."

"I'm okay," I answer, because the last thing I need is someone babying me. Besides, I crashed twelve other cars before this one. It's not like it's something new. "Thanks for the bandage."

I place my feet on the floor, breathing in.

"If those stitches open, I'm not sewing you back together again," she responds.

"Avani, darling, relax," Brooklyn says. "She only crashed her car into concrete."

"Step back," Avani says, frowning as Brooklyn rolls her eyes. "Or I'm going to…"

"Make me?" Brooklyn raises a single eyebrow.

Avani blushes a deep red, but Brooklyn does step back. My head still hurts, but at least I don't taste blood in my mouth anymore. My legs feel fine, but I'll only know for sure when I start using them again.

I walk toward the glass and ask, "Why am I inside a cell?"

Brooklyn grimaces. "I'm sorry, this is just procedure. We don't know if you're contagious."

"Contagious?"

"Plague," Avani says. "We'll probably have you out in a few days. I'm sorry."

I don't know what to say to this.

"So," Brooklyn says, turning to me. "Who the hell are you and how did you find us?"

I open my mouth, but I'm not sure where to start. So I begin with simple answers. "Clover Martinez." It hits me that I'm talking to another person for the first time in six months. "I heard your radio message."

Brooklyn grins triumphantly at Avani, who has moved to the lab equipment and isn't even looking at her. "Told you so. What did I say? The message works! It worked!" She looks at me again. "And now here you are, you magnificent bastard."

I shoot up an eyebrow, and Avani turns to me.

"Just ignore her," she tells me. "Everyone else does."

Brooklyn pretends that Avani hasn't spoken. "Can we call in the others?"

"No," Avani says, turning back to her equipment. "Don't overwhelm her. She's tired. And underfed." She turns to me again. "I think you have three broken ribs that haven't healed properly. I'm surprised you haven't died."

At least she didn't say that I was lucky.

"I'm going back to the messroom," Avani says. "Don't talk too much, and remember to breathe between sentences."

Brooklyn rolls her eyes as Avani disappears from my sight. Brooklyn stays, her green eyes observing me. Sputnik gives a small bark, pawing the glass again.

"How long did it take for you to figure it out?"

"It didn't take a genius."

I realize too late that this might be the wrong thing to say, but Brooklyn laughs it off. "Couldn't make it too hard. Never know who's still out there." Then she asks, "Do you want to eat? You look hungry."

I nod my head. My stomach grumbles on cue.

Brooklyn comes back a couple of minutes later with a plate of food. She slides it through a special cutout in the glass but doesn't open the door. I sit behind the glass eating spaghetti, my stomach rumbling. Brooklyn sits cross-legged in front of me and looks like she doesn't mind talking while I eat.

"So, this is the main lab. Usually this is Avani and Flint's area. We have loads more labs, of course, but this is the one we use most." She's doing a tour-guide voice, which makes me wonder if she ever used to give actual tours. It's strange to remember that people did different things, normal things, before the attack. "The compound can actually hold more than three thousand people, at full capacity. And, of course, they had it stocked with supplies to support three thousand people living here. Engineers, office people, pilots, military personnel, and whatnot."

I nod, because I feel like that's what I'm supposed to be doing.

"That's how we've been here for so long," she continues in the same tone. "We have enough supplies to sustain all of us for at least five more years."

I don't ask her if she's planning to stay locked up in this place for another five years. It looks like a fortress, which makes me wonder what kind of people really did live here and whether the stories about Area 51 were true. Whatever the case may be, they were right about something—we needed to be prepared for a possible alien encounter. Or in our case, an alien annihilation.

Not that they had actually *been* prepared. Although there is a vague military look to the place, it's clearly a basic compound to harbor scientists and technicians, and possibly some army officials.

"How many people are here?"

"There are seven of us," Brooklyn explains. "It's kind of a genius hub. I'm not a genius, of course, but the rest…" she says, gesturing toward nothing. "Avani's one of those weirdos getting a college degree at age seventeen. The rest aren't far behind."

When I finish my plate of spaghetti, Brooklyn slides something else through the cutout. It's a Kit Kat bar, which I regard with wonder.

"It's edible," she says, seeing my face. "It's no Milky Way, and it's a little stale… But still, it's chocolate." She gives me a bright smile.

I tear open the wrapper, afraid that this will turn out to be a weird nightmare and it will taste like dried passion fruit or something, but it doesn't. I bite into it, and the chocolate overwhelms me. I close my eyes for a moment. Ever since I heard Brooklyn's voice on the radio, I've been driving nonstop. There was no time for luxuries.

Brooklyn laughs out loud at my expression. "Guess you didn't find many candy bars on the road."

I shake my head. "No, not really."

Brooklyn lets me enjoy the rest of my chocolate in peace. My heart breaks a little when I bite into the last piece, knowing that this is probably a treat she's given me, and not a normal ration.

"So, who's this good boy?" Brooklyn finally asks, peering at the dog.

"He's a she, and the name is Sputnik."

"What kind of name is Sputnik for a dog?"

"What kind of person from New York is called Brooklyn?"

She rolls her eyes. "Like I haven't heard that one a hundred thousand times. My parents were from California. We lived there till I was eight, and then we moved to New York. And yes, kids pointed this out to me at every single school I went to." She barely pauses to take a breath. "Now, why Sputnik?"

Sputnik demonstrates by taking three quick turns around Brooklyn, sniffing from one side to the other.

"She kept following me around like that, always going in circles," I say. "And when I started calling her that, she listened."

Brooklyn nods. "Sputnik is actually masculine in Russian," she says. "But, you know. World's ended. Gender is a social construct built by a society that no longer exists. So who cares?"

Sputnik finally quiets down, sitting on the ground, her fur

spreading around her. She's still eyeing the glass, but at least she's stopped whining.

"How long have you been here?" I ask.

"Five months and one week."

"You got here fast."

She nods. "There wasn't much to stay for back home."

There's an awkward pause, and I'm not sure what to say. *I'm sorry? Yeah, same?* In a decent world, none of these words would have to make sense.

"So I came west," Brooklyn continues. "I hoped that there would be somewhere that was safe."

"Were there other people here when you came?"

I'm so curious about what happened everywhere else. All I know is my own horrible experience.

"A few," she said. "Most died from the plague. Flint, Andy, and Boss turned out to be the only survivors."

It feels like she's just throwing out random names.

"Boss?" I ask tentatively. "Is he an adult?"

Brooklyn turns her head to look at me, as if she can guess my thoughts. "No adults in this world anymore, Clover," she says. "You better get used to it."

My throat dries up, and I shift slightly. My head doesn't hurt so much anymore, and my lungs are back to breathing like they usually do.

"Where is he?"

Brooklyn laughs. "Boss is a she. She's on the outskirts, scouting our perimeter."

I nod. It makes sense—somebody has to keep the defenses up. It's a miracle that the aliens haven't found this place yet, considering how huge it is. They must have some kind of great security to go undetected, and it looks like much of the complex is underground.

"So," Brooklyn says. "How did you survive?"

I raise an eyebrow, surprised by the question.

She gets up, walks over to somewhere I can't see, and brings back two bottles of beer. She snaps them open with her teeth and then grins, dissolving all the toughness that had appeared a moment before. She puts one inside the glass opening for me. "It's probably the kind of story that deserves a drink, isn't it?"

I shrug, grabbing the beer. It's strange to be drinking and telling stories, something that normal teenagers would do. But I'm not a normal teenager. Not anymore.

"Nothing much to tell," I reply. It had been luck. That's how I survived. "Just pure…luck, I guess."

Brooklyn nods, her mood somber again. She takes a swig from her bottle. She doesn't look that much older than me—eighteen, maybe nineteen. She's a tiny thing, and she only looks tough because of the absurd amount of eyeliner that she's smudged around her green eyes. Her nose ring and the all-black clothing with band logos help, too.

"Guess there's a reason I'm named Clover."

Brooklyn laughs, and I wonder how she does it. I don't think I'll ever smile again. "I'll drink to that." She raises her bottle in a friendly gesture.

I don't answer her, but I take a gulp from my bottle. The beer tastes acidic and bitter at the same time. I can't see how people willingly drink this stuff. I set it aside.

Brooklyn smiles easily again, as if she feels right at home. She looks like this has been her home all her life, as if the outside world doesn't even exist.

"What about you?"

Brooklyn shakes her head slightly. "Not much to tell, either. My parents were in the Philippines."

"Oh."

"They were visiting Mom's parents," she adds, taking another sip of beer. "They left me at the apartment. I even went to class at NYU the day. Took a god-awful test on semiotics. When I got out, the whole world was falling apart."

"In my town, we were all on lockdown."

"I mean, it's New York," she said with a smirk. "No one was going to stay indoors for a whole week."

She shrugs, like it's no big thing. Like I don't know what she's *not* saying—that she never got to say goodbye to her parents. But at least she also didn't have to watch them die.

"I wish they would've warned us, you know?" Brooklyn says at last. "Then I wouldn't have wasted time studying for that test."

Unexpectedly, I laugh. It's amazing that in so little time, Brooklyn has managed to bring laughter out of me.

"You were in high school?" she asks.

"Finishing my junior year," I answer. "Almost there."

She eyes me closely. "You didn't bring any weed, did you?"

I snort, then shake my head. "No."

She groans, pressing her forehead against the glass. "Ugh, I hate you." She glares at me. "There's only cigarettes here, and I hate the smell."

"Sorry." I shrug.

"Nothing like aliens to cure bad habits, you know?"

Brooklyn fills the gaps in our conversation easily, telling me stories about NYU and how everyone expected the Asian kid to major in math. But she went into linguistics, which, as she puts it, is the mathematics of language. I observe her easygoing manner, her quick smile. She acts like everything that she left behind lies forgotten in a distant place.

When our bottles are empty, I look at her, waiting.

"Can you let me out of here?"

She gives me a tight-lipped smile. "Sorry, Clover. Higher orders. It's procedure. We're just making sure that you didn't bring anything with you."

"And if I did?"

"We'll find out soon enough," she replies. "Until then, you're supposed to stay in isolation."

I snort. I've seen isolation. I've been in isolation for the last six months.

"I promise I'll take good care of this girl," Brooklyn says, petting Sputnik. "I'll see you tomorrow."

I nod, frowning. When the lights go off, I force myself to breathe slowly and try to sleep.

CHAPTER 11

"It's a shark."

This is the first sound I hear as I open my eyes. The white lab lights are strong, and just in front of my cell, I see the boy I almost ran over. His skin is a deep brown, and glasses perch on the bridge of his nose. His hair is cut in short curls that sit close to his head.

He shakes his head and keeps drawing on a whiteboard.

"A whale?" Avani says. "A plane?"

The guy looks annoyed, gesturing to his drawing.

"A sea lion?" Avani asks, but then a timer goes off.

"It's a dolphin," he says. "Seriously? A plane? I'm amazed."

"This is difficult," Avani complains. "Don't blame me if you can't draw, Flint."

I swing my feet to the edge of the bed, knocking them on the frame as I try to rub the sleep out of my eyes. Avani and the guy named Flint look up sharply.

"Clover, you're awake," Avani says. "Good. That means your body is functioning properly."

I don't know what to say to that.

"Sorry if we woke you," Flint says. "There isn't a lot to do around here." He approaches the glass, eyeing me with curiosity.

"Given that I almost ran you over, I think we're even."

He gives me a big smile, full of white teeth. "It's fine," he says. "Good to be reminded now and then that we're still alive." His accent is British.

I look over at Avani. "Are you still examining me, or can I leave now?"

She purses her lips. "I'm sorry, it's really not up to me to let you out."

"It can't be that hard to figure out whether I'm contagious or not, with this much equipment around," I say, gesturing toward the lab.

"Your tests look fine," Flint says. "It's just that we need to review them with someone else."

"Boss?" I guess, remembering what Brooklyn told me last night.

Flint and Avani exchange a look.

"Yes," Avani finally answers. "Look, we're not even supposed to be talking to you this much right now. We need to be

81

certain that everything is all right before we let you out. Run more blood tests."

I cross my arms, getting impatient. "I can't stay in here forever."

"Look, it's not that bad," Flint says. "We can bring the TV around, if you want, and I'm sure that everything will be sorted out in a couple of days."

I don't approach the glass. I feel tense—I know that something is wrong here, but I can't put my finger on what.

A noise beyond my cell makes me turn, but it's just more people coming in. I recognize two of them, Brooklyn and the other girl I saw when I crashed the car, who thankfully isn't carrying her bazooka now. Two others are with them, a mousy girl with dull hair and glasses that take up half her face, and a boy; both are white. For a second, I can see Noah behind the boy's eyes, and it makes me shudder.

"Guys, come in." Brooklyn gestures to them, signaling for them to stand in front of the glass. "This is the fresh meat, Clover."

Six sets of eyes peer at me through the glass, as if I were an animal inside a zoo.

"She's the one who crashed the car?" the unfamiliar boy asks. "Nice job."

"Give her a break," Brooklyn snaps. "Clover, let me introduce you to the Last Teenagers on Earth. I see you've already met Flint and Avani. This is Rayen," she says, pointing to the bazooka girl. "Don't mess with her. This is Adam, our mechanic of sorts. Last of the rare species of white boys—first time they've ever been endangered." Adam rolls his eyes at Brooklyn. His smile is warm and his eyes fix on mine before I turn away. They're exactly the same gray-blue shade that Noah's had been. "And this is our resident nerd, Andy. Nobody really knows what she's doing here."

Andy gives me a small, encouraging nod and adjusts her blue-framed glasses on her nose.

They look at me expectantly, taking me in. There's clearly a reason that they're calling themselves the Last Teenagers on Earth. Just by looking at them, I can tell that I'm not the only one who has suffered losses.

"Right," I say, because I'm not sure what else I'm supposed to say. I wish I could blame my awkwardness on the lack of human interaction for the last six months, but the truth is that I've never had a lot of friends. It was strange that I had a boyfriend.

Ex-boyfriend, I remind myself. It feels weird to think about it in those terms, since I'd seen Noah get turned to dust.

Thinking about him makes my stomach churn.

All these introductions are overwhelming, forcing my mind to return to a time when I had lived with people other than myself. It's strange to be around people again, and the hardness in their stares, their eagerness for something that I can't pinpoint, makes me shrink from them.

"Nice to meet you," I finally say, hoping everyone will finally stop staring at me like I'm a zoo attraction.

"Good job on totaling the car," Adam says.

I freeze, and all the others sigh.

"Oh my god." Brooklyn shoves him. "Sorry about his manners," she says to me.

"Men are pointless," Rayen states.

"Ditto," Brooklyn agrees, rolling her eyes. "That's why I only date girls." She high-fives Rayen with a grin.

An uncomfortable silence falls again to the room, all effort of conversation gone.

"So," I finally say, finding my voice again. "Any chance that one of you might let me out of here?"

"Yikes," Andy says. "Not off to a great start."

Brooklyn turns to glare at the smaller girl.

"I know it must be hella uncomfortable being in there, Clover," Brooklyn says. "But that's just the way it is for now. We really can't let you out until we've gotten authorization."

"I swear I'm not dangerous."

"I mean, she did bring a dog," Andy says. "People who bring dogs aren't dangerous."

Avani shakes her head. "It's not our decision to make."

That seems to be the end of the discussion. When the Last Teenagers on Earth turn around to go, not one of them so much as glances back at me.

I spend the day locked in my cage, sometimes pacing back and forth, sometimes lying somewhere between sleep and wakefulness.

There's one good thing about being locked up—for the first time in months, I'm not afraid to sleep. Even though my nightmares still haunt me, it seems that between these walls, they're dampened, just like sound is. The only thing I watch is the clock on the wall, letting me know how many hours have passed.

When night arrives, Brooklyn comes in by herself with another meal.

"Hey," she says, sliding the tray to me. This time, she has a hamburger. "Sorry about this morning. Maybe that was a little too much too soon."

"It's okay," I tell her, though I don't know why I'm bothering to lie to her.

She sits down in front of me.

"How's Sputnik?" I ask.

"She's doing well," she answers. "Ate the rations we gave her. She managed to kill one of our chickens, too, so we'll be eating that for lunch tomorrow."

I can't help but laugh. Sputnik, though she looks like a very silly dog, has always been a good chicken chaser.

Brooklyn opens her mouth, then closes it again, as if she wants to ask me something but isn't sure how to do it. I don't know what she wants. I don't know what any of them want. They are as much a mystery to me as the aliens.

"Is there any good news?" I ask.

She breaks into a smile. "Your tests are all clear. I think you'll be able to get out tomorrow."

"That's good, right?"

She hesitates. "Yeah. I think so." She bites her lower lip. "We haven't had anyone new here in a while. Boss insisted on keeping you quarantined, just in case. After the plague…"

She falls silent.

"What plague?" I ask.

"It got half of humanity, after we started breathing the dust clouds," she says. "A bunch of people here suffered from it. Kept coughing their lungs out of their body. There were traces of bacteria. Adults who had left the compound brought the bacteria back here, and then kids started coughing, too. It's extremely contagious, so isolation is the least we can do to guard against it."

I'd seen a few blackened bodies on the road, early on, but I'd never been able to surmise that there had been a plague. I had shut myself off from the world entirely for three weeks after Malmstrom, barely able to keep it together. So I hadn't seen it happen.

I decide to change the subject.

"So, the radio," I say. "How long has it been running?"

"Since I got here," she says. "It's kind of like a beacon. That's what I'm hoping for, anyway."

"Well, it worked," I say. "It brought me here."

"It was an accident, wasn't it?"

I give the smallest of nods. "Yeah. I wanted to play a CD. But the port was jammed, so I pushed a radio button and there you were."

Brooklyn's smile gets wider at that, her green eyes sparkling. "Accident or not, you're welcome here."

I gesture to my cell. "Sure doesn't feel like it."

Brooklyn gets up, then shrugs. "I promise you, you'll be out of there tomorrow. Then you'll be able to enjoy the other side of Area 51."

CHAPTER 12

Brooklyn was wrong.

They don't let me out the next day, or the day after that.

Flint brings Sputnik to me, lets me see her and pet her through the cutout, and then he takes her away. My meals are regular, but I'm still not allowed to leave my cell. I haven't seen the sun in four days, and time is ticking by.

I wonder if they're ever going to let me out.

When Flint comes to get something from the lab on Day Five, he freezes when he sees me.

"You're still here?" he asks, in an incredulous tone.

"Well, no one came to let me out," I say.

I don't bother banging my fists against the glass or anything like that. I just stand, looking at him and waiting.

When I first arrived, I wanted to ask so many questions. I was so hopeful, because to me, finding other survivors meant one thing. It meant fighting back. It meant having numbers and resources, and it meant that we could learn things from each other.

It meant that we had a chance, something that, for six months, I didn't think we had.

But right now, sitting inside this enclosed glass cell, I can't think of a single reason to believe that they're interested in fighting back.

"I'm just…" Flint pauses for a moment. "I don't know what to say."

"I don't think it matters much," I say. "Unless you plan on letting me out."

He sighs. "We want to," he confesses. He shakes his head, running his hands through his short black curls. "I mean, none of us *wanted* to put you in there. The others didn't have to go through this when they arrived."

I take a small step back. Flint sits on the table in front of the glass, swinging his legs back and forth.

"Violet has very strict rules," he says. It's the first time I hear Boss's real name. "She was concerned about your arrival and wanted to do background checks."

"And you don't question her?"

He shrugs. "She's always run this place. She's the one who managed to keep us all alive."

I can't respond to this, because I don't understand what's

happening. I don't understand the dynamics of this group. I don't know who they are or how they work.

"And when will she decide to let me out?"

Flint sighs again. "Only she can say, Clover. I'm sorry."

I want to ask him to fight back. I want to ask him to release me. I want to ask so many things, but I keep my mouth shut.

He waves a small goodbye and leaves me alone in the dark.

It's late when I hear footsteps again.

Brooklyn doesn't care much about noise. She lights up the whole room and finds me sitting up, wide awake in my bed.

"I'm done with this," she says.

She walks up to my cell door. For a second, I think that I'm hallucinating, that she's just going to disappear in a puff of smoke, but she opens the door and steps inside.

She gestures behind her with a nod of her head.

"Come on," she says. "You're done here."

I follow Brooklyn in silence.

Sputnik meets me just outside, jumping on me and licking my face. I hug her and tell her to be quiet, because I'm certain that whatever Brooklyn is doing, she's not supposed to be doing it.

She guides me to the bunk beds where all the other girls are sleeping and points to an empty one in the far left corner.

"Here," she whispers, giving me a clean pair of pants and a shirt and sliding me Abuelo's gun. "We'll talk it over tomorrow."

CHAPTER 13

When I wake the next morning, Brooklyn is nowhere to be seen, but Andy is standing over me, staring at me with her bright blue eyes.

"You're on guard duty today."

"Guard duty?"

"Running the perimeter around Area 51," she says. "Come on. We can grab breakfast before you go."

I quickly change and pull on my boots, following Andy through the compound's corridors. I sneak curious glances into the various rooms that we pass while Sputnik follows me silently, still unsure about this new territory.

Breakfast consists of unappetizing cereal with powdered milk. Andy grabs the stuff from a huge pantry, and for a moment

I can't believe that they have working fridges. I eat in a big, wide messroom, with Andy watching me intently. Finally, I gather the courage to ask her about my release.

"Brooklyn didn't talk to Violet about letting me out, did she?"

Andy sighs. "No, and I assume that we're all going to be in big trouble."

"So Violet gives the orders around here?"

Andy laughs. "Yeah. Pretty much. Violet's always been bossy, ever since she was a kid."

I raise an eyebrow. "You've known her since then?"

She nods. "We grew up together. She's my best friend. My parents worked for her mom. Melinda used to be the boss of Area 51 back in the day, oversaw all the main operations and research. Violet inherited the post after she was gone." She shifts in her seat. "I mean, after the adults left for the last attack."

"They seriously just left the kids here alone?"

"It happened little by little," Andy answers, looking away. "It's not like they had a choice. The ones who went to fight and came back brought the plague with them." Seeing the look on my face, she says, "Okay, here's a crash course in the recent history of planet Earth. First, the aliens attacked, destroying all of Earth's defenses. Then they started wiping out people, apparently. They were turning humans to dust, and when survivors breathed in the dust, it caused some kind of sickness. It turned everyone's lungs black, and it was contagious, because a specific type of bacteria grew in the human dust. Some adults caught it when they were out fighting and brought it back here to

Area 51. By the end of the month, everyone except me, Violet, and Flint was dead."

One month. That's all it took to wipe out everyone here.

I bite my tongue so I won't say anything rash. "But how are we all still here? Why haven't they found the base?"

Andy shrugs. "Wish I knew the answers. I guess we're just very lucky."

An uncomfortable silence fills the room, and Andy doesn't look like she's going to be the one to break it. I eat the rest of the meal without speaking. When I'm finished, Andy gets up, guiding me toward another mysterious corridor.

"This is the only door that you can unlock to go outside," she says, pointing. It has a circular handle and looks like a vault door. Andy steps aside. "We barricaded all the others so nothing would get in. This one has a fingerprint scanner."

She presses her finger to the scanner. After a second, it lights up green. "I'm not sure when I'll put you in the system, but…" She digs around in one of her pockets and takes out a pair of gloves, handing them to me.

I take them, feeling stupid for not understanding what they're for.

"Oh, right!" she exclaims. "Put them on."

Even though her hands are smaller than mine, the gloves fit. She motions for me to put my finger on the scanner. The screen lights up green, and the name of the authorized person pops up: Andrea Walsh.

"I glued fingerprints to the gloves," she explains, smiling.

"That way, I can leave them on all the time when it gets cold in the winter. But you can keep them for now. They'll grant you access to pretty much everything inside the compound. Rayen is waiting for you just beyond the door."

She waves goodbye as the door closes behind me, and for the first time in days, I'm out in the sun. I blink in the bright sunlight, trying to cover my eyes. A figure approaches, and I flinch before I realize that it's Rayen.

"Hey," she says. She has the bazooka again, holding it firmly in her hands. A rifle is slung across her back and two pistols are strapped to her belt, along with ammunition. She looks like a brown version of Rambo. "Glad you could make it."

"Feels a little weird seeing the sun again."

Rayen grins, her hair moving in the slow breeze that offers the only relief from the desert heat. "Nobody else likes being outside. But I kind of enjoy it."

"There's no comparing natural light to indoor fluorescents." I shrug.

"Your dog is going to regret this idea in about five minutes."

She's right. Soon after we start walking, Sputnik goes back to wait in the shade, panting heavily.

Rayen motions for me to follow her, and we walk the perimeter of the compound. Her steps are sure as she traces our route with almost military precision, and I follow her in silence, my shoulders tense. After half an hour, she turns to me.

"They never show up here, you know," she says. "There's no need to be so worried."

"It's only a matter of time," I say. "No place is safe for long."

"Some optimist you are."

I can't help but laugh. "I prefer to deal with reality."

She gestures around the deserted grounds. "Because reality is so much better right now?"

I laugh again, and Rayen's face breaks into a smile. "You get used to it," she continues. "The shock is a bit much when you first get here."

"You didn't live here before?"

She shakes her head. "I'm from Fort Apache Reservation in Arizona, from the White Mountain Apache Tribe. Came here on foot."

"Wow. You heard Brooklyn's message?"

She shakes her head again. "I was the first to arrive, actually. Got lost in the desert and ended up here. Must've been luck. Six months and counting."

I don't reply. We all keep talking about luck. But is it lucky that we survived? Or are we the unlucky ones? Bitterness fills my mouth, and the cold metal of the gun on my back grounds me here.

Abuela used to say that God doesn't keep you alive unless He has a plan.

Right now, it looks like God's plan sucks.

"What about you?" Rayen asks. "How did you get here, besides crashing your car?"

She eyes me with interest, one eyebrow raised. For a second, I can see tension in her shoulders, and I don't get why it's there.

I shrug. "I wasn't doing much. A lot of walking around and driving. Got a plane off the ground in the beginning, but it didn't last."

She turns to me, surprised. "A plane? You can fly?"

"My abuelo used to," I reply. "Best pilot in the air force back in his day."

"And you?"

"Didn't have the chance. I wanted to go to college and try for NASA, but…" My voice trails off as I look up at the sky. It's bright blue, not a cloud or a spaceship in sight. But I know that they're still here—and as long as they're on Earth, the sky will never belong to me like it once did. It'll never be mine again.

Rayen looks up, too, as if she can sense what I'm thinking. For a couple of minutes, we just stand there, looking at the immense blue that covers our planet, that was supposed to protect us. But it didn't, and here we are.

Unable to take our feet off the ground.

When I'm finally done with guard duty, I'm hot and sweaty from spending the whole day out in the sun. Brooklyn shows me the showers. Sputnik follows me in, and for the first time, I feel like I'm washing away a layer of loneliness as I shower. Sputnik doesn't know what to think of the water, and I spray it on her while she tries to avoid it. I chase her around until I catch her, then shove her under the showerhead, using up all the shampoo without a second thought.

When I come out, it's almost an hour later, but I feel like a new person. Sputnik smells like wet dog, but she's a lot cleaner, her black fur shining and the blaze between her eyes flashing a snowy white. She wags her tail, forgetting my bath betrayal, when she sees Brooklyn at the door of the shower room holding something that looks like a giant bone.

"What is that?" I ask.

"I don't know," she answers honestly. "But it does look like dog food."

Sputnik doesn't give Brooklyn a chance to back down; she jumps up and steals the bone from her hand, happily bouncing around and then darting into a corner with it in her mouth.

Brooklyn looks a little concerned, but I've stopped worrying too much about what Sputnik eats or doesn't eat. Like me, she's found her own way of surviving.

"Come on," Brooklyn says. "We've all been waiting for you."

I follow her through the compound, still trying to learn my way around the corridors. We reach the messroom, where the tables have been shoved aside and a big banner proclaiming *Welcome Clover!* in bright green letters has been hung up on a wall. Six sets of eyes stare anxiously at me, waiting.

For a second, I don't know how to react.

"Is this a party for me?" I ask, still not sure that I'm grasping the concept.

"Hell yes," Brooklyn replies, shoving me forward and handing me a can of Coke. "You made it here alive! It's time to celebrate!"

They all clap me on the back, and songs from Brooklyn's playlist start blasting over the speakers. Avani offers me food, which she assures me has been made by Flint, the only person in the compound who can actually cook. They all talk to me and ask me questions, which I respond to in the best way I can, and Sputnik makes her triumphant return by trying to steal the chicken cooking in the oven.

"Sorry about the whole mess from before," Brooklyn says, gripping my shoulder. "Thought we'd make it up to you."

I nod my head in thanks and try to blend in with the others.

The party feels strange and thin, and I can't quite make out how I feel about this night. At one point, a very defiant Sputnik steals the Welcome Clover banner and runs around the messroom with it. It takes three people to catch her. Then the Last Teenagers on Earth make me sit, and Brooklyn brings out a worn game of Cards Against Humanity.

Brooklyn deals the cards, and everyone snickers. We play a few rounds, and Rayen ends up winning most of them with outrageous combinations that I'm not sure are even possible. I keep drinking soda, trying to ignore the strange feeling in the back of my mind that something about this feels wrong.

"This is unfair," Andy complains.

"Unfair is not getting to see episode nine of *Star Wars* because the world ended," Flint replies. "I wanted to see if Rey and Kylo Ren get together!"

"Rey and Kylo? No way!" Brooklyn says, punching him in the arm. "You were my brother, Flint. I loved you!" she teases.

They keep playing cards and get into another discussion while I sit quietly, not sure where I fit in this scenario, or even whether I can hold a normal conversation with them.

"Okay, next," Brooklyn announces, drawing a new card. "Okay, this one is good: 'I drink to forget…'"

We each put a card facedown in the pile to complete the sentence. Brooklyn shuffles them and starts reading them aloud.

"'I drink to forget… My SATs,'" she reads. "Avani, that's you for sure. You big nerd."

Avani rolls her eyes.

"'I drink to forget… Poor life choices,'" Brooklyn continues. "That's all of us. 'Nickelback.' Me too. 'Daddy issues.' Really?" When she gets to my card, she purses her lips. "Hey, this one says, 'Alien invasion.'"

She tries to make it sound funny, but the atmosphere gets heavier.

She looks up at me. "This one's yours, isn't it?" she asks, and I realize that everyone's eyes are on me.

I nod, slowly, not sure how to respond.

Brooklyn puts the cards down, biting her lower lip. "Will you tell us?" she asks.

I frown slightly. "Tell you what?"

"About the outside," Avani says, almost in a whisper. "What happened after."

I frown deeper, my eyebrows knitting together. Surely, with all the resources they have out here, they know. They've seen what happened.

"Just tell us," Brooklyn says.

And finally, I understand.

They don't know.

They only call themselves the Last Teenagers on Earth because it's a cool name that Brooklyn came up with. Because, before me, nobody ever showed up at their doorstep, and they're living their days as if nothing has changed. Andy told me about the plague, but that's all she knows. They think some of the planet got wiped out, but they don't know how much.

"There's nothing," I say carefully, my words measured. "There's nothing left."

They blink, expecting more.

"There's no one else out there," I say. "I went from Montana to Connecticut, Florida to Texas. It's been six months since I saw another living soul."

I can't read their expressions. Rayen turns away, as if she's suddenly thinking about something else, but I can see the anger in her deep eyes and her tightening jaw. Brooklyn looks stunned, Avani like she's about to cry.

"No one?" Brooklyn asks tentatively, as if she's hoping that I'm lying.

I shake my head. "That's why I was so shocked when I heard your voice on the radio." I try to explain things as gently as I can, but there's no good way to break this kind of news. "I thought you all knew."

"We haven't had any contact with the outside," Rayen says,

keeping her voice even. But she's not as good an actress as she thinks she is. "We know nothing."

"Well…" I say. "There's good reason for the name you go by. For all I know, the aliens have taken over everything. And we may indeed be the last surviving teenagers. We're probably the last human beings on Earth."

Brooklyn slams her fist against the table so hard that it makes me jump. Just as she opens her mouth to say something, she turns and freezes.

I quickly glance over to where she's looking, and I see someone in the doorway.

This girl is taller than the rest of them, and her blond hair falls in waves over her white shoulders. Her eyes are an icy blue, a color that I've only seen in the frozen lakes of Montana. Her jaw is set and her whole look gives off a dangerous, menacing attitude.

"Boss," Brooklyn perks up, her face betraying the emotion that she's trying to hide. "I didn't know you were coming."

The girl doesn't answer for a few seconds. She doesn't cross her arms or approach us. But I can see her alpha position from here—they all deeply respect her.

"I thought we had rules, Brooklyn."

"Sorry," Brooklyn mutters.

"She was supposed to stay in isolation," the girl says, emphasizing her words carefully.

Brooklyn doesn't respond this time. But I don't have to sit here while she talks about me like I'm not in the room. Whoever she is, I'm not afraid of her. I've seen far worse things than a blond girl with a bossy attitude.

"We need to talk," she says to Brooklyn. "And someone put this girl back in isolation, where she belongs."

"You can't just hide the truth from them," I say, turning to her and speaking before I can stop myself. I don't care who she thinks she is. "They deserve to know."

"I'm the one who gets to decide that," Violet replies.

I get up from the table and walk toward her.

"I don't know what kind of hellhole you're running here," I say, stopping right in front of her. Logically, my best shot would be to keep my head down, but in this case, I'm willing to part with logic. Because logic is also telling me that we need all the information we can get. And that means sharing. "You don't hide this kind of information. You just don't."

I glance at Brooklyn and the others, who are looking at me like they don't know whether to be afraid of me or to cheer me on.

I'm tired of being feared, and I'm sick of being alone.

And I know that I've already made my decision, even if I didn't mean to. Rayen's words had hit me—they really don't know anything.

"Let's talk," I say to Violet. "Alone."

CHAPTER 14

Violet's footsteps are sure and calm, echoing down the sterile halls of Area 51. Her boots are made of pure leather, and they're the finest I've seen in ages. I didn't raid any houses that had boots as nice as hers, and I'm willing to bet my own crappy pair that Violet wasn't a girl who was raiding houses in her spare time.

She turns and enters a room, and I follow her. I don't like acting like a meek dog, but whether I'm in trouble or not, these people have given me good food and a hot shower. That's better than what I had before.

I stand in the middle of what appears to be an office, waiting for her to say something. Her demeanor is very different from the others', so it throws me off. She sits in a comfortable chair behind a desk and trains her blue eyes on me. I don't intend to speak first, because I'm sure that's what she's trying to make me do—back down.

"So," she starts after we've been in an uncomfortable silence for more than a minute. "It's Clover, right? Brooklyn tells me that you made quite an entrance here."

I resist the urge to respond to her tone with a "Yes, ma'am." This girl isn't older or better than I am, and she has no right to order me around.

"Okay. You're not going to talk, so I will." She leans forward, her blond hair falling in waves of golden light. "You might not understand this yet, but we have rules here. Just like any other place on earth." She doesn't correct herself. "So if you want to stay here, you're going to have to obey the rules. First things first, you do not want to question my authority on any matter."

I know better than to interrupt her. This room gives no clues as to who she really is, or was, before the attack, which makes it harder to guess what she's like. But unlike the others, I feel like she's right where she belongs.

"I hope we're clear on that."

"Yes," I answer her calmly. "We're clear."

"Okay." She nods her head. "So no talking about the outside. Or what is happening beyond the compound."

"You can't mean to keep them in the dark."

Violet glares at me. "It's hard enough to keep hope alive without the outside interfering. I have a lot to deal with here."

"I hate to break it to you, but aliens invaded Earth, and the entire human population is dead," I reply.

For a second, she looks taken aback, but she quickly controls her face.

"The outside interferes," I continue. "You can't pretend that you're all on a fucking vacation."

"What's happening here is none of your business."

I set my jaw. I get what she means. Down here, the atmosphere is almost happy, like some kind of big summer camp. The thing is, it's not summer, there are no schools or camps or vacations anymore, and everyone else in the world is dead.

"Sit down," she says, and this time, I obey. I sit down and face this girl who doesn't take any bullshit. "So you want to leave?"

I don't know how to respond to that. After a moment, I ask, "How did you know?"

She shrugs. "I see you, Clover. You've been on the outside for too long. Being around people again? It isn't easy. It also means that you can't take an all-on-your-own approach to life anymore."

She looks hard at me, like she wants me to crack. But I know this strategy—it's the same one I'd use. There's a crucial difference between Violet and me, though. Nothing she has to say can bother me.

"You done?" I ask her with a straight face. "My turn. You, Violet, like to be in charge. I'm a wild card among your perfectly stacked little deck. I'm pretty sure you've already decided that you don't like me, but whatever. So here goes: you act tough, and you probably are tough, but my guess is that you haven't left Area 51 since the world ended. That's none of my business, but you don't get to tell me about the outside. I've been there. For the last six months. I don't know whose choice it was to hide the truth, but it wasn't a brilliant one. Pretending that nothing is happening is not a strategy. *The world fucking ended.* And we have to deal with that, and not stay sheltered in this happy little bubble."

Violet looks at me with her harsh blues. She doesn't flinch. "Are you done?"

"No," I answer, because I'm not and because I'm pissed off. "I'm willing to bet that you're an only child, probably raised by distant parents. So when they died, you thought you should follow their example—be distant and commanding, like you've got to protect these poor losers who look up to you. You're not wrong to want to protect them, but hiding the truth from them isn't a good policy. So I guess you have two choices: kick me out and risk being seen as an actual dictator, or let me stay. And deal with the consequences."

She doesn't seem offended, which doesn't really surprise me. I think I've figured out exactly who Violet is—someone too much like myself. And then she does surprise me. She smiles.

"You're good," she says. "But as much as I'd really like to kick you out right now, I won't. Do you know why, Clover? Because you need us. And I'm not so terrible as to deny you that."

I don't respond. The worst part is—she's right.

Because I've learned that there's a difference between being alone and being lonely. I had never been lonely before. I'd always had my grandparents. For a while, I had Noah. I had people who cared about me, and I never realized how much I would miss that until they were gone. Until the world turned to dust and I was the only one left standing.

"You can't keep hiding things from them," I say at last. "Even if you want to. I've already told them about the outside."

"Look, we've been on lockdown ever since the last adults came back and died here," she says. "We haven't had any news since then. The last they told us, people were still fighting back. Humans were still trying to win."

"How long ago was that?"

"Five months. All the others were already here."

That's why they were so hopeful. They'd watched the last of the adults die, and the other kids, too. But they still hoped that there'd be something left, if they just kept themselves really quiet and waited.

"So what's the plan?"

Violet raises a single eyebrow at me. "The plan?" she asks.

"Yes," I say, impatiently. It's been six months since the invasion started. They haven't been on the run—they've all been here together, safe. Surely they've been working on something to fight back. "The plan."

Violet blinks. "Clover, there is no plan."

For a second, I think I've misheard her. But Violet doesn't mispronounce words. She doesn't hesitate. Everything about her is calculated.

She's been on lockdown since the last adults returned. She's locked herself and the others away, for good.

I don't know what I expected.

"That can't be," I say. My tongue suddenly feels like sandpaper. "You have everything here. Resources, people. We can fight this."

"No, we can't," she replies. "We're just trying to survive."

"Of course we can. Surviving means nothing if we just stay locked up here forever."

"Then convince me how."

I see kindness and pity in Violet's eyes as she watches me process the situation. And I hate it.

I had hoped that someone here would have the answers. But they don't. Of course they don't.

No one does.

They'd all rather stay here and throw welcome parties and take showers and eat good food and not talk about aliens— screw the rest of the world.

Anger bubbles in my blood and tears form in the back of my eyes. We were supposed to fight back together. We were supposed to have *something*.

But once again, I'm left with nothing.

CHAPTER 15

Adam, the boy who reminds me of Noah, is waiting for me outside the door, Sputnik by his side. I quickly wipe the tears from my face, trying to pretend that they're not there. Sputnik circles around me three times, her tail brushing against my legs.

I crouch down to look at her, and she licks my tears, as if she knows that I want to wipe them from existence.

"You all right?" Adam asks. He stands there in his shy, nice-guy pose, which is cute but doesn't cut through my armor. "Was she tough on you?"

"I'm fine," I say, which doesn't really answer his question, but it'll do for now.

"Are you sure?"

I don't know why he cares. We barely know each other.

"Yeah. It was nothing."

"Brooklyn is really sorry she asked about the outside," he says. He seems hesitant, with his hands in his pockets, unsure of how to move.

"She shouldn't be." My voice has an edge of anger. "She has a right to ask. You all do."

He looks at me straight on, and it's unnerving how much he reminds me of Noah. Especially that shade of gray-blue in his eyes. I look at my feet.

"So is it true?"

"Yeah," I reply. "It's true."

"What was it like?"

I can tell that a part of him doesn't want to know. A part of me doesn't want to answer. But I owe it to all of them to share my knowledge.

"It's empty," I tell him. Because I walked for miles and miles and all I saw was blackened bodies in the streets and, where there were no bodies, dust in the air. Because I know that, unless there was some kind of miracle, we are indeed the last ones left on the planet. The ones who were forgotten. "Just like everyone went on a vacation."

There's a deep sadness in his eyes when I say this, and it's something that I've come to know.

He wipes some tears away, taking it in. He's probably wondering about the things that I've seen and he hasn't.

"I saw some of it," he says. "When I was making my way down with Brooklyn and Avani. I never thought I'd miss seeing houses." He pauses, taking a deep breath, then looks right into

110

my eyes. "But I do, you know? I miss seeing the blue sky and the landscape."

We fall silent.

"Want to see something?" he asks lamely.

Without knowing why, I nod. I follow him into a corridor, and he leads the way toward a distant staircase. Then we climb through the dark up a ladder, and when he finally opens a trapdoor, twilight greets me. Sputnik stays behind, whining.

We're at the top of one of the watchtowers. Here, I can see Area 51 in its entirety, its fences and barbed wires, and then miles of desert.

"I come up here a lot," Adam says.

I look around. I can understand why he likes it—maybe if he tries hard enough, he can pretend not to see the emptiness.

"I like it."

Adam sits on the wall, his legs dangling. I follow suit, letting the breeze rustle my hair.

For a moment, looking at the sky and feeling the wind on my face reminds me of airplanes, of how it used to feel when I could go up high and not be afraid.

"I couldn't salvage the car, you know."

I give him the smallest hint of a grin. "It wasn't the first one I've wrecked. I actually can't drive that well."

"How many?"

"Don't laugh."

"I won't."

"Thirteen."

Adam opens his mouth in a wide *O*, a caricature of disbelief. "Is there anything that you actually can drive?"

Looking at the sky right now hurts, like my heart is breaking at the sight of it. "Yeah. Planes."

"Really?"

I nod. "My abuelo was an air force pilot. He taught me."

He looks at me quickly, as if he's afraid to ask. "With the invasion?"

I nod. Sympathetic words are empty now, and he doesn't bother saying them. Silence is more comforting, because it's true. "Yeah. End of the world blows."

Adam nods, and for a moment, I let myself miss them.

"I wish I could remember them without the sadness," I finally find myself saying. "And only remember the good stuff." It feels good to let the words out, to let go of just a little control.

"That does happen, eventually," he says, and I wait for him to go on. "I lost my dad when I was eight."

I nod.

"He was in the army," he continues. "One day, he just didn't come home. They sent a medal in his place. They told us to be proud, that Dad had died a hero. But I couldn't understand how a scrap of metal could substitute for a person."

"Because it can't."

He nods. "That person will never come back. It doesn't matter how they died. They died. End of story." He sighs, and I understand perfectly how he feels. "After a while, you get used to it, I guess. Now I remember the good stuff. He used to make waffles when he was home, and he would always burn them. Mom and I would eat them and pretend that they didn't taste terrible." He pauses. "But sometimes, it hits again. The pain is kind of like the tide."

His voice fades a little at the end of the sentence. And in that moment, I realize what it's like to really relate to another human being. For a second, I understand Adam.

"So," he says, trying a smile. "What's your story?"

I'm taken aback by his question, because it's not like Brooklyn's or the others'. He really wants to know.

"Raised by my grandparents. I've only seen my mom in pictures."

"That must suck."

"Not so much. It's not like I can miss her." You can't miss something you never had.

He looks at me. "Do you ever wonder if…?"

I know where his thoughts are going. I've wondered this myself a couple of times in the last six months. If my mother were alive, would I recognize her? I don't even know if she was alive before the aliens landed. She came home one day with a baby in her arms and left during the night. No one ever heard from her again.

"It doesn't matter. She's not really my mother, you know? If she's out there, she's only a stranger." I pause. I don't pity myself. I don't pity my mother, either. "And if she's dead, I mourn for her like I mourn for the rest of humanity."

"And how's that?"

"A little. And sometimes not at all."

He nods, turning his gaze back to the horizon. And we just let ourselves stay there in silence, until we are engulfed in darkness.

CHAPTER 16

I don't see Violet after our talk.

I don't think she's avoiding me, but maybe she doesn't want to face the reality that I brought to her door. None of them do. They asked me about what happened out there, and then they promptly erased it from their memories.

I've been around almost all of Area 51 now—between patrol duty, the labs, feeding the chickens, and cooking and cleaning duties. It's peaceful, and even Sputnik has gotten used to the routine, even if she does constantly try to steal my place in bed when there are twenty other bunks available. Most of the doors have been locked for safety, and Brooklyn has taken me on a complete tour of the area, including the old compound where Area 51 first started, the chicken coop, the farming grounds, and the lounge.

Almost two weeks after my arrival, I decide to spend a day with Brooklyn and Andy in the computer rooms. There are rooms and rooms filled with the fastest processors the government could afford. Brooklyn explained to me that the base's generators were powered by nuclear energy, and they're supposed to keep going for years without interruption.

When I enter the room, Andy and Brooklyn are engaged in a fierce game of *Mortal Kombat*, each trying to punch the other out.

"Hey Clover," Brooklyn says without looking up from the screen. "Care for a game?"

"I haven't played in ages," I answer. I only ever played video games at Noah's house, and he used to get annoyed because I'd get sidetracked by all the quests in *Assassin's Creed* and never finish the main plot. "So this is what you guys do all day?"

"Gotta keep the radio going," Brooklyn says with a grin. "I mean, you heard it. There could be others."

"I heard it by accident."

"No need to be harsh," Andy says.

She beats the hell out of Brooklyn, who throws the controller on the desk.

"It's on a loop," Brooklyn says. "But I like changing the songs. I miss just listening to the radio."

"If anyone hears the *Hamilton* soundtrack one more time, they'll come all the way over here just to commit murder."

Andy leans back in her chair. In front of her are more than a few screens showing different areas of the compound. They keep jumping around between images, and I glimpse Avani and Flint in the laboratory running some experiment, and Rayen patrolling the perimeter again.

"Can you see everything from here?"

Andy looks up and nods. "Yeah, why?"

"Just wondering," I say. "What kind of security do you have in place? In case anyone else comes knocking?"

"It's secure," Andy says. "This is a secret government base. It doesn't get more secure than that. Half of the facility is underground. We've got traps. We've got missiles. We saw you coming from miles away."

Missiles won't do anything. I saw the devastation in the cities, saw the news when the TV was still working. There is no weapon that will stop them. But I don't tell them that, because it doesn't help me accomplish anything.

"What about the Area 51 archives?"

Andy turns in her chair. "Violet doesn't let us look at them," she says. "It's in the rule book."

"So you all just do everything she says?" I lean against the desk, and Sputnik sneaks in behind me. "No rules are ever broken?"

"Rules keep us alive," Andy says.

"Rules keep you misinformed, too," I say. I turn to Brooklyn, sensing that she's much more of a rebel than Andy is. "Didn't you ever look?"

"I got here the same week that the adults came back in," Brooklyn says. "Everyone was too concerned with not coughing their lungs out and trying to stay alive."

"And since then?"

"Since then we've stayed here," Andy answers. "Clover, did you just come here to annoy us into doing something that we *don't* want to do?"

"It was an honest question," I say, trying not to sound as annoyed as I actually am. "I'm just wondering why it's never occurred to anyone to fight back."

At that, Brooklyn laughs bitterly. "Fight back? Right. Clover, you're the one who's actually seen it out there." She shakes her head. "It's nothing short of a miracle that I'm alive. I'm not going to risk my life again for nothing."

"It's not for nothing."

"Of course it is," Brooklyn says, incredulity in her face. "I mean, when you were alone out there, did you fight back?"

She turns to me, and my cheeks burn. I know they're getting redder as she stares, her green eyes defiant.

"No."

"That's what I'm talking about," Brooklyn says, getting up. "You can't come here and ask us to do something that you weren't ready to do yourself."

She shakes her head and walks out of the room. I chew on the inside of my cheek as Andy adjusts her glasses and looks over at me.

I let out a sigh and sit in Brooklyn's chair.

Andy hands me the controller and changes the game to *Galaga*. She starts firing on insects as fast as they appear on the screen. I try to play along, but my fingers aren't as quick on the controls. Andy's solidarity is the silent kind, as if she doesn't know how to finish the conversation, either.

"It's not your fault," she finally says. We both keep our gazes fixed on the screen. "Violet told me you asked about the plan."

I look over at her and meet her blue eyes. "And?"

Andy shrugs, turning back to the screen. "I mean, what do you expect? We're just a bunch of teenagers. We're not some superhero force destined to save the world. We're just conserving our energy."

"But we're not alone," I say. "That's the difference. Together, we can do something."

"There were seven billion of us," Andy says, her voice neutral. "We still dropped like flies."

It's the way that she says it that gets me. It's the way that they feel like there's nothing worth fighting for. That we can't make a difference, because the others couldn't.

The difference is I am alive—*we* are alive.

The rest of humanity isn't.

CHAPTER 17

I can't fall asleep that night. After a while, I give up on the notion entirely and sit up in bed.

"Still have nightmares?" a quiet voice calls out in the dark. I turn and see Rayen, curled up in her bunk bed with a book. A small reading light is clipped to the cover, dimmed so as not to wake the others.

I nod, my vision blurred.

"Yeah. Happens to all of us," she mutters, nodding her head toward a shelf in the corner. "You can pick a book, if you want. Helps pass the time."

I look to my side and see Brooklyn's messy black hair. She sleeps soundly, her breath even. In, out, in, out. I get up and pad softly to the bookshelf. Andy turns in her sleep, shifting from one side to the other, probably plagued by nightmares, too. Avani's head is covered with blankets, like some kind of protective shield.

There isn't a wide selection of books to be had—mostly crime novels and old sci-fi classics, none of which really interest me. I pick a book at random, only to see that it's a *Star Trek* novelization. I grimace, sliding it back onto the shelf.

"Holy Saint Barbie of Rainbow Skittles." Andy looks up. "Just choose one."

"Shut up, Andy," Rayen tells her. Andy shakes her mousy hair, trying unsuccessfully to go back to sleep. "That's Andy's way of swearing. We've all picked it up."

"I tolerate the light, but not conversation," Avani hisses from her bed, uncovering herself and pulling her blankets away from her body. She wears a white nightgown that looks like it must have been handmade back in the 1920s.

I try not to roll my eyes. I pick another book and see that it's a Jane Austen novel, lost among all the other lowbrow titles. Criticizing society feels especially pointless now, but I think I can appreciate Austen's irony more than I can stomach hopeful depictions of benevolent aliens.

I take it back to my bed, but by now, it's clear that nobody is going to be able to go back to sleep. The only one who's still sleeping soundly is Brooklyn, who is snoring with her mouth hanging open.

Rayen slams her book closed, setting it on her bedside table. "What now?"

"Sleepover party?" Andy suggests with a huge yawn. "We could watch a movie."

"You have movies?" I frown, but then I remember that they have everything here, since they've stayed hidden and have their own power generators.

"Of course we do." Andy rolls her eyes. "This isn't the barn you grew up in."

Rayen and Avani both throw her a nasty look, as if warning her against something. I raise an eyebrow.

"What? Brooklyn did say she had a farm. Or something. Who cares?"

"Yeah, it was a farm," I say, my voice icy. "But we still had Netflix."

I try to shrug the whole thing off, but there's something about this need to be accepted into this new group, this need to fit in, that annoys me. I came all this way because I didn't want to be alone. This is what I've wanted for so long— someone else on this planet besides myself. But now that my prayers have been answered, there's still a part of me that would rather go back to the way it was. Me, Sputnik, and the road ahead.

Avani tries to calm me down, saying, "I'm sorry. Really. We know that you've just arrived and you're still adapting to a new situation. It's hard."

Brooklyn shifts, the noise finally waking her up.

"Well," I say, trying to control my temper. "Yes, it must have been *so* hard for you all to have to adapt to having nice things, like hot meals and movies and talking to your besties every day." My tone turns especially nasty at that last phrase.

Avani and Andy look at me, shocked. But I didn't make it all the way here just to keep my mouth shut.

"Clover," Rayen says, eyeing me like I'm a wounded animal. "That's not what she meant."

I don't want to bite back any of the bile rising to my throat, any of my disgust. I can't just forget the fact that they were all sitting on their asses while the world was blown to bits.

"I don't care what you all think of me," I spit. "The difference between me and you is that I survived out there. I'd like to see you all try."

Shoving myself back under the covers, too tired to go on like this, I ignore their outrage and my anger and try to sleep.

- - - - - - - - -

The next morning, I make my way through the silent corridors. When I enter the messroom, everything goes quiet.

My bare feet thud softly against the slippery floor. Brooklyn and Rayen have their eyes glued to me, but Avani and Andy are intent on pretending that they haven't noticed me come in.

"Morning," I say, out of politeness.

"Morning," Flint answers, oblivious to the tension in the room. "Sleep well?"

I don't smile. "As well as I could."

I sit down at the table, where they've set out cereal and cookies and peanut butter and even some bread that looks freshly baked. I grab some of everything, filling my mouth like a hungry scavenger. Flint watches me in amazement, probably wondering how much food I can actually stuff into my mouth at once. The girls continue to make an effort to ignore me.

I regret ever coming here.

"Who's on patrol duty today?" Brooklyn finally asks, breaking the silence.

"Me," answers Rayen. "Violet was supposed to be with me today."

I still haven't seen Violet since our conversation.

Finally, Brooklyn sighs. "Okay, Clover, what was that last night?"

Heads turn in my direction, and I catch Rayen glaring menacingly at Brooklyn. I've only been here for a few weeks, but I already know that Brooklyn won't shut up about this kind of thing. It's probably beyond Brooklyn to keep her mouth shut at all.

"Maybe you guys should tell me what it was," I reply, taking a big bite of bread on purpose, to fill my mouth. "I got the impression that you're the ones who don't want me here."

"I want you here," Andy offers, but her comment gets lost in the void that seems to be filling the room.

"Thanks," I mutter.

"Maybe the problem is that *you* don't want to be here," Avani says, turning her brown eyes on me, like she's trying to psychoanalyze me. I want to spare her the frustration and tell her that I'm too crazy to be put into one category.

"Maybe it is," I concede. "So what?"

Silence fills the room again. I realize too late that this was the wrong thing to say. It's been so long since I've had to worry about what's the right or the wrong thing to say. There's an art to making people hear what you want them to hear, to saying the exact words that will get you what *you* want. Sometimes it's about emotion, and sometimes it's about logic. It depends on who the person is and what you want from them. Even though I've never had a lot of friends, I always knew how to deal with this sort of thing when I needed to.

And I know that I've said the wrong thing.

"So what?" Brooklyn repeats, with an edge in her voice. I've hurt her. I barely know this girl, but for some reason I already have the power to hurt her. "Are we really so bad that you think the outside is better?"

"That's not what I meant."

"People skills, Clover," Brooklyn says. "Not very smooth."

"It's not about being smooth," I say, deciding to go with logic. You can't contest logic. You can fake feelings as much as you like, but there's no beating pure, simple logic. "It doesn't matter whether you want me here or not. What matters is that you aren't willing to do anything about this situation, unless it involves acting like total cowards."

They all stare at me, stunned, but I can see that my words have hit home. That's what I was going for.

"We can't do anything while—" Flint starts.

"Don't give me that bullshit," I argue. "Violet's already

tried. You've been here for six months. Six months, just sitting back, watching movies, doing God knows what, and not one of you has ever bothered to look at what's happening outside?"

"The satellites—"

"Still work," I say. "Or did they just fall out of the sky? You *chose* this. All of you did."

I get up, my hands balling into fists from anger. This is not on me.

I expected something different, and they haven't delivered. I expected to find *survivors*. I wanted a plan of action, a way to make sure that surviving was worth it in the first place. That I hadn't survived for six months for nothing.

"You don't have to stay here," Brooklyn says quietly.

I look each of them in the eye. I wish I could look Violet in the eye, too.

I feel their cowardice and fear and anger all mixed in the air, and a lot of unspoken words. I've seen it before, reflected back at me in the mirror. It's hopelessness, the same desperate feeling that has made me raise my gun to my head so many times.

I can't save them from it. I can barely save myself.

That night, when everyone is asleep, I get up. The other girls are breathing deeply, and the light is dim. I shove Sputnik off the bed, and she pads around quietly on the floor, understanding our need to be silent.

I pick up my bag and wait until I'm outside the room to

put my boots on. Andy's gloves are in my pocket, and Sputnik follows me down the hall. I stop by the pantry, packing up some food that won't spoil on the journey.

I slide on the gloves and touch the fingerprint scanner. It lights up green, but as I step through the door, I hear a noise behind me.

Rayen stands there in the dark. She emerges with the moonlight and the wind that passes through the door.

"So, you're leaving?" she asks.

There's something about the shadowy moonlight, or maybe it's the darkness hiding our faces, that makes me tell the truth.

"I can't stay," I tell her. "Not like this."

"There's nothing out there."

"There's nothing in here, either, Rayen," I say. "Staying here or going out there, it's the same thing. You proved that to me."

The clouds pass, and I can see her face again. She stands still, wearing a beaten checkered shirt.

"What do you hope to find out there?"

"Anything is better than this."

Maybe it works for them, staying here, suspended in time, just like the fate of the earth. It doesn't work for me. If I stay here, I'll just die faster.

Only one thing has kept me alive all this time: moving. I have to keep moving, to keep trying to find something else.

In a way, these people have given me hope. I found them, so maybe I can find others. Maybe all I have to do is look harder. I can make that my next objective, now that I know I'm not alone in the world.

I wait, breathing hard.

"I don't want to go out there any more than you do," I admit. "But as far as this place goes, it's nothing like I imagined it would be."

"Yeah. The world ended and people still suck." She shrugs. "That's the way it is. People don't miraculously get nicer just because the world ended. We keep on being who we are."

Rayen is brutally honest. She states everything with a simplicity that leaves no room for masking things with flowers and perfumed lies.

"We've been here for a long time, Clover. The outside isn't better. Human contact isn't necessarily better, either. But it's what you've got right now."

She has a point.

"I can't give you a good reason to stay," Rayen says. "But at least you know that this is what you'll get. If you choose to stay, you choose this."

"Choose what?" I ask, my voice biting in anger. "There's nothing to choose here."

Rayen gives me a sad smile, which tells me she knows I'm only putting up a front. She reaches out to squeeze my shoulder. It's the smallest of touches, and I freeze in place from her compassion.

"The chance to not feel alone anymore," Rayen says. She slowly turns away from the door, making her way back inside.

I don't reply. If I stay, it means dealing with all this. We're each individuals, but we're either together or we're alone. That's what she means.

I have a choice to make. Either I walk out of here right now, take Sputnik, and go, or I stay. Stay and give them a good reason to wake up. A good reason to fight, to break free of this apathy and hopelessness that has overcome us all. We can't just keep waiting until the day we turn to dust.

I can't leave them.

Not yet.

Not without giving it my best shot.

And I know what I have to do.

CHAPTER 18

I find Adam in the garage the next morning, working on the car that I rendered useless. His big hands are covered in grease, and I watch him intently as he works underneath it.

"I thought I destroyed that thing," I say, and Adam jumps, hitting his head pretty hard against the metal. "Sorry. Should've knocked or something."

He gets out from under the car, massaging his head.

"You busy?" I ask.

"Not really," he says, gesturing to the wrecked car. "Why? Are you planning to bring in more cars?"

I laugh. "No." I pause and choose my next words carefully. "I'm sorry about yesterday."

He wipes his hands on a towel, looking at me. "That's okay. It was all in the heat of the moment."

I nod, biting my lower lip, trying to finding my way around this conversation.

"Brooklyn told me to find something that I like to do," I say casually. "And I hear that you're the one to see about airplanes."

Adam's face lights up. "Yeah, of course," he says. "Let's see what we have."

I almost feel guilty as I follow him, the wheels of a plan turning in my mind.

Almost.

We walk through the halls of Area 51, dark and silent. This place is supposed to be welcoming, a refuge, but it's nothing of the kind to me.

"Is there something specific that you're looking for?" Adam asks, looking back at me. "I mean, I've only been down here once. I'm not sure what all the models are."

I shrug. "Not really. I just want to see them again," I tell him. "Just to remember."

It's not a lie, but it's not the truth, either.

Adam stops in front of a huge gate. It's different from the other doors in the building—triple the size, built to fit vehicles larger than a small truck. My heart beats fast when I look at the huge door, as if I can sense what's behind it.

He puts his hand over a panel, and it blinks green.

The doors slide open, and I take in the biggest underground bunker I've ever seen. Just ahead of me are rows of military trucks, loaded down with weapons.

I don't realize that I'm running until I feel the adrenaline rushing and my heart hammering against my chest. And then I stop.

Beyond the trucks, more rows of machines await. Machines I know. My heart breaks when I think about who would love to see this right now. But Abuelo is dead—and I have to enjoy this for the both of us.

Rows and rows of planes sit beyond a yellow line. I can see Lockheed A-12 prototypes that should've been destroyed years ago. Rows of F-15 Eagles greet me like old friends. There are MiG-31 Foxhounds, F-16 Fighting Falcon, F-22A Raptors and an F-111 Aardvark, exactly like the one Abuelo used to fly in the air force.

I don't hesitate.

I approach the nimble Aardvark and touch my fingers to the metal. And it feels like I'm home again.

This is a stupid idea and I know it. Adam stands in the other corner of the bunker, oblivious to what I'm about to do.

I leave the Aardvark and head for the plane that I know will get the job done, a legendary, unbeatable jet. It's a Lockheed SR-71 Blackbird. Major General Eldon Joersz and Lieutenant Colonel George Morgan broke all speed records with it in 1976. Only a total of thirty-two were ever built. The program was terminated in '89, due to Pentagon politics, not because the craft was obsolete. It was reopened briefly but shut down for good in

1998. Some of the models ended up in museums and some were lost. I'm not surprised to find one of them here, stashed away in the biggest collection of fighter jets that I've ever seen.

Abuelo took me for a ride in an F-15 Eagle at Malmstrom last year, for my sixteenth birthday. I've never been in a Blackbird. But I have to believe that this is going to work.

Hanging on the wall near the plane is a G suit, which I quickly put on—the plane isn't pressurized, so I'll need the suit to handle high altitudes. I climb my way into the cockpit. Settling inside it, I turn on the comm unit and start up the plane. Adam has clearly realized what I'm up to—I see him waving his arms and shouting—but I can't hear him over the roar of the engines.

This is my only chance.

I put on the helmet and test the controls. A smile tugs at the corner of my mouth. I place my hand on the joystick and don't let myself think as I maneuver onto the runway.

Adam's yelling frantically now, but in a few seconds, he's lost from sight.

I let go of the joystick for an instant and allow a squeal of glee to escape my lips. I press the button that opens the bunker's sky hatch. The plane flies through the hatch in the ceiling unscathed. I have this under control.

The hatch closes behind me. I risk a look from the window and, seeing the whole area covered in dust, I'm impressed by how well the camouflage system works. If I didn't know better, I would never guess that there's a hatch there.

The plane easily breaks the wind. I can feel its power beneath my fingers, power that can only be wielded if you know how to do it. I can't help but think about how much I've wanted to fly one of these and how different these circumstances are from what I always imagined.

The wind rushes past and I cut through the air, spinning. An orange button starts blinking on the instrument panel, and I open the intercom channel, preparing myself for the outrage that awaits me on the other end.

"Clover!" Adam hisses. "What are you doing?"

"Testing something."

"Get back here, or God help me, I'll…"

I grin. Being in the sky again makes me feel like I can defy the whole world. "You coming to get me?"

Another voice chimes in over the intercom. "Who the hell is in that plane?" asks Andy.

"It's Clover."

"Holy Mother of Sweetened Peas," she says. "Those planes are supposed to fly with a pilot and a navigator!"

"We're a little short-staffed."

"Bring that thing down, now!" she orders. "Are you crazy?"

I look at the radar. There's nothing yet. My fingers grip the joystick, and I breathe in and out.

"I know what I'm doing," I tell them. *I do*, I tell myself.

"The plane hasn't crashed yet, so I hope you're right," says Adam.

"I'm tracking you," Andy says.

"Don't!" I shout and the plane shudders. "Don't! They might track the signal back to you."

Andy mutters a curse on the intercom. Adam is silent.

This is taking too long, and I'm starting to wonder if my theory is wrong.

"Oh my God," Adam says over the intercom, and I can guess what he's seeing.

"I've got you on screen through a satellite," says Andy. "Are you insane? Come back!"

"Andy, shut up and look at the screen," says Adam.

Another curse follows. This is a stealth plane, but it doesn't manage to evade the aliens' attention. I can feel the force of an incoming shot, and I dodge it with a quick dip of my wing. The laser beam hits the ground with a boom, and I dive as low as I can, practically grazing the desert.

"Clover," Andy mutters. "There are two of them on your tail."

I look at my radar. "Yep. I can see 'em."

"*You can see them?* Is that all you're going to say?"

I should be afraid, but all my fear is gone. I'm back where I belong. They can't take this feeling away from me.

The two spaceships on my tail confirm what I've suspected. Any plane that tries to fly will be taken down. I could drive a car for days on end, but they'll go after a plane, or anything airborne, within minutes. Why? Why do they want to take down our aircraft so badly?

I don't have time for questions. I need to dodge the aliens

first. I pull up and gain altitude. They're trying to pick up on my contrail, but their ships were made for the stars. My plane was made to fly here on Earth, on *my* planet. And they're not going to beat me on my own turf.

I speed up, rising to the clouds. The Blackbird can reach an insane Mach 3.3, but I'm not crazy enough to try that without a navigator. And although I can't shoot the aliens, I can slow them down. It's time to play a game.

I open the missile hatch. Adam and Andy will want to murder me right now. I press the button anyway and grin as the missiles lock on their target.

They're right on my tail now, so I release a burst of chaff, which hits the air like metal confetti, to confuse their radar. Their guns start shooting at me and I make evasive maneuvers—spinning around two, five, seven times—as the plane climbs higher.

The two spaceships keep chasing me through the endless, empty sky as I go up and up toward the stratosphere, turning the plane over so many times that I don't know up from down.

They accelerate and boost their engines as they prepare to cross the stratosphere—they think that I'm heading to outer space. They're catching up, and I wait until they're almost on me.

I breathe.

I kill the engines.

The plane hurtles toward the ground in a full-blown dive. The spaceships can't do the same—the aliens are saner than I am. I have nothing to lose.

I count to ten. Breathe in, breathe out. The plane continues to fall.

And then, just when I think I'm going to lose it for good, I turn the engines on. The response is immediate, and the plane is back in my control. Roaring and fighting to stay alive, just like I am.

I accelerate as fast as I can.

"I'm heading for some caves I saw up ahead," I say over the intercom. I press a button and send over the coordinates. "Come pick me up."

CHAPTER 19

It takes a few hours for my ride to arrive. I've hidden the plane inside one of the caves. I lean against the metal hull of the Blackbird, sweating, my gun at my side.

I recognize the war truck when it arrives, but I keep my gun raised until I get visual confirmation of the driver. Adam gets out and walks over to where I'm standing.

He doesn't smile.

"Put it away," he says, nodding toward my gun. All friendliness has disappeared from his voice. I shove the gun in the back of my pants. "What the hell were you thinking?"

"I was thinking that we have an advantage over the aliens," I say, not backing down. "I needed to find a reason to stay and fight. I have it. Right here."

"They could've killed you!"

"They didn't."

He shakes his head, and his face is a deep red.

"What did they say back at the base?" I ask, carefully.

"Do you even care?" he replies, his tone harsh. I don't say anything to contradict him. "Violet is furious. Rayen and Brooklyn think you're Christ reincarnated. Avani wants both your head and your personality tested."

He shakes his head again. The others' reactions don't surprise me. But I've disappointed Adam, and I do feel bad about that.

"You could've put us all in danger."

"I know," I say, meeting his eyes.

This is all part of the plan.

He sighs, his shoulders sagging. "Just help me attach this to the back of the truck."

We work in silence. Adam is pretty strong and so am I. We wrap metal cables around the plane, and I wheel it forward to the platform of the truck. Once we've finished attaching it, I hop in the front of the truck next to Adam.

We drive in silence for a long time before Adam finally speaks. "Violet said that you knew exactly what you were doing when you asked me to show you the planes. Is that true?"

I don't even blink. "Would it make you feel better if I admitted that I'm a manipulative bitch?"

He laughs, in spite of himself. "Yeah. Yeah it would." He glances at me. "You could have just told me what you wanted to do."

"You wouldn't have agreed to let me do it."

"How do you know that?"

"Because you're too nice, Adam."

He doesn't say anything to that. I have to tread carefully with Adam.

"What were you even thinking?" he asks, his knuckles white on the steering wheel. "One wrong move and it would've been over. All of it."

"I wanted to test something."

"Something worth risking your life for?"

What life? I want to spit back at him. What we're doing isn't living. Not really.

"Yeah," I finally say. I cross my arms, eyeing the road.

A few minutes pass, but Adam isn't one to give up. "So what did you want to test?"

I hate explaining stuff to people. I can never find the right words. "You're driving this truck, right? And you've been doing it for forty minutes."

Adam nods, furrowing his eyebrows.

"Notice any spaceships following us?"

He tenses up and his hands grip the wheel even harder.

"There aren't any—you can relax," I tell him, and he does so, visibly. "But it took me less than ten minutes in the air—in a stealth plane—to get two of them on my tail."

"So you knew that they were going to come after you, and you took off anyway?"

I nod, my face serious. "Avani said that we don't have any

advantages," I begin, finding my voice even though my throat is parched. "That we don't know anything about the aliens. That there's no point fighting back because we can't win. But I knew that if I went out there in a plane, they would come after me."

I pause for a moment, letting Adam process my words.

"They're predictable," he says.

I nod. "Look, I understand. I understand that no one wants to fight back. I understand that it's going to be hard and that it might cost us our lives. But I can't live like this. We aren't *living*, Adam. None of us are."

He stays silent for a long time. I watch the road and the desert, the rock formations on the horizon. I miss Sputnik's company.

Just when I think that we're going to spend the rest of the trip in complete silence, Adam speaks again. "So what are you suggesting?"

I look over at him. "I'm saying that we can find a way to fight this."

He nods slowly. "So that's your plan?" he asks. "Use yourself as bait to draw them out?"

"Yeah. I just needed to test the theory."

"How did you figure it out?"

"They never go after cars. I drove across the country, and they never attacked me once. But the second I got an airplane off the ground, they came after me," I explain, adding, "I like to actually drive the vehicles before I render them useless, you know."

He laughs at that, and the tense atmosphere begins to dissipate. "Quick thinking. Crazy, but quick."

"Yeah. I always know what I'm doing."

He narrows his eyes. "Always?"

I nod. "Pretty much."

"No emotion involved?"

I smile, then shrug. "Call me calculating, but yeah. I think stuff through."

"That sounds like a harsh way to live, though," he says after a while. "Don't you think it's sad?"

The truth is that sometimes I do. But at the same time, this is how I've survived.

"Not really," I say. "I guess it's what's kept me alive all this time."

"What do you mean?"

I don't know how to put it into words. So I launch into another bad explanation. "It's just... Anyone who is too emotional wouldn't survive out there."

"I don't get it."

"Okay," I say. "Take Snow White. Sweet and soft and kind. Put her in the middle of nowhere. Take everything from her. Then tell her that, for all she knows, she's the last human being on the entire planet." I glance over and see that Adam isn't smiling anymore. "Does Snow White make it or does she break it?"

He doesn't answer because, really, there's no point. We both know what happens.

"Is that really how you felt?" he asks.

I nod my head.

"How did you do it?"

"There wasn't much to it," I say. "Put one foot in front of the other. Hold your gun to your head a couple of times." I shrug. I still don't know I did it. "Life goes on."

He doesn't say anything for a while. But the question he comes up with next almost makes me smile.

"What do you have here, then?" He taps the left side of his chest.

I know the answer to that one.

"This little red organ," I tell him. "It's called a backup brain."

Adam smiles, like he knows a secret. Like he knows that whatever I say about how tough I am, it isn't 100 percent true.

CHAPTER 20

When we get back, Violet is waiting for me.

She has a look of pure fury on her face that I haven't seen before. Her eyes are filled with an icy anger that freezes everything around me, and she barely gives me time to get out of the truck before she's on me.

Adam moves to follow me, but Violet shakes her head. He steps back, and I follow Violet in silence.

We reach an area of the base that I haven't been to before. At the end of the corridor, she opens a door that leads to an impressive-looking office. It must be part of her personal quarters.

"In." She gestures, and I don't hesitate.

She closes the door and I look around. This office has fancy chairs that match a cherrywood desk with detailed carvings of leaves. The lush green carpet sinks when I step on it, and I wonder if I should take my boots off or if doing that would make Violet think that I'm not taking this seriously. Leaving them on, I sit in one of the chairs in front of the desk as Violet sits down behind it.

I know I'm about to have a serious talking-to, a sermon to rival our priest's back in Montana. I used to sit in church on Sundays and hate having to listen to the pastor talk about some old Bible passage.

I complained about it to Abuela once, and she only had one thing to say: *Take it up with God.*

So I did. That's how I used to spend my time during Sunday mass. That's why I whispered to Abuela's rosary after she was gone, talking to the one person who was supposed to hear me. But talking to God always felt an awful lot like talking to myself. There's only silence in response.

Maybe the aliens have taken Him, too.

"What were you doing?" Violet asks, and I snap back to attention. Her voice is surprisingly calm.

"You told me to convince you that we can fight back," I say. "This is me convincing you."

"I told you to blend in!" Her voice rises, her words unflinching. "I told you to stay put. That you were welcome here. And you repay me by putting us all in danger?"

"I knew what I was doing."

She barks a laugh. "Funny how that doesn't take into consideration everyone else here. You're not alone anymore, Clover.

You can't just do whatever you want. There are more people to consider. We are eight." She breathes in, trying to calm herself. "*The last eight.* Doesn't that mean anything to you?"

I breathe, too, steadying myself. Adrenaline is still rushing through my blood. A few hours ago, I was up in the sky, where no one had the power to stop me. Where I truly belong.

"It does," I finally say. "But I don't want to just sit around here and waste my days away. I don't want to spend the rest of my life in this compound doing nothing, just waiting and waiting and waiting, until we die off, one by one." I take a deep breath, steadying my shoulders. "Violet, I can be the bait. We might not know what these aliens are, or why they came here, but I can be the bait. They're predictable. They don't attack cars, but they do go after anything that's airborne. They're looking for something. And we can set a trap, so that when they come looking for me, we can capture them, and then we'll find a way to win this fight."

My voice breaks as I finish, my throat parched. I'm exhausted to the bone. I don't want to keep fighting.

But it's the only thing I know how to do.

I'm not looking for redemption, for some kind of forgiveness for having survived while others had not. I don't need to atone for my sins. Abuela taught me to believe in many things, but what she always said the most was to never regret anything. Maybe that has made me a bad person; maybe I still have to suffer for the things I've done. But I know how to pick my battles, and I can't let regret keep me from doing what needs to be done.

"You're in the safest place on earth right now," I say, indignation seeping into my voice. "The last remaining sanctuary. You have technology and electricity and goddamned hot showers. Stuff that's been in my dreams for months. Don't tell me that you don't have tech or resources. Don't tell me that you don't have any advantages on your side."

I look at her, breathless. Everything that I've been holding in for months after the invasion has come pouring out, spilled on the table like hot coffee.

"Clover, this is not some sci-fi movie. We're not in some magical reality where Will Smith comes sweeping down from the sky and saves us all."

I don't want to give up. I'm not allowed to.

An idea creeps into my mind. I take out my gun and lay it on the desk for a few seconds. Picking it up, I click the safety off, and a bullet slides into the chamber. For the first time, it doesn't feel heavy in my hands. I put it against my temple, then lay it on the desk again, pointing the barrel at Violet.

"There are easier ways to give up," I say.

Violet looks at the gun with widened eyes and then back at me. All I can do is offer her a simple choice, a choice between surviving and living. Because at the moment, we're not doing either.

"That's exactly what you're doing," I say. "You're putting a gun to your head, but you don't want to pull the trigger."

Violet keeps staring at me, half-stunned.

"Ask me how many times I've put that gun to my head."

Her eyes are wide and blue.

"I'll tell you," I say, when she doesn't speak. "Nine times. Nine times I've loaded that gun and waited. But I couldn't pull the trigger." She doesn't blink. "You might think it's because I didn't want to do a disservice to my grandparents, after everything they sacrificed for me, or because I thought I was the last human left." My voice catches in my throat, and I breathe. "I don't pull it because I'm a coward, and that's the only thing stopping me."

I click the safety on again and slide the metal barrel back into the place where it feels more comfortable. Violet keeps her eyes on the gun the whole time.

"What I'm asking you is this," I say. "Do you want to die a coward like me?"

She doesn't answer.

"I'm not a leader, Violet. I'm just some random girl who showed up on your doorstep. All I'm saying is, please, let's give ourselves a chance."

On our own, we are nothing. Together, we're the Last Teenagers on Earth. Together, we are Earth itself.

I get up and walk out before the tears come.

CHAPTER 21

"Rise and shine!"

This is the first thing that Brooklyn shouts as she comes into the dormitory. I frown at her, still half-asleep. Andy pointedly ignores her, continuing to play a game in her bed. None of us move.

"Come on, let's go!" Brooklyn shouts, like a PE teacher on a cold winter morning.

There are protests all around the room, but we get up all the same. She leads us to a room that I recognize immediately: the war room. It's large, with high ceilings and a huge metal table set up for meetings. Behind the biggest chair is a map of the world that covers the entire wall.

Brooklyn sits next to Avani, which doesn't go unnoticed

by me. I sit next to Andy. The boys are already here. Rayen is the only one who seems relaxed, but that girl isn't afraid of anything. Sputnik sits with her head on my lap, and I pet her absentmindedly. After last night, I'm not sure I'm in the mood for whatever this is.

"Good morning," Violet says as she strides through the door, making all of us jump. "Thanks for coming."

"It's not like we have anything better to do," Brooklyn mutters.

Violet throws her a pointed look. "So," she starts. "Before we begin, is there anyone who would like to say anything about yesterday?"

Violet gives us time. Flint looks at me and shifts uncomfortably, while everyone else avoids my gaze, except Adam, who offers me a small smile.

Andy's hand shoots up.

"Yes, Andy?"

"I couldn't find the powdered milk. It isn't in the pantry."

Violet gives her an exasperated look.

Andy shrugs. "What?"

Violet ignores her. "Fine, if we're all settled, then we can proceed. I have big news. You might be wondering why I called you to the war room for a meeting."

"Not really," says Rayen, which earns her a glare of her own.

What a bunch of idiots. I wonder if the Universe regrets leaving Earth to us.

"This is serious," Violet says. "I know that we've been asking a lot of questions, and we still don't have the answers to most of them. And I need to ask for your forgiveness." She looks at me. "Instead of looking for the answers that we needed, I shut them out. I made a mistake, and I apologize."

The whole room seems stunned by this, myself included. I didn't take Violet for the apologizing type and, apparently, neither did the others. That probably makes her a better person than I took her to be.

She looks at me again, nodding slightly, like I owe her something. But I owe her nothing, and I don't want her to think that I do.

Brooklyn, as always, is the first to express herself. "Are you actually saying that you were wrong, or did we just end up in some kind of freaking apocalypse?"

No one laughs at her joke.

Violet doesn't look amused, but her face is a picture of placid calm. "Are you done?"

"I am. Please go on, Your Bossiness."

"What I'm trying to say is… Maybe we've been sitting in here for too long. And Clover is right. Maybe it's time we find a way to fight back."

The room is silent.

Andy turns to me, alarm on her face. "You can't mean that," she says, turning back to Violet. "We're safe here."

"We're safe here," Violet repeats, and for a moment, I think she's going to forget everything she just said. A shadow passes over her face and then clears. "We're safe. But maybe not for long. I think it's time we use what we have around us, the resources that we've been left with. It's time we fight for our world. Or die trying."

There's silence again.

Then Brooklyn starts clapping, a smile on her face. "Great speech. Not keen on the dying part, but other than that, very good. I give it an A-plus for effort."

"It doesn't need a grade." Beneath her irritation, Violet is smiling. "All I need to know is whether you guys are with me."

We all exchange looks. There's no need for me to say I'm in. And as I look around at these people, so different from one another, I can tell that they're in, too. Andy is the only one who looks uncertain.

"I'm in," Flint says.

"I'm in," Avani echoes.

Rayen shrugs. That means yes.

Adam nods.

Brooklyn responds the only way she can. "Hell yes."

We've all lost something along the way. But among this group of strange misfits, I can't help but feel like we've found something else. Something that's worth fighting for.

Earth, I guess, reflects us. We're broken and, frankly, beaten. But we're also still standing.

So I say, "Count me in."

Violet smiles. "Okay, that's eleven percent of a plan," she says briskly. "But before we go further, I think we should follow this age-old advice." She looks at each of us in turn. "Know your enemy."

CHAPTER 22

Violet presses a button, and a large screen rolls down in front of the wall with the map. It's absurd how easily I've gotten used to things like this again, after surviving for months without electricity. Area 51 is a fully equipped government facility, and it looks like we're finally going to see what kind of resources it has to offer.

The screen lights up, and Violet starts typing on a keyboard.

"I'm gathering the archives that are stored here," she tells us as she pulls up a hard drive. "We should be able to get more information about the invading alien force."

The way she says it sounds so professional. When I say it, it sounds like something out of a bad Tom Cruise movie.

"Here goes," she mutters under her breath, and several different windows pop up. A warning message appears, blocking them, and my heart sinks as I read it: ACCESS DENIED.

Violet looks over at Andy. "Come on, Andy," she says. "Open it up."

Andy makes no move to help. "You told me we wouldn't have to," she says. "You told me we would be safe—"

"You are safe," I cut her off, and Andy turns her widened eyes to me. "But for how long? We can't hole up here forever."

Andy looks like she's about to argue but stays quiet.

"This was not Clover's decision," Violet speaks up, glancing quickly at me. "This is my call."

"But—"

"This is an order from your commander. Open it up."

Andy finally seems to grasp the urgency of the situation. She starts connecting cables from underneath the table to her laptop, and in a matter of minutes, she gets a progress bar going. Everyone seems to hold their breath as the bar slowly reaches 100 percent. The warning disappears, and an instant later, a new message pops up: ACCESS GRANTED.

I'm not prepared for what happens next. Hundreds of folders appear, full of files on research projects, experiments, prototypes, and who knows what else. Within a few minutes, it's obvious that it would take a team of professionals years to sort through all this information. We're just eight teenagers who are running out of time.

The amount of data overwhelms everyone in the room, and even Violet looks shocked as the hard drive continues to vomit its contents on the screen, opening more and more folders by the minute.

The sight makes me sigh wistfully because there is so much here that I wish I had the time to read. It's simply too much, and I know that we won't even be able to get through half of it. That would be impossible. My heart sinks again, knowing that we're going to need more luck than I thought.

"Okay." Violet recovers, and she's back in command. "Look for any relevant information, starting with the most recent files. We're looking for archived reports, charts, satellite images, anything that can give us some insight into what we're dealing with. Stick to your areas of expertise."

A few people grunt in response, and the table lights up as a screen appears in front of each of us. I don't have a specific area—I'm not a genius like half of these kids seem to be—so I'm not sure where to start. I'm good enough at math, good with physics, and I liked history. But I'm not an expert on anything, except for the one thing that they've taken from me forever—flying.

I settle down to my new challenge: digging deeper into the lives of the things who stole mine.

It's hours later when we start fidgeting in our seats. Flint is the first one to break, yawning loudly, which earns him one of Violet's looks.

Unperturbed, Flint yawns again, starting a chain reaction of open mouths all around the room.

Then Brooklyn lets it all go. "Do you know what I would really like?" she asks, but it's a rhetorical question. "A magical robot that could filter all this data and give us the answers. I'd just say, 'Hey robot, do you know how to defeat these aliens?' and the robot would be like, 'Yeah, sure thing. Throw eggs at them.'"

Avani makes a face. "Eggs? That's your idea?"

"Yeah. Why not? Have *you* tried throwing eggs at them?"

"No." Avani rolls her eyes, pursing her lips in disdain. "But it doesn't seem plausible."

"They're aliens—everything is plausible," Brooklyn points out. "It's a theory. We should at least test it out."

"A theory requires a scientific hypothesis."

"Okay. Hypothesis: aliens might be vulnerable to eggs. It's formulated."

"That's not scientific at all!"

"Of course it is. I'll write it down and everything."

Avani looks like she's about to retort, but a glance at Violet stops her.

"Cut the bickering," she scolds both of them.

"Are you sure that NASA doesn't have one of those robots stored somewhere?" Brooklyn asks.

"They don't."

"Pity."

Brooklyn turns back to her reading, but she's distracted now and, consequently, everyone else at the table is, too. Then she looks up again. "What about a bomb?"

Violet sighs loudly. "They've tried bombs. We have video footage of it, if you want to see it. Bombs are useless, except for hurting us. They don't hurt them."

"But the aliens still survived," Flint responds. "Bombs don't work."

"Even if they're DNA-oriented?" Brooklyn asks. "You know, like a biological weapon. What if we could explode a whole species at once? Attack them with a virus?"

Avani shakes her head. "That's just a hypothesis, and practically speaking, it can't be done. Supposing that we could build something like that—and believe me, scientists have tried for years—we'd have to get a sample of their DNA and decode it. From there, we'd have to create a virus that could take out their species—and their species only. In the end, it can't be done anyway, so don't bother with that idea."

Andy fidgets in her chair. We try to get back to the archives, pretending to pay attention, but it's obvious that we can't concentrate anymore.

"We should be asking ourselves real questions," Flint says. "Like how did they get here?"

"Oh yes," Brooklyn replied. "Chatting with aliens. The perfect plan."

Rayen snorts. "What were we supposed to say when we saw the aliens? 'Dagot'ee, welcome to our planet. How long are you staying? Can we get you anything?'"

Adam laughs, and Violet tells us all to shut up and get back to reading. By then, it is too late.

"Enough," says Rayen, with so much conviction that Violet doesn't even question her. "We're not going to get all this reading done in one sitting. Let's be realistic and organize this."

She gets up, retrieves a whiteboard from the corner of the room, and brings it up to the front. For a second, I'm reminded of school and realize that, if everything were normal, that's exactly where I'd be sitting right now. It's November—or at least, I think it is. I've lost count. In July, I even forgot my own birthday.

I let myself wonder what it would be like if I were in school. What classes I'd be taking. Whether I would have met with the college advisor. And on my birthday, Noah would've bought me cake and Abuela would've made tamales for dinner.

My daydream sends me into a guilt trip. I'm reminded of how kind Noah could be, when he wasn't being an asshat. I wonder if, eventually, I would've fallen for him. My biggest regret isn't that he's dead; maybe it's that I didn't love him enough to mourn him. To regret living and leaving him behind.

I'm far too attached to myself for that. And it doesn't matter anymore. They're all dead, but I'm still here.

Rayen slaps her hand against the whiteboard, bringing me back to reality. She takes a marker and throws it at Adam, but Sputnik sees it first, grabbing it in midair. Rayen chases after her.

"Give it back!" she shouts at Sputnik, but the dog is far out of her reach. She dashes through the door and is gone in a second, the marker still in her mouth.

Rayen sighs and finds another marker, then hands it to Adam. He gives her a quizzical look.

"You have the prettiest handwriting," she tells him, and Adam walks awkwardly to the board.

"Brainstorming time," Rayen announces. "What do we really need to know?"

We all look at each other.

"Who are they?" Violet speaks first, and Adam dutifully writes her question on the board. The words shine in bright red marker.

Brooklyn perks up in her seat. "The Annunaki!"

Flint groans from the other end of the table.

"What?" I ask, frowning.

"Here we go again," Rayen mutters.

"Shape-shifting reptile aliens who have been here for centuries. They ingest human blood to keep themselves alive. They came down from the heavens and took prominent positions in government organizations."

I stare at her, mouth open.

"Just ignore her," Flint says. "Brooklyn is obsessed with conspiracy theories."

"Look," Brooklyn says. "Aliens have invaded. So for the first time, the conspiracies actually make sense."

"Except that these aliens blew humans to dust and don't drink blood!" Avani shouts back.

That shuts Brooklyn up. We turn our attention back to the whiteboard, waiting for someone to add another question.

Avani goes next. "What do they want?" she asks.

"How did they get here?" Flint suggests.

"And how the fuck do we kick their asses back to where they came from?" Brooklyn chimes in.

Adam writes that one down in a less explicit way.

We contemplate these four questions—they're essential. If we find out these answers, then we'll have an advantage.

And right now, I'll take anything I can get.

"That seems to cover it," Rayen says. "There are smaller questions, but I guess they can be answered within these four big ones." The room goes quiet. "Any ideas for the first one?"

Brooklyn hesitates, then says, "They're from another planet?"

Rayen snickers and Violet knits her blond eyebrows together. But Brooklyn is, in fact, right.

Violet opens up a new folder on the screen that appears to contain files on the alien landing back in April.

"This is all the information we have here at the base," she says. "Basically, it's all the government knows, so it's all we know as well."

"Not exactly," I point out. "When was the last time that was updated?"

Violet looks at her screen. "Almost seven months ago. When the attacks started."

"So we have more information than that," I say. "We're seven months ahead. The things we've learned can't be for nothing."

"Clover is right," Avani says.

"But how many close encounters have we had?" Violet asks.

Brooklyn frowns. "Second kind, third kind, or fourth kind?" She opens her mouth as she thinks. "Which one was Spielberg? I always get them mixed up."

Everyone ignores her, and for a few minutes, no one speaks.

"One," Avani says, breaking the silence. "They…" She swallows. "I hid."

We look at each other, shifting uncomfortably. Andy has her head down, probably pretending that she can't hear us.

"Have you…" I begin. "Have you never talked about this?"

The silence that fills the room is damning.

"We avoid all alien-related subjects, all right?" Flint says eventually. "It's not like we enjoy talking about this over tea."

"This is ridiculous," I say. "Not talking about it doesn't mean that it never happened."

Avani looks at me sadly. "Not all of us like to talk about our feelings."

"This is not about your feelings!" I slam my hand on the table and my voice rises. "This is not about *anyone's* feelings. Literally no one cares about how you feel. Everyone who cared is dead now."

I breathe hard. Wide eyes stare back at me, but I don't care. I'm not finished.

"People have died. More people will die, if there's anyone left out there. And the thing is, this is not about you. Frankly, it's not about any of us. But as Brooklyn puts it, we're the Last Teenagers on Earth. So we either suck it up and put the past behind us, or we're dead. Dead like the rest of them."

The room is quiet when I finish. I don't need them to be moping right now—I need them to be wide awake. I need them to understand what's at stake.

"Once," Brooklyn says finally. "When they came out of their spaceships. I ran and didn't look back."

"One time," Adam says, nodding. He doesn't add more.

"One time," Flint echoes.

Violet shakes her head. We all know what that means. To my surprise, Andy also shakes her head. I had assumed that a run-in with the aliens was the reason behind all her fear.

"Twice," says Rayen, and the others nod their heads respectfully. I nod too. I know what it feels like. "First when they got my family. Second time when I was on the run."

Now there's only one person left, and they all turn to me.

"Four times," I say, my throat dry.

"Four?" Brooklyn says in horror. "Four times? And you escaped?"

I nod, numbly.

"You are indeed one lucky leaf, Clover."

"It wasn't luck," I mutter, and they all turn to me again. It's now or never. The moment of truth. "It was something else."

Brooklyn raises her eyebrows expectantly, and I go on. "The first time, I was with my ex-boyfriend. They were chasing us. They caught up to Noah, and they shot him." I pause. "But they ignored me. And it was like…"

"You weren't even there."

I look up sharply to see Avani with her dark eyes fixed on me. "How did you know?"

She doesn't hesitate. "Because that's exactly the same thing that happened to me."

CHAPTER 23

The whole room is stunned, and I can't bring myself to speak. Brooklyn spins in her chair so fast that, for a second, I think she might fall.

"You never told me this."

"Well, I didn't want to sound like a complete freak of nature," Avani says defensively. "Why would I tell you?"

"Oh, hell," Brooklyn exclaims. "Because it's the exact same reason I survived."

Adam throws the marker on the table. "Yeah. I mean, I ran through my town when they attacked. They shot everything that moved…except me. It occurred to me later that it must have been because I was somehow invisible."

We all nod—we've all reached the same conclusion.

"So we are all freaks," Rayen says, and I can't wrap my head around the fact that they've been through the same things I've gone through. "Good to know."

Violet is quiet. Andy doesn't move.

That's when it hits me. They don't know if they're immune.

"We're all weirdos," Brooklyn concludes. "But what makes us weirdos? Was it our clothes?"

I shake my head. "I was wearing different stuff at each encounter. It's definitely something else."

"I could run some tests," says Avani. "Take blood samples and run them through the lab to see if I can find anything."

"Are you sure that's a good idea?" Andy speaks up.

"Can't hurt. Besides, I guess we know our advantage now."

"Bloody things can't see us coming." Flint grins and fist-bumps Brooklyn.

Violet shifts in her seat. "That *would* be an advantage, if we knew how to destroy them. Which we don't. We don't know anything about them, and all these archives are useless." She sighs deeply, and I can see that she's frustrated. "We don't know where they're from, we don't know what they want, we don't know how to break their armor. We don't know how their technology works or how they stay alive. We're shooting in the dark."

"My egg idea is still up for grabs," Brooklyn offers. No one finds this worth an actual response.

Adam gets up and picks up the marker. He walks back to the whiteboard.

"We don't know a lot," he says. "But we do know some things."

He starts by writing down "excellent sight/hearing," then moves on to "impervious to bullets." Those are the things that he knows, and I wonder if Adam, who looks like the star player of the football team, had the same idea I did of shooting them.

Suddenly we're all shouting things out.

"Six stable legs."

"Their guns beep before they fire," says Rayen, and I'm glad that I'm not the only one who noticed that.

"Incredibly fast."

"Always in twos."

"No verbal communication," says Brooklyn, which is an interesting point.

Adam dutifully writes down all of our observations.

"They come out at night," I point out. "Their guns wipe out all human matter."

"These are all valid points, but we're not getting anywhere," Violet says. "Maybe it'd help if we actually thought about the other questions. What do they want?"

I don't know, and I haven't figured out their strategy. They came in a massive invading force and started wiping us out. But not with bombs. One by one, like they wanted to look each person in the face before killing them. I can't see any plan behind their attack.

"Food?" Avani suggests.

"Electricity?"

"Resources?"

"To colonize our planet?"

"To destroy Earth so they can build an intergalactic highway?" offers Andy, and we all glare at her. "Sorry."

"I'm out of ideas," says Brooklyn. "I mean, why would they want to come here?"

"There must be something about Earth," Violet muses.

Brooklyn cocks an eyebrow, looking around the room. "A bunch of losers? No offense, but that's all we have available at the moment."

We fall silent.

"For how many movies I've seen, you'd think I'd be able to come up with an answer," Brooklyn says, sighing.

"I hear you," says Flint. "This is the end-of-the-world scenario, and we haven't even got Will Smith."

I smile. For a second, I can almost believe that we're just a bunch of kids discussing alien movies. The kind I liked to watch with Abuelo, before my life turned out to be like one.

"There aren't all that many possibilities," says Rayen.

"We've been through the main ones," Andy says. "*War of the Worlds, Arrival, Alien, Independence Day, Battlefield Earth, Pacific Rim…*"

"My God, woman, how many alien movies have you seen?" Flint asks, turning to her.

"Some." Andy looks guilty for a moment. "Enough." She looks down. "Okay, maybe all of them. Don't judge me."

"Guys," Violet says loudly. "We need to take this seriously.

Forget the movies. Forget about everything else and concentrate. We need to figure this out."

We go silent, staring intently at the whiteboard. It doesn't have the answers, though, and they're not going to magically pop up anytime soon.

"We use the airplane," I say. "Lure them out of hiding."

"Are you sure that they would come after you?" Violet asks, concern written all over her face.

I nod. "They will. We just have to find a way to bring down their ship."

"So what you're saying is…" Brooklyn starts.

"We use the plane as bait," I say. "We capture one of them. And then we learn exactly what our enemy is searching for."

CHAPTER 24

We discuss all our ideas at length: how to lure them out, how to capture them, how to react if this or that were to happen. We come up with at least ten backup plans, but the real problem is that our main plan might not work, even if everything goes perfectly.

Eventually, the others decide to go to bed. There's been enough discussion for one day, not to mention a hundred ideas floating around for what we'll need to do to prepare.

There's one thing that I want most of all. I want to be able to go up in the sky again without being hurled out of it. Ever since the aliens arrived, that's the only thing I've wanted. To go back to the place where I belong, where I feel like I'm complete. Maybe then, I'd find that I still have something to live for, even if everything else is gone. I could still honor the Martinez legacy.

I stay up in the kitchen. I'm unable to sleep, even though I know I'm safe. My body is completely exhausted, yet I can't close my eyes without seeing memories flash by. Sputnik has no problem sleeping, lying down in the middle of the kitchen floor and snoring as I try to read the most recent archives.

They aren't very useful. They mostly contain the same information that we already know, with one major exception: the government had figured out that something was coming two months before it hit Earth. They'd written tons of reports about the astonishing number of spaceships directed at our planet, and how it seemed impossible to stop them.

They had explored ideas—atmospheric shields, atomic bombs, and so on—but none of them were viable. When the aliens landed, they tried everything, but nothing had worked.

They'd been able to capture and study one spaceship, but they still couldn't find answers. Their ships are made of a metal not found on Earth, a smooth, thin, malleable metal that, once shaped, becomes so dense that nothing can get through. They tried moving it, but it proved impossible.

Mainly, though, the government had focused on dealing with peoples' reactions—subduing the rising panic, suppressing alarmists and weird alien cults, reassuring the public that there was nothing to be worried about. But in the end, it didn't matter. The aliens sent out forces that were too strong, too fast, too efficient. There wasn't one big spaceship to attack, but a million little ones. Their strength was in their numbers, and we had nothing to fight that. So we perished.

The government estimated a force of fifty million invaders. Fifty million indestructible invaders who, in a matter of days, broke us in half. They destroyed our air bases first, so that we couldn't fight them in the sky. Once people started turning to dust, and other people started breathing it in, they started dying, too. Blackened lungs and blackened bodies, like I'd seen on the road. And then there was no one left to tell the tale.

"Can't sleep?" comes a voice from the doorway, and I turn to see Flint standing there.

I shake my head. "Not really."

He walks over to the coffee maker on the counter and presses a button. The drink comes pouring out. He fills two cups and brings one over to me.

"Should we really drink coffee at this hour?" I ask.

"You're not going to sleep, so what difference does it make?" he replies, shrugging as he sits down.

I thank him with a nod. The coffee tastes good.

"It never goes away, does it?" Flint examines me. "That sensation that you have to stay awake."

"No. Not for now, anyway."

"You don't get used to it." He smiles.

"I thought you were one of the kids raised here."

He nods. "My parents came over four years ago and brought me along. Dad worked with Violet's mum in the research department." He takes a sip of coffee. "I never lost the accent. The rest is history."

"Did you ever get used to living here?"

He shrugs again. "It was difficult. But you've got to admit, your father working at Area 51? That's brilliant. Only problem is you can't tell anyone."

"And the kids here are unfazed." I crack a smile.

"So unfazed."

We sit quietly for a moment. The archive files overlap on the tablet in front of me, and I discard some of them with my finger. I don't have time to sort through them all.

"But you did see them once," I say carefully, and his dark eyes glow. "How did that happen?"

"Not one for small talk, are you, Clover?"

"I just really don't see the point of talking about the weather." I smile. "I'll ask you another question, if you want. Do you believe in God?"

Flint smiles. I like that about him.

"I'll take the first one. That's a lot easier to answer." His smile fades. "Kids were starting to get really sick from the plague. The adults were either already dead or just taking that turn for the worse, after the last expedition. So we said, 'Hey, let's call for a doctor.'"

He pauses and takes a deep breath. Like he's trying to convince himself that he's just telling a story, one that's not about him.

"So we went. A group of ten of us, thinking that we'd find a doctor in the next town. Little did we know, everyone there was already dead." His voice is dry. "We arrived in town and, of course, it was empty, so we started arguing about what to do next. Some of us wanted to split up to cover more ground, but others wanted to go to the hospital and try to find someone there. Voices were raised, and that was all it took. They came. None of us had seen them up close before. They started shooting. I froze." He takes a gulp of coffee. "I mean, I didn't know what to do. I thought for sure I was dead. So I stood there, glued to the ground. They shot all the others, and then they left. The end."

I nod. There's no use saying I'm sorry. He knows how I feel.

"Fun times," Flint says with a smile that doesn't reach his eyes. "We go on. I guess that's what matters." He looks at the tablet in my hands. "Find anything interesting?"

"Nothing worthwhile."

"Yeah." He nods. "Just reports going back to the fifties, and they didn't believe that aliens were real."

"On a scale of one to ten, how satisfied are you that the United States government was wrong?"

Flint laughs. "Oh man, I'd like to say ten. But then again, I really wish that they'd been right." He finishes his coffee. "You won't find anything. I've had a look."

"You have?"

He nods. "The only strange thing is that there was a blackout about twenty years ago."

With another weary smile, he gets up and leaves. But something about the blackout that he mentioned intrigues me, and I get lost in the archives again.

CHAPTER 25

The next day, everyone seems to wake up with a mission. Avani, Flint, and Adam are busy digging up all the stuff that we're going to need to knock out an alien, once we've captured one. Brooklyn takes our blood samples to test our invisibility theory. Andy is monitoring the computers, and Rayen is on patrol outside. Violet has shut herself inside her room, and I think she's probably studying the plan to make sure that nothing could go wrong. We've given ourselves a week to prepare; I just hope it's enough time.

Everyone looks very busy, and for a second, I feel bad for not contributing. I know too little of the facility to be of much help, and besides, my part of the plan doesn't lie here.

So I sit down next to Andy in her computer room and continue to search through the archives for any scrap of information that we might have missed. Following up on Flint's tip, I look through the reports from twenty years ago and find that one whole week is missing.

"Hey, Andy?" I look up from my screen. "What happened here twenty years ago?"

"I don't know," she answers absentmindedly. "Why?"

"There's a week of missing reports," I tell her, showing her my screen. "My best guess is that they got wiped somehow. Can you do anything to track them down?"

She studies my screen for a minute, then frowns. "Probably not," she tells me. "I believe that they were digitizing all the old archives at that time. This week probably got lost in the shuffle. There's a blackout reported and everything." She shakes her head. "Interns, I swear."

She returns to her various computer monitors. She's got a movie playing on one, a game of *Skyrim* on another, and the security cameras on the rest. I have no idea how she can concentrate on all of them at once.

"But don't you think this is important?" I ask her.

Andy turns to me. "Frankly, Clover, I don't know. This could be nothing or it could be everything. But right now we also have a death plan to get through."

I feel like she's blaming me for all the changes. For getting them to finally move.

But we all decided this together, and we all have to find a way to be part of the plan. So I leave to check on the others.

When I get to the lab, Avani, Flint, and Adam are already there, studying some papers that are spread out on the table. Sputnik comes trotting up behind me, her tail swishing from side to side as she sees the others.

"What have we got?" I ask, leaning over the table.

Avani sighs deeply.

"All right, so, here's a map that the government compiled of where all the spaceships landed," Flint says, pointing to the little dots on the map. Across the whole world, almost all of the land is covered. According to a new scan Avani presented, we're looking at a little more than five million shells. Then I notice a few empty spaces.

"They didn't go to Antarctica?" I ask.

"Well, they've got a population of about two hundred during winter," Flint explains. "All shipments stopped after the invasion, so…"

He doesn't need to say what we all know: with no supplies, it's likely the population didn't survive.

"A couple of ships landed there," Adam says. "But they're different than the ones that landed here, like they're prepared for the extreme cold."

"So our hypothesis is that their bodies can't take the freezing temperatures," Avani adds. "We think that we can build some kind of freezing chamber with the materials that we have here. At best, the alien will essentially be sedated."

"And at worst?" I ask.

"At worst, we're all screwed," Adam says, sighing. "The

alien is unaffected by the cold, gets out of containment, and kills everyone."

Avani takes a deep breath, wiping sweat off of her brow. She's wearing a white lab coat, and her thick brown hair is piled on top of her head.

"None of this is really giving me any confidence," she says. "We don't know what these things are. For all we know, they're invincible. And I'm pretty sure that they're not just going to walk voluntarily into a cryogenic chamber."

"They aren't completely invulnerable," Adam says.

We all look up at him.

He clears his throat, his cheeks blushing red. "When they came to my town, my house was being remodeled," he explains. "The whole house was torn apart, and there were wires everywhere. When they came, I panicked. And I turned on the circuits."

"You fried one of them?" Flint asks in disbelief.

"No, not fried," he says. "It was more like a short circuit, of sorts. I'm guessing that those metal legs have to be wired to their bodies somehow. I managed to delay it, that's all."

"So with a big enough electrical current, we could disable one for long enough to get it inside the chamber," I say. "I mean, it's not the best plan, but it's a plan."

Avani breathes deeply again, fanning herself with her hands. "Am I the only one who is hot in here?"

"Yes," Brooklyn says, grinning as she walks into the lab. "What are all you nerds up to?"

"We aren't nerds," Avani snaps, blushing. "Technically, we're saving your ass. What are you doing to prepare?"

Brooklyn stops and greets Sputnik, scratching behind her ears. "I was trying to help you, but then I got distracted."

Avani gives an exasperated sigh. "Then let us get back to work. We're the ones getting that thing into a cryogenic chamber. We're inventing solutions from scratch. Like *real* scientists."

"Go ask Rayen if she has any stun guns," Adam says to Brooklyn. "We need one that can create short circuits."

"Fine. Where would you guys be without me?" Brooklyn says as she waves goodbye.

"A lot quieter, that's for sure," Flint replies. He turns back to us. "So, Clover draws the aliens out with an airplane. Then we short-circuit one of them until we can get it inside the chamber and study it to discover its weak points. We have one problem: How do we get them out of the spaceship?"

They all look at me.

"Both times that I flew, they tried to take me down," I say. "Both times, they came after me in fighters. Not shells."

Avani frowns. "What's the difference, again?"

"The shells are the ships they arrived in," Adam says. "They're pear-shaped, closed up, and useless, I'm guessing. They're still around?"

I nod. "They aren't designed for flying. Just for landing."

"And the fighter ships?" Flint asks.

"I think there are one or two aliens piloting each one," I say. "They're bigger than the shells, the size of a small plane, and highly maneuverable. Plus they're equipped with weapons to take me down."

Flint lets out a slow whistle.

"We could use an electromagnetic pulse," Adam suggests. "It could work. But there's no way to test it on their ships."

"That means that my plane has to be fast enough to outrun the pulse, so that my electronics won't get scrambled," I say. "We've got a few in the bunker that would work."

I look around at the others, and I already feel a bit more confident. We don't know much, but these ideas are better than nothing. They're better than what we had before.

And I'm willing to do whatever it takes.

CHAPTER 26

The next day, I head to the bunker to clean out the plane that I've decided to use. It's got a powerful motor, and I check again and again that everything is working, running all the tests that Abuelo had taught me to do ever since I was a kid.

"You ready?" Adam asks as he comes through the bunker gate. Sputnik barks at him, doing her usual circles around his legs.

"Yes," I answer, though I'm lying through my teeth. "Does anyone need me over at the lab?"

"You can't think you're that essential to building Avani's machine."

I turn to him.

"I'm kidding," he says, putting his hands up. "You know, I never got to thank you."

I meet his gray-blue eyes. "What for?"

"You stood up for all of us," he says quietly. "I would've stayed here for a long time, not realizing that I was missing something. Not realizing that we could do this."

He offers me a sincere smile, and it disarms me. He is so much like Noah that it almost hurts to look at him.

But he's not Noah, I remind myself.

I step away from him.

"So, I kind of owe you a favor," he says. "What are you doing right now?"

"Besides focusing all of my energy on this plan?"

"I could teach you how to drive."

I laugh, despite myself. "Do you have some ulterior motives?"

"Maybe." He laughs, breaking that grin that makes his eyes sparkle. "I mean it, Clover. You can't keep crashing cars."

"It's the end of the world. I can do whatever I want."

"Yeah. But what if you die in a car crash? What will we put on your tombstone? 'Clover…'" He waits for an answer.

"Martinez."

"'Clover Martinez. One of the Last Teenagers on Earth. Fought aliens. Died in a car crash, though.'"

The way he says it makes me want to laugh—it does sound absolutely ridiculous. "Strangely enough, there's a bigger chance of getting killed by aliens than of dying in a car accident these days."

Adam smiles again. "You owe your tombstone to humanity. It should say, 'Died fighting aliens.' Or something epic."

"I'd rather sit through a root canal."

"Come on, Clover. Be a good sport."

"I hate sports."

But somehow, Adam convinces me. He pulls a truck over to where I'm standing, near the entrance gate, and points out that there's only one way I can go, in a straight line down the runway to the opposite end of the bunker, where there's an empty space that's barely visible from here. Five minutes later, I'm sitting in the driver's seat with Adam riding shotgun, my hands gripping the steering wheel. Sputnik sits in the back, a seat belt over her fur.

"Okay," I say, when I think I'm ready to go. The truck is military-grade, so it's a lot bigger than any other car I've driven, which feels weird, like I have a bear in my control, instead of a small dog. It also has a manual transmission, and I'm used to automatics. "Are you sure about this?"

"Look at it this way," Adam says. "You've never crashed an army truck, so your record is clean."

My lips are set in a thin line. Driving this truck feels like a worse idea than taking the plane out for a ride.

"You've got this," Adam says, and it feels strange to be trusted. I have crashed thirteen cars, and this guy sits here and tells me that he still has faith in me. "Now push the clutch pedal all the way down, start the engine, and put it in first gear."

The problem isn't the driving itself. It's that five seconds after we start, I'm already thinking about something else. My brain seems to have completely forgotten that I'm supposed to be concentrating on driving.

At Adam's instruction, I release the brake, press the gas pedal with my right foot, and, feeling the clutch engage, slowly lift my left foot up. The truck starts rolling forward. Adam seems delighted by this, and I wonder how long it's going to last.

It never felt like a bad thing that I couldn't drive, or that there was something that I wasn't really good at. Plenty of people are bad at plenty of different things. You don't usually go around telling them that they should do it anyway.

Unconsciously, I shift the truck into second gear. It starts going faster, but of course, we're still inside the bunker. We're not supposed to go fast. Up ahead, I see a solid wall.

Or at least, I see something that looks like a solid wall. It's similar to the others, but somehow, from this angle, it doesn't quite line up right.

"Are you seeing this?" I ask, pointing to the wall.

Adam frowns. "Clover, maybe you should stop."

Now I notice a slight crack in the wall. And the closer I get, the more visible the crack gets.

I've looked at the blueprints of this compound a dozen times. I've memorized them by now. Right there, there's supposed to be an exterior wall and nothing more. The biggest bunker in Area 51 ends here.

But my instincts are screaming that something is wrong. I check Adam's seat belt and I check mine, and before he can tell me to stop, I shift into third gear and accelerate down the last stretch of the runway.

The front of the truck hits brick and a cloud of dust rises up into the air.

I grab the key from the ignition. There's rubble in front of us, but there's also something else. Something shiny and metallic.

I take off my seat belt, and Adam scrambles to release his and Sputnik's. I jump out of the truck to investigate. The dust from the crash starts to settle, and a room beyond the wall takes shape.

Adam strides angrily to my side, but he stops ranting when he sees what I've hit.

Beyond a false wall, sitting right in front of us, is a spaceship.

CHAPTER 27

"Are you kidding me?" Adam asks in disbelief. "There's a *space-ship* in our *basement*!"

Sputnik is the first to go through the hole I've made. She runs through the debris happily, padding her paws over the dust and barking.

"Jesus," Adam says, gasping again. "This changes—"

"Look, you can't tell the others," I say, stepping in front of him. "If Violet finds out, she'll cancel the mission. We can forget about fighting, and we'll be stuck wasting our lives away in here."

Adam looks reluctant but doesn't say anything. I move forward, stepping over the debris so I can get a better look, and he follows me.

This ship is different from the shells that landed all over the world. I've only seen spaceships similar to this twice—on the day I flew to Malmstrom and the day I got the Blackbird to fly.

But this ship isn't a pursuer. The fighters that tailed me were small, sleek, and fast. This one is bigger. It's made from the same type of metal, though, and I can see our reflections in its hull. Sputnik steps forward and, before I can stop her, she licks it.

"Sputnik!" I shout, running toward her. I open her mouth, but there's nothing there besides her terrible breath. "You silly dog. Do you have to lick everything you find?"

I stand at my full height next to the spaceship, and I realize how large it really is. It's more like a cruiser than a pursuer, definitely built for longer distances, and I think it could easily hold thirty people.

I walk around it, examining it. There's no visible door on the outside, like all their other ships. I can't figure out a way to get it open. I tap against the sides. Nothing happens.

I sigh, stepping away. My fingers are coated with dust. In fact, the whole spaceship is covered in a thick layer of dust—too thick to be from my wild crash. This ship looks like it hasn't been moved in months.

No, not months. Years.

This ship was here before the invasion.

"Clover?" Adam asks. "What is it?"

I turn to him, shaking my head slightly. "This thing is old, Adam. Older than it should be."

He frowns. "What do you mean?"

"This looks like it's been sitting here for ten years. Maybe more."

I turn to the wall to inspect the spot where I crashed. From here, it's easier to see the crack that divides this room from the rest of the bunker. This wall was built later, to hide this ship. I pick up a small brick and shove it in my pocket.

"We've gotta tell them," Adam says.

"We will," I reassure him. "But not yet."

"Why not?"

I sigh. "We have a plan to catch these things. And then we find one of their spaceships sitting right here under our noses. Something that isn't supposed to be here." I look at him expectantly.

"We don't have enough information yet," he says.

"And?"

He hesitates a little. "Violet will call it all off."

I nod. The spaceship remains quiet in the room. It doesn't even buzz.

"They're going to find out anyway," he argues. "Look at the size of this hole you've made. And the security cameras…"

I check the angles of the cameras in the bunker, and there's no way that they could have caught my crash on video. They can't see this room. Besides, this area is isolated enough that no one will find anything here unless they come looking.

"Help me keep this hidden until we know more about it," I say.

Adam nods.

There are too many pieces to this puzzle, and none of them fit. The aliens, the blackout, the planes, and the spaceship. There's some element that unites all of these together, I'm sure of it. But I'm missing it—the answer is just out of my reach.

I meet Adam's eyes. "If I find anything useful, I promise I'll tell them."

He looks comforted by that. My word is not worth much, but it's all we have. "I'll hold you to that," he says.

I nod. Adam looks at the spaceship again, as if waiting for it to answer our questions. It doesn't move.

"Let's go," I say.

He nods, accompanying me back to the somehow undamaged truck. We work together to clean up the debris, and Adam parks the truck in front of the hole in the wall. I really don't think that anyone is going to come all the way down here besides us, so our secret should be safe.

At least for now.

CHAPTER 28

We only have a few more days until we go through with our plan. I have to find answers, fast. I need to talk to Flint, and I know where he'll be late at night.

Flint is sitting at the table in the kitchen, nursing his coffee and looking over some schematics for the cryogenic chamber. He was holed up in the lab all day helping Avani build it, making sure that everything would work.

"How was your day?" he asks.

"Boring. Yours?"

"Better stay boring," he says, with a wink in my direction.

I smile, sitting down across from him.

"You do realize how stupid our plan is, right?" Flint shakes his head, looking back down at the schematics. "It's just... There are a lot of flaws. There isn't one single aspect of it that feels like a sure thing."

"They can't see us," I remind him.

"You willing to bet your life on that?"

"What's my life worth, anyway?"

He looks up sharply. "Your life is not worthless, Clover."

"I know," I answer evasively. "But I just think… My abuela used to say this to me all the time: 'When our time comes, it comes. Don't fight it.'"

"You think she meant the aliens?"

I laugh. "If I were with her when they attacked, she probably would've," I answer. "She'd want to murder me for this plan."

"So would my mum," Flint replies, nodding his head. "'Flint Nelson Rogers, who do you think you are to fight aliens?'" he says, imitating her voice. "'Let the white folk go out there and fight those things. You stay right here and finish your chores.'"

I bark out a laugh. It's too similar to what Abuela would say: *Chores always come first. Be home by sundown. Don't mess with stuff that ain't your business.*

"Yours too?" He raises an eyebrow.

I nod my head slightly, a smile crossing my lips. "You never think that's going to be the stuff you miss, you know? Them ordering you around all the time."

"With both my mother and my father in the compound, I couldn't put a toe out of line." He smiles, lost in the memories.

"Well, it hasn't been our time to go yet," I say. "There has to be a reason that we've survived this long. So I guess we might as well do something useful."

"Might as well get ourselves killed, more like," he replies, but his smile doesn't fade. It's like the spark of life in Flint hasn't gone out, no matter how hard the last seven months have tried to take him down. It's like Abuela told me when the aliens first landed: *We do what we always do. Survive.*

"What can I do for you, Clover?"

"How did you guess?"

"You might find this surprising, but people don't usually seek me out unless they want something."

"Shocking."

"I know," he replies, laughing easily. "What do you need?"

I pull the piece of brick out of my pocket. It isn't damaged much, and it's not recognizable as being from the bunker.

"A rock? You shouldn't have."

"I just want to know how old this is." I hand it to him, and he picks it up, turning it in his hands.

"Is this an emotional rock? Are you attached to it?"

Without warning, Flint puts the brick near his mouth and licks it. My eyes widen, and I make a disgusted noise. Flint grins at my expression.

"Is that standard procedure?" I ask, bewildered.

"No. I just really wanted to see the look on your face. It was worth it." He coughs and rubs his tongue with his finger, as tiny pieces of debris fall to the floor. "This is disgusting. But it tastes like a pretty regular brick to me."

I'm half-disappointed, and it probably shows.

"What I could do," he suggests, "is take it up to the lab. See if I can find anything specific on it. Can't make any promises, though."

"That would be awesome, actually."

I just need a date. If he manages to analyze the age of the brick, then there's a chance I can figure out when that wall was built, or when that spaceship arrived. It's a long shot, but it's all I've got.

"It'll take some time," he says. "But we have good lab equipment, and I should be able to do a radiocarbon-dating analysis."

"That's fine," I answer. "I owe you one."

"Oh, I'm counting on it." He smiles, then shakes his head. "I suppose that whatever this is, Violet isn't aware of it?"

I give him a very sweet smile.

"I thought so." He sighs, rolling his eyes.

"Thanks, Flint. I promise I'll repay you."

"Anytime."

When I get to the laboratory the next day, Avani is flitting about, her hair flying everywhere, and it's clear that she's barely slept for days. Rayen and Flint managed to find the electromagnetic pulse in one of the labs, so the only thing we need to worry about is building the machine that will confine the alien. In the corner of the lab sits a prototype with a transparent ball full of electricity that blinks in different colors and buzzes like a hive of bees.

"Is that it?"

She nods.

The machine is like a glass coffin. It's small enough that it will fit in the back of the smallest truck we have. There's a piece on the side that looks like a scanner, a lit-up grid panel of some sort.

"What is this?"

Avani looks up, blinking and then frowning at the buzzing thing. "An idea I had about the aliens. Maybe they can't see us because they perceive the world differently."

I raise an eyebrow at her. "What do you mean?"

"Like ants, who use their antennae," Avani explains. "But in this case, I was wondering why they can't see *us* specifically. Bats and snakes don't use regular sight—their vision is built from the sounds they hear."

"I made a big racket one of the times I encountered them," I reply, not wanting to dismantle her theory, but not wanting to lie, either.

Avani smiles at me. "Me too. I tried to hide in a cabinet with a bunch of pots and pans, and they all came crashing out. Which doesn't explain how they don't see us. So I wondered if what they actually see might be brain waves, which they use to, you know, target humans. We vibrate in a specific frequency, and we can be differentiated from animals and static things like houses. Technically, the whole world is written in wave frequencies. Like a radio. Tune in to a different station…"

"And you can't hear it anymore," I say, catching on. "That's actually a really good idea. So you're basically saying that our brains are defective?"

Avani shrugs, raising her hands. "Maybe we vibrate in a frequency that they can't read."

"What about the blood samples you took?"

Avani groans. "They got us nowhere. The machine is broken, and they all showed up the same."

"What?"

"All the scans are of Violet's blood," she tells me. "And we haven't all got the same blood, obviously. So the machine probably just repeated the same DNA pattern for every sample. As I said, broken."

I chew on the inside of my cheek, not knowing what to say. This could be a big clue to what makes us different, why the aliens killed everyone but could never see us.

Avani smiles at me, putting her hands on her waist. "Anything else I can do for you?"

I remember why I came in here in the first place and nod. "Yeah. Adam. Is he here?"

"Yeah, in the back," Avani says. "He's fixing up the truck."

I find Adam in a back corner of the lab trying to fix what looks like a bunch of giant metal ropes.

"Hey."

He looks up and grins. "Hi. Come here looking for the handsomest guy in Area 51?"

"Yes. Where is Flint? I didn't see him when I came in."

Adam gives a hearty laugh, shaking his head. "It's hard to win with you. So what do you need?"

"Your help breaking in somewhere."

Adam's face falls. "Is this about the spaceship?"

"Yes. C'mon. What are you afraid of?" I tease him. "There are no cops to arrest us for breaking and entering."

Adam gets up with a sigh, rolling his eyes at me. He comes closer to the workbench I'm leaning against, and I can smell his sweat. He turns to me, and a faint blush creeps into his cheeks.

I should tell him that these feelings won't be returned. I should just get it over with, but he might hate me if I tell him the truth, and right now, I'm tired of feeling alone.

"Meet me at midnight," I say.

"You do realize that we should be sleeping," Adam says. "We have an alien to catch in a few days."

"Aren't you curious at all to find out what happened in Area 51 and what they were trying to cover up?"

"I'm more curious to know when I'll be able to act like a normal guy again," he says, looking at me.

I know that look—it's one that Noah used to give me sometimes, when he wanted to ask a question that he didn't dare ask.

I decide that it's best to brush it off. "You're the last of the white boys, Adam. You're going to save the world. Female survivors will be lining up to be with you."

"One can dream, right?"

"Yeah. Hollywood did it all the time."

He laughs at that. "Hypothetically, we're the last humans

on Earth," he says. "We might be responsible for repopulating the whole planet."

"We might. We could also just let humanity die. I mean, we put up a good fight."

"Yeah. Still, we have a responsibility."

"My family had diabetes for generations. My genes are no good. Might as well kill off humanity now."

Adam chuckles. "We watched too many movies."

"We did," I agree. "Why did teenagers get to be the ones who survived? We have no sense of responsibility at all."

"Speak for yourself."

I narrow my eyes. "If you had a kid today, and you could exchange it for a brand-new Pokémon game, would you?"

Adam looks at me bewildered, opening his mouth in offense. Then he shuts it, unable to come up with a response that lets him keep his dignity.

"That's low."

I find myself smiling at Adam's disappointment.

"Come on, Clover. You would sell out the human race for a game?"

I snort. "I'd sell all of you if the aliens told me they had Ben & Jerry's ice cream. I wouldn't even blink."

Adam tries to look hurt, but we both just end up with goofy smiles on our faces. It feels easy talking to him, and I wonder if this is what it's like to have real friends.

The end of the world is cruel. But it can be kind with the smallest of things.

CHAPTER 29

Adam's footsteps are surprisingly light for a guy his size. When I ask him about this, he says that his mom had really strict curfew rules. I can almost imagine him in a simple but tastefully decorated house, sneaking through the hallway while his mom sleeps. His high school experience must have been completely different from mine. And yet, we both ended up here.

"You sure about this?" he whispers as we approach the door to Violet's office. "This is a bad idea."

"You afraid of a little girl?"

"Hell yeah. And Violet isn't little, she's taller than me." I consider this, and it's true. She has a model's body, very tall and lean. "And calling me a coward won't get the job done." He looks slightly irritated, putting his hands in his pockets.

"Yeah. But did I annoy you enough to do it?"

"You did. Congratulations, Martinez."

"Just doing my job."

The door, of course, is locked. I could break in by myself—after spending six months on the outside breaking and entering, I'm practically a professional. But this mission could take hours, and I think Adam is good company.

I break through the lock a moment later and quietly slip inside the old office.

The lights turn on automatically and I freeze, but the room is empty, and I force myself to relax. Adam comes in after me, clearly uncomfortable.

"What exactly are we looking for?" he asks as his eyes sweep the room.

I point to the badly concealed door near the right corner of the room. I noticed it the first time I was here and have wanted to explore it ever since. It's unlocked. We enter a confined space that feels a lot like a broom closet. I'm relieved to see that there are only four file cabinets inside, which should make our search easier than I thought.

"Any file that fits the time frame of twenty years ago is relevant," I tell him. "In June, to be exact."

"What happened twenty years ago?"

I shrug.

"So you don't know what we're looking for?"

"There's an information gap in the archives that Violet got us. The reports from the first week of June are missing, and we know that there was a blackout around that time."

He makes a face but doesn't tell me what he's thinking.

I frown at him and turn back to the files in front of me. I pull them out methodically, one by one, taking a quick look at the contents for anything that stands out. Most of the files are about half-finished projects that don't interest me. But they all seem to have been signed by the same person: Melinda Deveraux. Violet's mom.

After a few minutes, I realize that while I've gone through five files, Adam has just been staring at me.

"What?" I ask him irritably.

"Just you. It's like you go looking for trouble. Why didn't you just ask her about this?"

"Because I have a hunch."

"Hunches can be shared."

"I just don't want to," I tell him. "Not until I know for certain."

"Why?" He's staring at me with those gray-blue eyes that remind me uncomfortably of Noah.

"Because I hate being wrong," I tell him. Mostly, I just really hate when people point out how wrong I am.

Adam looks incredulous. "Seriously?"

"It's a character flaw. Sue me."

Does this make me proud and arrogant? Sure. It also makes me smart. I turn back to the files.

Adam shakes his head like I'm a hopeless case and starts looking through files, too. I work faster than him, flipping through pages, scanning for dates. It's a tedious job, but someone has to do it.

"What makes you think these reports are so important?" Adam asks.

"It's too much of a coincidence. A whole week missing after decades of meticulous reports?"

"You think someone wiped them out on purpose?"

I nod without turning to look at him. I'm on my third drawer now, barely glancing at the documents, except to look at dates.

"Why would they?"

"I don't know," I say, but I have a gut feeling. "I saw something, though. It was on the reports for two or three weeks before they go missing."

"A spaceship?"

Now it's my turn to look at him, surprised.

"I can put two and two together, Clover."

"I'm glad you were an exemplary student," I say, and he brushes off my comment with an eye roll. "But yeah. An unidentified flying object, heading straight for Earth. The reports are pretty steady, and the size described is close to the one downstairs."

"And after that?"

"Nothing."

"Which makes you wonder."

"Exactly."

We both go quiet. We're used to having aliens around now. But if that spaceship really did land here fifteen years ago, that changes things. It means that we've dealt with this before. It means that these aliens are not the first of their kind to visit Earth.

I look at the next file and a name catches my eye. ANDREA WALSH is written in black capital letters, along with some other names I don't recognize. Behind it are a couple of other files, one on a project for a new satellite launch and another file labeled INSIDER.

I take it in my hands just as Adam whispers excitedly, "Found it!"

I almost jump at his words. I scoot over and Adam hands the file to me. There are no names on the front of the folder, which is strange.

I open the file. On the first page, there is a date. I turn the pages and hold my breath. There are more than fifty pages of a thick manuscript, and another attached file.

I recognize three things immediately.

First, Melinda Deveraux's signature is on every page of the document.

Second, a faded photo shows what looks like a meteor but has a strange shape to it.

And third, every single page has been redacted.

CHAPTER 30

On the morning of D-day, while everyone is getting ready, I separate some water and rations for Sputnik. She keeps circling around my legs, her fluffy tail beating against my jeans, as if she can feel the tension in the air.

I eat breakfast while Avani and Rayen review their checklists. My pulse is electric in my veins. Rayen guides us to the armory and shows us our options. We pick up pistols, rifles, and anything else that might be useful. We're each equipped with three powerful stun guns, in the hopes that we can short-circuit the aliens before they attack. Rayen gives me bullets for Abuelo's gun and a rifle, in case I need them.

Sputnik follows me back to the dormitory, her paws padding softly against the floor. I put food in her bowl, but she sniffs it and doesn't touch it.

"You be good," I tell her, crouching down and putting my hands behind her ears, cradling her big face with my hands. "No jumping or scratching at doors."

She wags her tail.

I need to move, but I can't.

Sputnik has been with me since Week Five. That's when I found her, in the garbage, trying to find something to eat. Her eyes were hungry and desperate, but there was something about her that caught my attention. And ever since then, I've never left her behind. She's often the one who kept me from going over the edge. She always managed to pull me back on time.

She circles around me, like the satellite that she is, and waits for me to say something else.

For the first time, I consider that maybe this plan really is stupid, that maybe we're all going to end up dead because of me. I put this plan in motion, but I might not be the one who gets to see Sputnik again.

"Hey," I tell her, my voice breaking just a little. "It's going to be okay. It's going to be all right."

She licks my face. I can't go back now. I hug her neck, squeezing it tight, my face against her fur, but I don't let go.

"Everyone is waiting for you." Adam steps inside the room, his hands in his pockets.

I get up, my throat tight. "I was just finishing up," I tell him.

He looks over at me and Sputnik and steps closer.

His eyes meet mine for a second, and there's tension there, the same tension I so often felt with Noah.

I don't want to be the same way with Adam as I was with Noah. I want things to be simple, and for all of these people to like me, flaws and all. I want to feel like it doesn't matter who I am or that I'm an outsider—I just want to belong here. I want to be friends. I want to *have* friends. I want Adam to joke around with me and Brooklyn to flash that crazy smile of hers. I want to bond with Avani and Flint over science, play video games with Andy, and have target practice with Rayen. I realize that even Violet is part of this—she's the boss, but she's more like me than any of the others.

"Hey, Adam?" I say, looking up. My fingers pick at my newly washed jeans.

"Yeah?"

"Can I be one hundred percent honest with you?"

He looks startled for a second, and I can hear my rational side telling me to shut up. But I also feel like I might regret it for the rest of my life if I don't take this leap right now.

"Okay. Go ahead."

I almost wince. "You know this thing? Whatever you think is going on between me and you? It's not happening." I might as well have punched him, by the look on his face. My stomach churns.

He nods. "Is this because of your ex-boyfriend?"

I bite my lip. "Yes… No." I sigh. "I don't really know."

Adam nods again, trying to understand. "Do I remind you of him? Did you love him?"

"I don't know." I give him an apologetic smile and look at

my feet. But there's nothing to apologize for—there's only the truth that I'll never find out.

When I look up again, Adam is laughing. "I thought you knew everything."

"Seriously?"

"Yeah. How can you not know? Why did you two even go out in the first place?"

I laugh. Noah and I were the unlikeliest of pairs, and I think that's why we became such good friends in the end. "He wanted to steal my homework. So he asked me out."

Adam wriggles his eyebrows. "And you accepted?"

"It was…" I can't finish the sentence. Conflicted feelings are roaring inside me. "I wanted to know what it was like. Everyone has this thing about finding love, everyone wants that romantic thing so desperately… And I wanted to know if Noah was my chance at that."

Adam listens silently to my confession, nodding. I struggle with the words and the explanations and the feelings that, after all this time, still haven't settled.

"I never felt that romantic connection with Noah. But I've never liked *anyone* that way," I say, motioning with my hands. "Sure, I've thought guys were hot before. Girls, too. It wasn't a big deal. But feelings never had anything to do with it."

I find my fingers behind Sputnik's ears. She helps ease away the anxiety burning in my brain. I've never told anyone these things before. I've never discussed them out loud. But when

I look up at Adam, he's still paying attention. He doesn't look weirded out.

"And so?"

I shrug. "I never felt anything more for him than just being friends. We broke up a month before the aliens attacked." Silence fills the room for a moment, then I continue. "But it was really hard to do, because he was just so nice. How could I tell him that I didn't love him the way he loved me? I thought I was broken somehow. I realize now that it wasn't really about Noah—I'm just not into romantic relationships. With anyone. I guess I just need people who I can call friends."

I give him a small smile, and he nods. Maybe he understands, maybe he doesn't understand at all. My feelings about Noah are still conflicted. I enjoyed his company, but he was needy all the time. We almost never agreed on anything. He was my friend, yes, but he wanted us to be something that I don't need. And deep down, the meanest part of me still thinks that he should've run faster. A part of me is just glad that it was him and not me.

There isn't pity in Noah's eyes. *Adam's* eyes. And for the first time, I can see the difference between them.

"You couldn't have done anything to save him," Adam says. He's levelheaded about it. "You know that, Clover."

"I do," I say, and I mean it sincerely. "I just wish that I could feel bad about it. I *should* feel bad about it. So I just keep running the scene over and over and over again in my head."

And it never changes. Not one single thing. I always watch Noah die.

"You don't have to feel bad about it."

"I should, though."

He shrugs. "Who knows? I mean, it's not our fault that we survived the end of the world. We're just the losers who got forgotten. We spend enough time feeling sorry for ourselves. I don't think we should have to feel damn sorry for everybody else, too."

"We're fucked up."

He laughs. "Yeah, we are."

"I just wanted to be honest," I finally say. "I like you, Adam. Enough that I felt like I could tell you the truth."

"And what's the truth?"

"That I'm a horrible human being?" I shrug. "Maybe that's why the aliens spared me."

"I hear that," he says, and I can tell that there's some meaning behind it. I don't know Adam well enough to know what he's done in his life. But I know human beings, and we're all capable of doing our worst.

Maybe Adam is more like me than I thought.

Maybe all of them are.

I look at Sputnik again, my heart hammering in my chest. As scary as that was, I'm glad I got it out. Because even if we have the advantage of being invisible, I've still got a bad feeling about this plan.

I scratch behind Sputnik's ears one more time.

"One of us has to come back here, okay?" I say to Adam. "I'm not going to let this dog starve."

He stretches out his hand, and I grip it.

"I promise you, we'll *all* come back," he says. "Promise me you'll come back fine."

"I'll come back fine."

We shake on it.

"You ready?" he asks.

I nod.

I'm not. But I can always lie to myself.

CHAPTER 31

The drive is bumpy. Adam, Rayen, and I ride in the truck that pulls the plane. This time, I leave the speedy Blackbird behind, choosing the reliable F-15 Eagle, which can be flown with one pilot and is highly maneuverable. It's equipped with eight missiles and an internal machine gun that fires from the right wing. I've flown in it once before, when Abuelo took me for a ride for my birthday, which reassures me that I'm not going to mess this up.

Ahead of us are Brooklyn, Avani, and Flint in a jeep that carries the electromagnetic pulse machine. Leading the way are Violet and Andy, keeping a steady pace in a big jeep with the cryogenic chamber, designed to contain the alien's body.

Adam taps his fingers rhythmically on the steering wheel. Rayen pretends not to be irritated by it. I pretend that everything is fine and that I'm not worried, even though my stomach keeps knotting up.

I go over the plan in my head one more time. That makes it even worse, since every time I examine the plan, I find a hundred little flaws in it that depend totally on chance. I just hope that I'm living up to my name, so that we'll at least have luck on our side, even when nothing else is.

We approach our coordinates, and Adam slows down until we come to a full stop. I wipe my sweaty palms on my jeans. My heart is pounding in my ears.

Adam and Rayen get out first. Dust rises when they jump down, and the whole desert is empty. The others park a little ahead of us, and we all get to work unloading. Adam and Rayen help me unhook the plane from the back of the truck. Flint and Avani heave the enormous electromagnetic pulse machine out of their jeep. It's about the size of a tiny car, and it pulses blue with electricity. When everything is in position, we gather around to hear Violet's last-minute instructions—she's still the boss.

"Okay," she says, her voice firm. Her blond hair is tied back in a braid, and the desert sun makes her blue eyes stand out even more. "We all know what to do. Don't miss your cues. We've only got one chance."

We all nod.

"Andy, get inside the jeep," Violet says, and the smaller girl looks relieved. "We might need to get out of here fast, so I'd prefer to have one driver at the ready."

Andy climbs into the driver's seat.

"Clover, after we fire the first electromagnetic pulse, you'll be unprotected for eight minutes while the machine recharges," Violet says grimly, bringing me back to reality. She conveniently leaves out the fact that I might be unprotected the whole time, if the first pulse doesn't work. "You good to go?"

I look up to the sky for reassurance. It's a perfect day for flying, with a bright blue sky that's clear for miles. Somehow, my fear vanishes. I've flown before and I'll fly again. I'll rise.

"To your posts," Violet shouts.

The F-15 has twin turbofan jet engines and can fly up to nine hundred miles per hour at low altitude, reaching Mach 2.5 at high altitude. It's damn fast and I'm dying to try it out. I'll have a good speed advantage over the spaceships. Their fighters are not as fast as mine. I guess it's the difference in the atmosphere—our jets were built for these conditions, but their ships were designed for outer space. Still, even with that advantage, I have to count on Rayen to not miss her shot with the pulse machine.

I put on my G suit, climb into the cockpit, and strap myself in. I turn on the engine, slowly but surely, and the plane starts warming up. I put in my earphones, then put on my helmet.

"Test, test," I say over the mic.

"Clover is a motherfucking alien slayer!" Brooklyn's voice crackles over the intercom. "Oops, sorry, Violet. But yeah, we can hear you, Clover."

"Good," I say. "I'm ready for takeoff."

My adrenaline pulses as I realize what I'm about to do. For the first time in seven months, humans are ready to fight back.

The plane slowly starts moving forward, and in a few seconds I have the acceleration to take off. Suddenly, I'm in the air, fighting against the wind as I gain altitude.

This time, the aliens are onto me much faster, as if they were expecting me.

I won't disappoint them.

"I've got them," I say over the intercom. My radar beeps twice as they appear on the screen. "Two showing up on my radar."

They're speeding up.

"I see them," Violet confirms. "We're ready to go. Set?"

"Set," Avani and Rayen respond at the same time.

I grip the joystick harder as I hold my own speed. Any second now, they'll catch up to me and start shooting.

But the shooting doesn't come. And I know I've made a mistake.

"Shit," I say out loud.

"What?" Violet shouts. "Clover, talk to me!"

"They should be shooting," I say, "but they're just staying steady on my tail."

"That's bad?"

"They're scouts," Adam says for me. "I think they were waiting for Clover."

And sure enough, there's a third beep on my radar. Something else has arrived.

"Fuck," Brooklyn says. "That ship is *big*."

I can't see it through the window panels, and I can't afford to turn my head to look at it properly.

"Change of plans," Violet announces. "We take the big one out first. Clover, what's your guess? How many are in there?"

"Hold on."

I spin the plane around in a wild swing toward the ground. The scouts drop from my line of vision just enough that I'm able to take a look.

My heart stops. It's huge. It must be three times the size of my own plane. It's not as big as the cruiser hidden at Area 51, but it's obviously a destroyer. They're not taking any chances with me this time.

I've got two scouts and a destroyer after me. I force myself to breathe.

"I see it," I tell them. "It's a big destroyer, but it's probably not crewed by more than four of them. Maybe six, tops."

Violet groans over the intercom. "That's probably more than we can handle."

"We either handle them or we're dead," Flint says quietly.

This ship was clearly sent here with the mission of taking my plane down. I don't want to say it out loud, but at least half of that big-ass ship is loaded with weapons.

"Take the big one out first," I hear myself saying. "I'll take the scouts myself."

"Are you sure?" asks Adam. He sounds worried.

"I'll take care of the two scouts," I say again, more firmly this time. "You guys handle the other ship."

A second later, the destroyer fires its first blast. My radar starts beeping faster as it approaches, and I spin the plane madly to avoid it. This is nothing like before. This is heavy artillery that I'm not prepared to take.

But I'm taking it anyway.

"Be ready," I warn the others as I narrowly avoid another blast. I'm doing insane maneuvering, but I'm limited by the scouts, which stay close beside me.

I point the plane down, heading directly for the ground, but before I hit, I pull the joystick and the plane turns over, its belly to the sky. I'm spinning under the big ship. It's too close to drop a bomb or blast, so it tries to follow me, but it's too big. It hovers in midair and tries to turn around. It's only for a few seconds, but that's enough.

There's a flash behind me as the electromagnetic pulse goes off, and I speed away from it across the desert, the other two ships right on my tail.

There's a gasp over the intercom, and, for a second, I'm afraid that we've failed, that the pulse didn't work and we're all going to die.

I turn my plane around, and it's like everything in the world has come to a stop. Then I see the spaceship that towered over the desert a moment ago, now slowly falling toward it.

It lands with a tremendous crash, raising a huge cloud of dust. I can feel the impact from the sky, where I watch, almost too stunned to react.

"Go, go, go!" shouts Violet over the intercom, and I know it's make-it-or-break-it time. "Spread out."

I wish I could be down there fighting with them, but that's not my job. I snap out of my stupor and speed up, the two scouts following close behind me.

I pray that they're too dumb to call for reinforcements.

I hear shouts over the intercom, but I ignore them. I have to if I'm going to get through this. It's evident that Rayen isn't going to be able to shoot the pulse a second time, so I tell myself what I already know: *I'm on my own.*

The scouts blow past me, pressing me on both sides. It looks like they're not carrying weapons—probably to make them lighter, so they can keep up with me. This is my chance to take them out. Surely and speedily, I lead the way across the desert toward a group of treacherous canyons.

The glare of the sun is starting to blind me. I have no idea how the scouts can see my plane, with the way the sun must be glinting off of it. What if they can only see me on their radar?

That gives me an idea.

I can still hear static and shouting and the blast of guns in the background. But nobody is screaming yet, which I take as a good sign.

"Andy," I say over the comm unit. "Do you have your laptop with you?"

"Do humans breathe oxygen?"

"Do me a favor," I tell her. The scouts are still on my tail. "You think you can fake a radar signal for a plane?"

She doesn't respond for a minute. Then she answers, "I think I can. What do you need me to do?"

I quickly explain my plan to her. I can hear the faint sound of typing.

"Will that work?" she asks. "Won't they see your plane in the sky?"

"They're relying mainly on their radar. If I kill mine and you set up a fake signal for me, we should be good."

The scouts are speeding up, closing in on my signal. I'm far away from everyone else now, so if they take me down, there won't be any collateral damage.

"The destroyer's signal is back online," says Andy triumphantly. And there it is again, a beep on my screen, as if it never went down at all. "One more to go."

I'm getting closer to the canyons. A part of me is sad that I'll be responsible for destroying some of them, but another part of me is relieved that there's still something left on Earth to be destroyed.

"Okay, got it," says Andy. "You ready?"

"Give me a minute."

"Are you sure this is gonna work? Their ships are indestructible."

"Damn it, Andy, how should I know? I'm a pilot, not an engineer."

The canyons are very close now. I speed up and head straight for them, the rock formations looming larger as I approach. It feels like I'm going to hit them. The scouts are close behind me, still pressing me, trying to corner me.

The rocks get closer.

And closer.

I'm on them.

"Now!" I shout as I bring the plane up and up toward the sky, coming so close to the canyon wall that it almost scrapes the belly of the plane.

There's a thundering noise as the two spaceships hit the wall, and I escape just as the structure collapses into a million pieces of rock. I turn on my stealth mode.

"Keep the signal up," I say to Andy. "Take it north. If they survived the rocks, they'll go after it, thinking that they're following me."

"Righto."

"I'm coming back around."

Over the intercom, I hear an explosion and an earsplitting scream that makes the hair on the back of my neck stand up. There's a lot of indistinct shouting. I try to pinpoint a voice, one that can tell me what the hell is going on.

"Avani?" I try. "Can you hear me?"

More shouting.

"We can't get through," says Brooklyn. "The ship is down, but not the weapons system."

"Can they see you?"

A pause. "I don't think so."

"Can you see them?"

"Yep. Five total. One of them is outside the ship, gun at the ready."

My mind races. "Take that one first," I say. "That's the one we're bringing back with us."

I can still hear shooting. They know that they're under attack—they just can't see it coming.

I approach their position and can see the whole scene from my vantage point. The spaceship is wrecked, with one wing completely destroyed. Our team is spread out like tiny ants on opposite sides of the spaceship. And right in the center, a lone alien shoots randomly in one direction.

"Two minutes," I announce. "I'll cover you."

"Roger that," Violet says. "Prepare for fire!"

I count to two minutes under my breath. My blood pulses fast through my veins. And then I position my plane and pull the trigger, like I'm in a video game.

A round of bullets springs to life, and the noise is continuous as they pummel the ship, each bullet ricocheting against its hull and dropping to the ground.

It's enough of a distraction to allow the team to move in. I circle the plane above the scene, bringing it to the lowest speed without making it crash but still being able to be a part of the battle.

Avani moves forward with Rayen and throws an electric disk that's meant to electrocute the alien. The alien fires his gun without aim, and Rayen swerves away.

"I'm a bad bitch," she shouts. "You can't kill me!"

Rayen advances, throwing the disk. It hits the target, and the alien sways, its legs tangling as an electric spark works its way up its body. The alien drops its gun and writhes on the ground.

Then Rayen aims her stunner rifle and even though I'm firing a hundred rounds per second, I can almost hear her shots.

One, two, three.

It goes down.

Avani and Flint rush forward to carry it to the cryogenic chamber, but the window I've created isn't enough to stop the other aliens from coming out of the ship.

The odds have turned.

"Shit," Brooklyn says. "Cover Flint and Avani. They're the priority."

I turn the plane around and fire again, but my bullets are useless. Rayen's ammo is electrified, and each time it hits, the aliens jolt. My bullets make no impact, like it doesn't even matter that they should've been tearing through flesh.

One of the aliens drops its gun, and Rayen is quick to pick it up. Adam and Brooklyn move in, raising their own rifles. But their bullets seem to be as useless as mine. They've probably already wasted their own stun guns.

"Damn it, Rayen," says Brooklyn.

"Aim right between the eyes," Rayen shouts as she avoids another shot.

The aliens are blinded. They seem to have lost their bearings and start huddling together, unable to see who is attacking.

"Hold on," I hear myself shout. "I have an idea."

"Your ideas are bad!" Flint somehow manages to shout back between gasps.

"Do you want to make it out of here alive or not?" I ask stubbornly.

There are groans, which I take as a yes.

"Back off and take cover," I tell them. "Three minutes until impact."

They don't ask what's about to happen—they just run. I circle around to give them enough time before the impact comes. I point the plane down and kill the engines, then pull the ejection levers.

I don't have time to think about the fact that I've never jumped with a parachute before. I don't have time to think about anything before my seat is ejected backward with such extreme force that it feels like every bone in my body is going to break and my muscles are going to tear apart and split me open. I panic, but an instant later, the chute opens automatically.

It all takes less than three minutes. I watch as the plane turns downward, falling directly toward the destroyer. I can feel the crash before it actually happens—the jet breaks nose-first against the spaceship.

The rest of the plane crushes on top of it, burning red against silver as it comes undone in a smoky black cloud. The engines hit and the whole world goes red.

I'm blown back by the explosion and the visor of my helmet flies up. Launching debris shreds my parachute. Burning-hot shards cut through my G suit and my face, and I taste blood mixed with traces of iron and gunpowder.

It tastes disgusting. But it also tastes like freedom. Miraculously, my intercom survives, and there's a faint buzzing noise in the background.

"Go!" yells Violet. "The explosion has you covered."

I half hear her as I crash-land into the rocky ground, doubling over in pain as my body takes the impact and I roll to the ground. It takes a few seconds for my vision to clear as the thick smoke rises, filling my lungs with charred air.

I pull off my helmet and hear a shot, and I know it isn't from one of our guns. I raise my head, get up on my scraped knees, and look up to see the two jeeps driving away.

Then everything falls apart.

There's one alien left, and Violet is standing right in front of it.

The difference is obvious—even from here, I can tell that it can see her. It clinks its metal legs and raises its gun. I watch, paralyzed, frozen to the spot where I landed. The gun beeps.

"Violet, get down!" I shout, but there's barely time.

The alien shoots, and I watch as Adam shoves Violet down and swings his rifle up.

But the laser catches him in the side.

A scream fills the air, and I don't know where it's coming from. It takes me a few seconds to realize that I'm the one screaming.

One second he was there, the next he was only a cloud of dust.

The alien looks around, then raises its gun again and heads toward Violet, who is still on the ground. I don't even think as I rise and pull my grandfather's gun from the pocket on the leg of my suit.

I fire.

Again and again and again, until the chamber is empty and I'm sliding another round of bullets inside.

I move forward, my hands trembling, and I don't stop shooting.

Oh my God, Adam, I think. *Adam is gone.*

Adam is gone.

I'm running toward the alien now, still firing. Violet scrambles to the truck while I keep it distracted. It doesn't fire back, and I can taste blood in my mouth as I fight to stay conscious.

"Clover, let's go!" I hear Violet's voice near the truck, and then she grabs me, dragging me along and pulling me inside. She slams the door shut, hits the gas, and speeds away.

Not Adam.

Not again.

I breathe hard, tasting the bitterness and feeling the ache in my throat. Then I let out the tears that I've been holding back for so long.

PART III

ON TOP OF THE WORLD

CHAPTER 32

I'm supposed to be grateful.

Grateful that I survived, grateful that we captured an alien, grateful that six of the others got out alive, too. We completed our mission. Instead I sit here, wondering if it was asking too much for Adam to have made it back here with us.

It's been three days. Avani and Flint have been down in the lab examining the thing, but I haven't gone there yet. We're all quietly mourning, not saying the words that we can't seem to find anyway.

My legs dangle from the parapet of the watchtower. I consider the fall from here. I'd probably break my neck. It wouldn't be too painful.

"I thought I'd find you up here."

Violet stands over the trapdoor. I wipe my nose on the sleeve of my jacket. I haven't cried since Avani stitched me up when we first got back, but it feels like there's always a lump in my throat. Sputnik, sitting outside under the shade of the watchtower, wags her tail when she spots Violet. But even Sputnik can feel that something is wrong.

"Did you need something?" I ask.

Violet shakes her head. I'm not sure what she's going to do, but I won't be able to bear it if she asks me how I'm doing. Instead, she swings her legs over the low wall and sits next to me.

"I wish I could thank him," she tells me. "I didn't realize that they could see me. I thought... I thought that because the rest of you were safe, I was safe, too."

"It doesn't matter."

"Of course it does," Violet says, turning to me. "I'm alive because Adam took the hit for me."

She goes quiet. Then, almost imperceptibly, she wipes a tear from her eye with the back of her hand. Knowing that we were invisible made us feel powerful, but we hadn't tested the theory on Violet and Andy. It made us feel unstoppable. But we all forgot one thing.

We could still die.

I sit there looking at the horizon, not knowing what to say. Adam's promise has stuck with me. He believed that he was going to return. He believed me, when I promised things that I couldn't deliver. He believed in fighting back, and he died for it. Just when I'd told him the truth and he hadn't turned me away.

"It's my fault, too," I finally say, grinding my teeth. "If we'd stayed…"

"If we'd stayed, we would be dead soon anyway," Violet replies, turning to face me again. "We both knew the risks. Adam knew the risks, too. We all agreed to fight." She swallows hard. "Before you arrived, I had everything prepared. In case they invaded. I had cyanide capsules in my room. I just thought that… It'd be less painful. That I could spare the others." She pauses but doesn't expect an answer. "But I couldn't make that decision for them."

Violet shakes her head. Then she does the unthinkable—she presses her hand to my arm, squeezing it gently.

"It's not our fault," she says. "I miss him, too."

Her words are comforting. The lump in my throat rises. My instinct is not to speak, but I'm tired of silence. I'm tired of not knowing how to bridge the gaps between me and the others. I take a deep breath.

"Adam reminded me a lot of someone," I say. "My ex-boyfriend. I couldn't save Noah, but I thought maybe I could save Adam."

"Noah died in the invasion?"

I nod. "I know Adam wasn't Noah. I know that. And I know I couldn't have done anything for either of them."

But there's that lump in my throat again.

I'm done with staying quiet. I can't run away from my demons forever, because no matter where I go, they keep chasing me.

"I wish I could've done something," I say. "I wish I could've had more time."

All my wishes are given to the wind, blowing away as soon as I speak them. My wishes mean nothing now.

"He was your friend," Violet says. "He was mine, too. And he still will be. Even if he isn't here."

She smiles at me, and I try to smile back.

"We just have to find a way to keep going," she finishes. "We can't change the past."

I feel a tear falling down my cheek.

"All we can do right now is miss him," she says simply. "And thank him for what he was willing to do for us." She pats my shoulder and swings her legs back over to the watchtower floor, landing gracefully. "We need you downstairs. We still have a planet to save."

CHAPTER 33

After my talk with Violet, I finally convince myself to head to the lab to see what's happening. I don't know how much help I'll be, but I have to at least try. There's a dark shadow over every face I see, but I know that everyone is trying to go on.

It's what Adam would have wanted.

Sputnik follows me to the lab, blissfully unaware of how much has changed. She still chases the chickens around and finds a way to play with everyone. It's a good distraction for us. It's a chance to be more concerned about stopping the force of nature that is the Bernese mountain dog than about the fate of the world.

When I get to the lab, Avani is just coming out of the cell, where the alien is being kept in its cryogenic chamber. She wipes her eyes quickly, but I know that she's been crying.

"Hey," I say for a greeting. "Can I help you with anything?"

She swallows hard. "I'm good, thanks."

"You sure?"

Avani pauses for so long that I'm not sure if she's ever going to answer me. I realize that in my own grief for Adam, I forgot the others. I forgot that Adam spent seven months here, seeing them every day. I arrived only one month ago, and it's been painful enough for me. I can't imagine what this has been like for them.

"I'm so sorry, Avani," I tell her. "You shouldn't have to be doing this. We can just—"

Avani wipes her eyes again. "I'm okay, really," she says. "I want to be here. This is one of the only things I know how to do. This is the best way I can help."

I'm not sure what to say. I put a hand on her shoulder and squeeze it. "You built this machine. You did better than all the other scientists out there. You figured out how to stop them, and you're keeping that thing locked up."

She nods, slowly. "I know. I know. But I didn't…" She looks away, shaking her head. "This is the least I can do now."

I try to guess her feelings, but there are too many of them. And I don't know Avani well enough to guess.

"You don't have to do this," I say. "Not by yourself."

"You don't get it," she says, stronger this time. "I didn't fight back." Red burns on her cheeks—shame. "I could've done something. But I didn't fight. I thought I had everything under control."

"It's not your fault."

She brushes my hand off her shoulder, turning away.

"I'm not like you guys," she says. "I'm not brave." Her lower lip trembles. It looks like she's about to cry again. She takes a deep breath. "I wanted to do something. Every single day for six months, I stared at the walls of this compound and wondered if this was what the rest of my life was going to be. Staring at these walls, forever. Not knowing what happened on the outside. Not caring what happened. Until you showed up."

"I ran away for six months," I tell her. "That's what I did. I went from town to town, running and never looking back. The day the aliens attacked, I ran away when my only friend went up in dust." I swallow. "I didn't try to fight them."

"But you want to now."

"Yes, because I think it's the best option we have," I say quietly. "It's not because I'm brave… It's just… It's just what we got."

Avani is calmer now, and the redness in her eyes is starting to clear. "I wish I could do things like you guys can," she says. "Handle weapons. Fight. But that's not who I am. I'm just the science girl, you know?"

I shrug. "And I'm the girl who crashes cars. There's nothing wrong with that."

Avani looks back at the alien, still locked inside the cold cell, its chamber covered in frost. The machine is beeping, running scans.

"Adam and I came here together," Avani says, her lips in a

tight line. "I met him first, two days after the aliens attacked. He offered to help me, even though he didn't even know me." She smiles at the memory. "We met Brooklyn a couple of days later at a gas station. And he offered to help her, too. That's when I knew that the three of us would stick together. He never minded the driving. Brooklyn had this crazy idea about going to Area 51, and Adam never said no. He just said, 'I'll take us there.'"

I appreciate her sharing this memory with me. As if sensing that she's in pain, Sputnik walks up to Avani and sits next to her. She smiles down at the dog.

"That's just who he was," she says. "He never questioned what we wanted to do, or whether we would even find anything here. He had more faith than all of us put together. And he never gave up on me." She looks up, wiping her tears away. "I'm going to miss him."

"Me too."

I think about Violet's words and how much they ring true. I can't change the past. I can't change the fact that aliens invaded or the fact that they took my grandparents, Noah, and now Adam. They've taken too much from me.

All I can do is thank Adam for his sacrifice. Thank all of them for their sacrifices.

And make sure that none of it was in vain.

"So, do you want some help or not?" I ask.

This time, Avani gives me a smile.

"Yeah," she says. "I think I could use it."

CHAPTER 34

I spend the next day helping Avani and Flint in the lab.

It's easier than I thought it would be. The frozen alien doesn't bother me much. Avani starts figuring out ways to take it apart, and we discover that they're not as unbreakable as we thought. We're able to remove pieces of their metal legs with lasers, but no such luck with the upper body. The brain scans seem to be working, and slowly, Avani studies and analyzes the data. She doesn't like to share what she finds, and we all respect that.

On the fifth day after we captured the alien, Rayen convinces me to ask Violet about the alien gun that we stole. It's not like we have anything to lose by asking.

When I get to Violet's office, the door is ajar. I'm about to push it open when I hear voices.

"You promised me."

I know from that statement alone that it's Andy. I peer inside and see her and Violet standing on opposite sides of the desk.

"I know what I promised," Violet responds. "But things change, Andy. We can't just stay here until we starve. You know that. We'd be killing ourselves, the slow way."

"Well, not Adam."

The jab hits home, and Violet winces. I straighten up, my back to the door, and hold my breath. Andy's words are more than just angry—they're cruel. Cruel in a way that I never thought she could be.

"None of us meant for this to happen."

"He's dead because of you," Andy spits. "You promised me."

"And I kept that promise for as long as I could," Violet snaps back, her voice rising even as it breaks. "I waited seven months. I thought you'd come around."

"I'm not going to come around. Those things killed everyone. *Everyone*. I'm not going to try to play hero now, when everyone else is dead."

"We're not trying to be heroes."

Andy snorts. "Yeah, right," she says cynically. "We were safe!"

"We weren't!" Violet bites back. I take another quick glance inside. She sits in her chair now, massaging her temples. "We've never been safe. Security isn't enough. We got lucky. And our luck isn't going to last forever." Violet looks up at Andy. "I'd rather face them on my terms, Andy."

Andy's jaw is set, her hands balled into fists. I decide to make my entrance, before they catch me listening. I knock on the door, and they both jump.

"Sorry to burst in like this," I say. "Rayen is asking about the alien gun."

Violet drops her attitude, sighing heavily. "Sure," she says, pointing to a box in the corner of the room. "But it isn't working."

I pick up the box. Glancing between the two, the tension is obvious, and I move back toward the door. Before I shut it, I can hear them taking up their argument again.

"You promised me that I wouldn't have to," Andy says quietly. "You promised me."

"I'm doing what I can."

"It's not enough."

When I get to the lab, I find Flint engrossed in his work, analyzing some of the metal that he and Avani managed to take from the alien's legs.

I drop the box with the gun on top of the table. Sputnik sniffs it with minimal interest, then trots off.

"Did Violet just let you take that?" Flint asks, frowning.

"She was in the middle of an argument."

"Let me guess. Andy."

I raise an eyebrow. "How did you know?"

Flint puts down his scalpel and raises his safety glasses, resting them on top of his head. "It's not the first time they've argued. I mean, I've seen worse. Back when there were still adults here."

"This looked pretty bad," I tell him. Andy's words were sharp and edged, like knives.

"You should've seen them before. They'd have full-on shouting matches," Flint says. "There were about forty kids here at the base, but those two were always like sisters."

"Andy said that we're trying to play heroes."

Flint looks up at me, then shrugs. "Aren't we?"

"I'm not doing this to look heroic."

"Being a hero isn't just about looking heroic, Clover," he says. "Sometimes it's just doing what you think is right. Even when it'll get your arse killed."

He meets my eyes, and I know that we're both thinking about Adam now. He saved Violet. He pushed her out of the way. Even if he wasn't trying to be a hero, he still wound up as one.

"Don't see it as something bad," Flint says. He adjusts his glasses back over his face. "It's just the way things are."

He's right. I look over his shoulder at his work.

"So what exactly are you doing?"

He sighs. "Decomposition of elements. But Avani says the machine isn't working…"

"This one?" I ask, pointing, and he nods. I look it over. I might not be the best with scientific equipment, but there doesn't seem to be anything obviously wrong with it. "It looks fine to me. Give me your blood sample."

He frowns, looking up again. "Say what?"

"Blood sample," I repeat. "Come on. Gotta be quick."

"I just said that it isn't working."

"Well, Avani won't mind if we test it twice."

Flint heads to the medical part of the laboratory and finds two syringes. He draws his blood first, then I offer him my arm so he can take mine.

I put both tubes into the machine and ready the analysis. "Very simple."

Flint doesn't bother responding. He shakes his head and goes back to his metal sample.

Rayen walks in, plopping down on a stool and dumping a huge weapon on the table. It's bigger than a bazooka, and I can't even begin to fathom where she finds these things.

"No guns on the table," Flint says.

Rayen glares at him, her brown eyes daring him to contradict her. "So?" she asks. "Did Violet let you take the gun?"

"Yeah, it's over there." I point to the box. "She says it isn't working."

Rayen curses. "I'm tired of things not working."

"Get in line," Flint mutters.

She rolls her eyes, then goes over and sits up on the workbench, next to Flint. She pokes him in the arm, and he looks up, irritated.

"What's going on?" Rayen asks, eyeing the microscope. "What have you got?"

Flint's whole manner changes, as if Rayen has just said the magic words.

"The aliens' legs are just metal," he says excitedly. "No organic material. It's stronger than anything I've ever seen. But it turns out that it's not immune to lasers. That's how I got this sample."

Rayen cocks her head. "You sawed off its leg?"

Flint nods. "Yeah. You know what's even more fantastic? It's a one hundred percent pure material. They have no nerves or anything that would allow them to control how they work," he says. "Of course, this led me to theorize that the legs might not have been part of their original species design. I've been discussing it with Avani."

Rayen and I exchange a look.

"Has he been like this all day?" she asks, unimpressed.

I nod. "Yesterday, too."

"They've altered their own species to make it better, Rayen," Flint says, like a little boy at Christmas. "How brilliant is that?"

"So what?" She shrugs. "I have six tattoos and I don't see you getting excited about that."

"They're scrap metal," I say.

"Exactly," Flint replies, completely missing our tone. "Which makes me wonder if they haven't altered the rest of their bodies, too." He gestures toward his face to indicate the strange human faces that the aliens wear.

"Why would they want to look human?" Rayen asks. "They could be like the Terminator, and they choose to look like us? Makes no sense to me."

Flint shakes his head. "I don't know. But it's interesting, because they're controlling their legs remotely. The metal is full of smaller articulations, but it's motorized. That's why we're able to short-circuit them. I'll have to cut it up to find out where exactly the motor is."

The day passes easily. My blood samples are still being processed, and I don't want to rush the results. Maybe that machine really is broken. Flint picks apart his alien leg sample until he has all the pieces laid neatly on the worktable. He was right—the entire thing is made of wires and metal.

He slides open a machine to analyze the metal, and sitting inside it is the brick I gave him. I blink in surprise. With all the events of the last week, I'd forgotten about this. Adam was the one who had been helping me hide it.

Flint tosses the brick to me carelessly. "There you go."

I turn it in my hands. "Find anything?"

"Nothing at all," he says. "Regular brick, through and through. About twenty years old. Can't be more specific than that."

Twenty years old. That places the false wall in the same time frame as the information blackout. But this might be enough to piece together my theory.

I keep turning the brick in my hand. Then I notice that Rayen is watching my face closely.

"Spill it," she commands.

"What?"

"You have the same expression my brother used to make

237

when he was hiding candy in his room," Rayen says. "Sweet Jesus of Spaceships, Clover, if you're hiding a Milky Way bar, I will *kill* you."

I shift my weight. "It's kind of bigger than that."

Flint, who has only been half listening, looks up from the worktable and asks, "What?"

There's no other way I can put this.

"There's a spaceship in our basement."

Flint drops everything he's holding.

CHAPTER 35

Flint and Rayen stare openmouthed because, of course, there's no other way to look at a spaceship that's sitting in your basement.

"It's fucking huge," says Rayen, as if those are the only words that she can actually think.

"Bloody hell," Flint says. "And you found this a week ago?"

I nod my head. "Adam and I found it." Saying his name feels like a forbidden reminder.

"You should have just told us, " Rayen says, her eyebrows scrunching together.

Flint seems stunned. He taps the spaceship, then moves his hand over its smooth underside.

"So interesting," he mutters. "It's made of the same material as their legs. But somehow…" He shakes his head. "You said that brick came from the rubble?"

I nod. "Yeah. The ship was hidden behind this wall the whole time."

"So this has been here for twenty years." He exhales in awe, pushing his hands through his hair, leaving it a mess of black curls. "Twenty years. This bloody changes everything."

I nod my head. It does. They were here before. And someone made sure that we wouldn't find out about it, because all the reports were wiped out. One week, twenty years ago, was redacted from our history, and we'll never know what happened. There are no remaining pieces to the puzzle, because the house caught on fire and burned to ashes.

"It doesn't have to, though," says Rayen quietly. "It doesn't change the fact that they came and annihilated us."

Flint nods in agreement.

"But if people had known that aliens came here all those years ago..." I pause. "If we'd known, we could've prepared. We could've been ready for the attack that was coming, and we would've been able to fight back."

Silence falls. Flint mutters something unintelligible as he knocks his fingers against the spaceship.

"It's not the same," he says, turning to us.

"What?" I ask.

"This is not one of their spaceships."

"What do you mean?" Rayen asks.

Flint just shrugs, as if the answer has been right in front of us all along. "It's not one of their spaceships."

"Explain yourself," demands Rayen.

He nods. "I've seen enough of them by now that I can tell the difference. This ship is made of softer material. Not to mention how much bigger it is than all the others. Right, Clover? The aliens' ships have very practical designs, without a single shred of elegance. They're built to be effective and fast. Beginning with the wings."

I nod slowly, starting to see what he's looking at. Flint has immediately pinpointed what had felt vaguely wrong to me. The design of the wings, the curve of the nose—this ship has style.

"The ships that invaded and attacked us... They look like an imitation of this one."

Flint nods. "Yes. And now that we know that these things are willing to change their bodies in order to improve them, why wouldn't they copy spaceship designs for the same reason?"

I evaluate the ship, cocking my head. "Considering the shape and the wing design, it would make sense. If this thing can fly"—I jerk my head toward it—"it's going to be a hell of a lot faster than any jets that we have."

"Not only that," Flint says. "The material is different, not as hard. The aliens have made their metal *look* the same as this, but it's not. The metal on their ships is the real deal, though. It's bloody impenetrable."

"So what are we looking at?" Rayen asks. "Two different alien species?"

Slowly, Flint nods. "Looks like it. Two alien cultures that have had close contact for a while. Maybe thousands of years, for all we know."

I narrow my eyes. "What are you saying?"

Flint turns to us, his dark eyes indecipherable. "What if the owners of this spaceship are still here?"

There's something deeply unsettling about not knowing what lurks in the dark.

Before, I knew they were out there, waiting for me to be careless or make a mistake. Now, there are more of them. An unknown species that may or may not be hiding out on Earth.

The spaceship is proof enough.

After making Flint and Rayen promise that we'd talk about this later, that we'd tell the others about the spaceship and what it means, I head to the dormitory.

It's empty when I get there. I'm dying for a shower, so I grab some clean clothes, and just as I'm heading back out, Andy comes in. She looks exhausted, and dark circles are visible under her eyes.

I remember the argument earlier.

"Hey," I call out. "You okay, Andy?"

She takes a deep breath before answering. "Yeah." She narrows her eyes. "You heard us arguing?"

I shrug slightly. "Sorry about that."

"It's fine," she says, but she doesn't look like it's fine. "It's just another stupid argument. I told Violet that this was dangerous. But she didn't listen to me."

"Andy, we can't hole up in here forever."

Her eyes flash a darker color. "I am aware. You didn't shut up about it till you got your way. Happy now?"

I shift my weight, taken aback. "Don't you want to find out what our enemy is like?"

"I already know what it's like. And that's all I need to know."

She turns away and sits on her bed, the light of her laptop illuminating her face.

I leave, not knowing what else to say.

CHAPTER 36

When I get to the lab the next day, everyone is already there.

"Surprise meeting?" I ask, eyebrows raised.

Violet acknowledges me with a nod. She has her blond hair in a tight braid, and her sharp eyes examine everything in the room. "Actually, yes." She gets straight to the point. "So, good news. Avani's brain scans work. Bad news…"

"We need medical supplies to keep the alien sedated while I run more extensive tests," Avani says. "We're practically out of morphine, and I don't want to risk it waking up."

"But it's in a cryogenic chamber," Rayen says. "Shouldn't the cold keep it under?"

Avani shrugs. "I'm starting the brain scans now, and I've been injecting the morphine directly into its eye to keep it totally under, but I want to have everything we might need at the ready."

Flint nods in agreement.

"I thought we might get supplies for everyone," Violet says. "Just in case…" She goes quiet for a moment, then continues. "I want to make an expedition. Me, Brooklyn, and Flint head to the town of Caliente. It's a one-day trip, maximum. They have a hospital that might not have been raided."

"Isn't that dangerous?" Rayen asks. "You can be *seen*."

Violet blushes a deep red but does her best to hide her consternation. "I know, but I don't want anybody else to leave."

"I can go," I blurt out. "It's no trouble."

"No offense, Clover, but I'd rather have you here," Violet says. "You don't know the area like we do. Brooklyn and Flint can cover my back."

She says that last part like she's trying to reassure herself, instead of us. An unnerving feeling creeps into my stomach. I don't like the idea of splitting up.

"Maybe we could wait and see how the scans go," I suggest, but I know that my argument is weak.

Violet shakes her head, like I knew she would. "We've all sacrificed a lot to get here. I'm not going to let this opportunity go to waste. If Avani says we need more supplies, we go get them."

Then I understand what she's thinking. It's dangerous for her to go, of course. But she feels guilty about the fact that they've stayed here for so long—and she doesn't want to be responsible for anyone else's death but her own.

"I don't like this," Rayen says, shaking her head. "It's stupid exposing yourself this way."

"I'll be driving," Violet says. "That's all."

I look at the others. Flint has his mouth set in a straight line, and I can tell that he's no more pleased about this than I am.

Finally, Rayen nods. "All right. But you're taking ammo and the short-circuit disks," she turns to Flint. "Those will work, right?"

He nods. "They'll buy us enough time to escape."

Violet nods again. "That's all I need." She turns to Rayen. "You're in command here while I'm gone. Stay on full alert. And Avani, don't you dare leave that thing's side."

We all nod. The orders are simple enough. Violet and Rayen leave the room talking about the best guns and truck to take, and Flint follows them.

Brooklyn and Avani exchange a significant look. Then Avani mouths "go" to Brooklyn, and she leaves. Avani pulls me aside.

"Hey, Clover?" she says calmly. But her eyes dart from side to side, as if she's nervous. "You remember the blood-scanning machine that we were talking about the other day?"

"Sure," I say, my hands in my pockets. I never came back to check the results. "Why?"

"Someone used the machine," she says. "It wasn't you, by any chance?"

"No." The lie rolls easily off my tongue. She's acting so strangely that I really don't want to tell her that I was the one who double-checked her on this. "Isn't it broken?"

Avani shifts her weight to her other leg. "Something happened. The analysis worked—it showed two different sets of DNA."

"But that's good, isn't it? Maybe we can do the tests again and isolate the factor that allows us to be invisible. Right?"

"Yeah…" But she's distracted. There's something in her eyes that I thought was tiredness at first, but it's something else entirely.

I freeze when I realize that I know what it is.

Fear.

"There was a problem with the analysis," she says.

"What happened to the blood?"

"It looks ordinary. But once I broke down the DNA coding and filed the genetic profile…" She goes quiet.

"Avani?"

"Well, you see…" she says dryly. "It wasn't human."

CHAPTER 37

My blood. Flint's blood. It can't be.

I'm not sure what to believe anymore.

My blood isn't human.

But I *am* human. I know this. I am as human as can be.

A doctor cut my umbilical cord when I was born. I learned my first words. I lost my first tooth while eating a hamburger at Wendy's. I got my period when I was twelve. I had my first kiss at fifteen, the same year I lost my virginity, both with Noah. All parts of me are entirely, and completely, human.

That machine is lying.

Something must have happened, or something must have changed. The blood in that machine is not mine.

I ran away as soon as Avani told me, leaving her to the alien creature, trying to wrap my head around this new information.

Now I stand in the room with the spaceship, my head spinning. It doesn't make sense. Sputnik sits by my side, waiting, as if she knows that I need her. I burrow my hands into her fur, hugging her tightly next to my body.

A noise behind me makes me turn. Rayen stops next to the pile of bricks, her expression indecipherable as she looks at the ship.

"Strange, isn't it?" she finally says. "Seven months ago, I wouldn't have believed in life beyond Earth."

"You didn't?" I ask.

"You did?"

I nod. "The universe is too big to not be hiding things."

Rayen smiles at that. She has her hands in the pockets of her hoodie. "That would almost be poetic, if it weren't for the present circumstances."

"This is the first and only time that I've regretted being right."

Rayen laughs, the sound echoing through the room. Then she looks at me. "You okay?"

I nod, slowly. I don't know if I'll ever be okay. Maybe I'm getting there. And I'm going to get my answers. "How are things down at the lab?"

"Avani is running the brain scans," she says. "We should head back. It's not like we're going to be able to open that spaceship just by staring at it."

The moment she says that, though, something changes. The reflective surface that I was so intently staring at gives off a strange, multicolored wave, then settles back to silver.

"Did you see that?" I jump to my feet.

Rayen raises her eyebrows, which means that I'm not going crazy. I hold my breath. The wave of color feels familiar somehow, like a signal boosting in the back of my mind.

I approach the ship carefully, pressing my ear to the hull. The silence that had always penetrated this room is interrupted now by a low humming.

I turn to Rayen, and she nods. She can hear it, too.

I walk beneath the spaceship, Sputnik following behind me. I concentrate on the sound, which gets louder and louder as I work my way toward the rear. The humming gets even louder, and I'm almost running now.

Rayen is right behind me, the dog between us, and we both spot something that wasn't there before. It's a glowing panel on the bottom of the ship, pulsing with energy.

I touch my hand to it and bite back a scream. "It burns!"

"Do you have something you can touch it with?"

My hand hurts from the shock, but I search through my pockets. There are a couple of keys and some gum that I stole from the pantry. I dig deeper and pull out Andy's gloves.

My heart pulses with adrenaline as I slide the gloves onto my hands for protection. They're soft and cushioned and, slowly, I press my hand to the panel.

This time, there is no burning shock. Instead, the panel lights up, and I step back, blinded by white light.

I hear Rayen say something, but I'm disoriented. It takes a minute for my eyes to focus as the light fades. Then a sleek, silver ramp slides from the spaceship down to the floor.

I glance at Rayen. She looks as stunned as I am, and Sputnik starts barking in the direction of the ramp. Neither of us hesitate as we move closer and climb it.

The spaceship is even more impressive from the inside. The ramp leads into what appears to be the main control room. There's a big chair in the center, with six smaller operating stations, and countless panels and lights. The whole thing is made from the same silver material, but here it bursts with a hundred different colors—as if, beneath all the silver, hues of red, pink, and blue are dancing.

A panel lights up before us, all white and blue. This is technology like I've never seen before.

"Interuniversal identity print complete," a voice says. Somehow, I know it's not speaking English—but my brain understands it. "Welcome home."

I hold my breath and look down at the gloves I'm wearing, the gloves that hold a secret.

And everything spins—the spaceship, the blackout, the aliens, and, at the center of it all, the one girl who doesn't fit.

I don't totally understand, but I think I have an inkling of what's happening.

Suddenly, Rayen's walkie-talkie crackles on.

"Avani," Rayen says. "You have to see something—"

"Whatever it is, it's not important," Avani cuts in. "I need you!" Her voice is panicky.

"What happened?"

"I think the brain scans woke it up," she says.

"It's awake?" Rayen exclaims.

"Shut up!" says Avani. "That's not the problem. The scans are."

I snatch the walkie-talkie from Rayen's hands. "What the hell, Avani?" I demand. "What's going on? Is it out of containment?"

"The brain scans, Clover," she says. "They show that these aliens are not individuals. They're a hive."

The line goes quiet.

"They have a *hive mind*," Avani repeats frantically. "The rest of them are probably coming here right now."

CHAPTER 38

I grab one of Rayen's stun guns on our way to the lab. My heart is beating so fast that I think it might burst out of my chest any second.

We arrive to find Avani in a panic, and it's obvious that she's not going to be able to take charge here. A plan is already forming in my head.

"Avani, hole up here in the lab," I tell her. "Stay with Sputnik. We're going to take care of this."

I look at Rayen. She looks tough enough to take on a hundred aliens.

"Any ideas?" she asks me.

"Me, you, and Andy take this thing to the old compound." I gesture with my head toward the alien that's lying in its chamber. "Barricade ourselves in. And don't let these fuckers get in our house."

"The warehouse," Rayen says. "It'll work."

I nod. Avani takes Sputnik by the collar, bringing her inside the lab. I can't let myself get emotional about leaving her again. Rayen grabs the alien gun, and it lights up in her hands. We don't have time to be surprised that it's suddenly working.

Rayen grins at me. I find myself grinning back at her.

Andy barges in a few minutes later as Rayen and I are wheeling the alien out, still holding it in the chamber. We probably won't be able to plug the chamber in once we're inside the warehouse, but it should stay cold for a couple of hours. There's no time to wrap my head around whatever just happened with the spaceship, so I push it out of my mind. Right now, we have to get ourselves out of this crisis.

"We have ten minutes until they get here," Andy announces. "Where are you taking this thing?"

"Old compound," Rayen and I reply in unison.

Rayen picks up fifteen or so short-circuit disks, but that won't be nearly enough. Then she hands Andy a stun gun.

"Why are you giving me this?" Andy asks, half whining. "You know I can't shoot."

"Well, Andy, it's time to play some real-life *Counter-Strike*," Rayen says as she hands her another gun.

Andy looks terrified. I just hope that she doesn't shoot herself, or us, in the foot.

And then we're out of the lab, running, wheeling the alien

in its cryogenic chamber through the corridors as fast as we can. It doesn't look like much of a menace anymore, with half its legs cut off. Andy guides us with her tablet in hand, accessing the security system and locking doors, trying to put as many things in our favor as we can.

The warehouse is darker and even older than I imagined it would be. It's filled with row after row of shelves and metal racks that are at least fifteen feet high, each of them holding dozens of boxes.

Rayen closes the door behind us and Andy taps a button on her tablet. The metal locks slide together, and we're shut inside with the monster.

"Sealed all the entrances," Andy confirms, clutching the stun gun and opening something else on her tablet. "Three minutes."

She types rapidly.

"One minute," she says. "They're heading straight toward the signal. I also set up a program that reproduces sound and brain waves, so they'll be a little disoriented. Let's hope Avani's brain-wave theory is right."

"Awesome," I say.

"Turns out there's actually an advantage to having a nerd in the group." She turns to us. "Just don't get me killed."

The tablet's screen lights up. There's a countdown going.

Ten. I blink, my heart racing. *Nine. Eight.* I empty my mind. *Seven.*

I've been here before. I know how to fight this.

Six.

I'm not afraid.

Five.

It's true.

Four.

I release the safety on my gun.

Three. Two. One.

I can hear them coming, or maybe it's my imagination. But I'm highly attuned to the sound of their metal legs clicking on the ground.

This time, I'm ready for them.

The warehouse door is blasted open by something similar to a bomb. I shield my eyes from the sudden explosion of light, and Rayen signals for us to split up. Silently, I tiptoe to the left.

I glimpse the broken door and the glint of metal just beyond it. Five aliens stand in the doorway, and there's no other way out of here. But we can't risk them breaching the main compound— our home.

They walk inside and I hold my breath. They split up, taking their time. I try to track them with my eyes, but now I can only see two of them, their expressions completely blank. Maybe Andy's device works, and they really are disoriented.

I still don't understand how they think. The one that we kidnapped is obviously sending brain signals for help. The only thing I can hope for is that they don't know our numbers or where exactly we are.

If all their knowledge and thoughts really are shared, then

we've been compromised, and Avani won't be safe for long. I cross my fingers that that's not the case.

I turn my head slowly, only to see one of them standing close by. I take a sharp intake of breath, squeezing myself against the racks. The alien looks straight at me, and I don't dare move or breathe. This one has a teenager's face, which makes it creepier than the others. Its eyes seem to be focused on me, but I'm not sure if they can actually see anything.

It continues down the aisle toward me, its six legs moving slowly, turning it in all directions, as if it's homing in on a signal. I squeeze myself tighter, trying to make myself smaller as it walks past me.

I slide one of the short-circuit disks out of the pocket of my jacket. Without taking my eyes off the alien, I turn and aim at its legs.

A terrible screech echoes through the compound as the circuit buzzes, frying all the wires inside its legs. The creature screams again as its legs give out, and it falls to the floor. But there's no movement in its mouth or eyes, and it's like I'm only hearing the screeching inside my brain.

It screams louder, and I recognize a distress signal—it's hurt. It occurs to me that the aliens can probably repair themselves. If they can alter their own biology, then I'm sure there's a lot more that they can do. This is my only opening, and I need to take it.

I rest my stunner rifle on my shoulder and aim straight for the middle of its head. It falls back from the impact, and for a second, I let myself breathe. It's out. They are not invincible.

They have a weak spot. I approach it carefully, as silently as I can. Its legs are still buzzing with electricity.

"Rayen," I whisper over the comm unit. "I think mine is dead."

As soon as I say it, I hear that clicking sound. One of its legs tries to pin me down. For a moment, I think that it can see me, but it screeches again, opening its arms aimlessly, trying to blindly grab me.

Another scream pierces the air and I tumble to the floor, my gun falling from my grip. One of its metal claws slams down on my leg, stabbing right through my flesh. The pain is intense, and I let out a scream as I try to get out from under it, my blood splattering the concrete.

Then I hear Rayen. I freeze, and she aims her gun at the alien and shoots.

Its skin goes up in a burst of dust. It looks like the blast has burned off its skin and face, revealing a structured skeleton— exposed organs, cradled by metal and wires.

The alien screeches, but Rayen doesn't give it any time to react. She shoots again, aiming for the strange pulsating organ in the middle of its belly. There's a burst of green, and then it falls back on the floor, motionless.

The alien's metal legs don't fit with its upper half—the cage around the green blob has a strange, constructed look. Its organs spill onto the floor, tainting it with a gross, thick liquid, but all the other parts look like they've been made. It looks like Frankenstein's monster, if the monster had been built from a hundred different species.

Rayen looks at me. "You okay?"

I touch my leg and the wound, then I nod. Blood is still flowing freely, so I tear a piece off my shirt and wrap it around my leg. I can fix this later. Rayen picks up the alien's gun and hands it to me.

"There's another one in this direction," she says.

"Let's go."

I make my way past the dead alien. Rayen signals for me to go right while she heads the opposite direction. I turn at the end of the aisle, my leg throbbing.

I hear shots behind me, and there's no time to lose. I raise the alien gun and keep it aimed as I turn around and come face-to-face with another one. It looks around, as if it can feel a presence near it, and I risk a glance up, where I see Andy sitting, fifteen feet high on the top rack, wedged between cardboard boxes and storage material.

I don't have time to tell her to get her ass down here or even to scream at her to ask her what the hell she's doing. I point my gun at the alien and pull the trigger. Its skin bursts into a cloud of dust, and I'm reminded of the people who I've seen burst like that. Its skeleton is exposed, and I see that pulsating organ again. I know exactly what I have to hit. The alien screeches, an inhuman noise that chills me to the bone. But it can't see me to retaliate. I am its invisible enemy, and it should be the one to fear me.

It runs forward, legs clicking on the concrete as it raises itself up to its full height and opens its monstrous mouth. I freeze in place as I aim my gun and shoot straight at that little green spot between the metal. The organ bursts. The alien drops dead at my feet, and it's not so scary now.

"What the hell?" Andy says from up high. "How did you do that?"

"Get the fuck down from there," I tell her, but she's already making her way down. "Rayen has the other three."

And the one that is supposedly in a coma. I don't let myself think about that.

I run toward the other end of the warehouse. Andy is close behind me. We're the only things echoing around the old compound now, and I shut down any thoughts of what might have happened. Nothing happened. Nobody is dead.

We find Rayen backed up against a wall, the remaining three aliens surrounding her. She has no way out. They can't see her, but she's been backed into a corner. If she moves, they'll know she's there, and they'll shoot in her direction. At least the captive alien is nowhere to be seen.

Rayen sees me coming and we lock eyes. She looks at the gun in my hand and nods. From here, I could hit her just as easily as I could hit one of them.

I don't stop to think about it.

I raise the gun and shoot.

The alien nearest to Rayen explodes in a flash of dead skin and dust, and for a second, I'm stunned. Two inches to the right and I would have hit her.

The distraction gives Rayen enough time to get away and

shoot one of the other aliens between the eyes. It staggers back, and Rayen and I move to back each other up.

We have to hurry—they're bigger and faster than us, and now they're scrambling together, trying to find their targets. I hear one of their guns charging up and point my own at the third alien, before it manages to shoot. Its skin blows to pieces, and I take aim at the green spot. The alien approaches, and I shoot without thinking twice. The blast ricochets off its metal cage and hits the wall. I curse. Rayen hits the one near her, and its green organ explodes. I turn my back, and the second alien comes hurtling toward me.

"No!" I hear a shout as Andy launches herself onto the alien's back and it throws her off.

Suddenly, the alien isn't interested in me. It turns to Andy, all metal and organs, and freezes.

I shoot it. The green blob explodes, tainting the walls. Rayen has finished off the third alien, and Andy lies on the floor. The impact from being thrown off has clearly knocked the wind out of her.

"Where's the other one?" I ask.

Rayen runs and wheels it over. It seems to still be asleep, shackled to its chamber, but it's not fooling me. Its brain is fully active, sending a homing signal right on us. I hope that the aliens are idiotic enough to think that if the signal stops, it means that the others have found him.

I shoot its skin off and the green organ appears behind the cage. But before I can shoot it, Rayen stops me, holding her arm up. I look at her, confused, and she silently takes a syringe out of her pocket. It's full of a transparent liquid, and she screws the needle in. Slowly, she puts the needle between the metal bars of the cage, pierces the organ, and injects the whole thing. It stops glowing and gray tissue spreads all over. The green blob shrivels up.

"What the hell is that?" I ask.

"Morphine," she says. I wait for her to explain why she's carrying a full dose of morphine around in her pocket.

She looks up and meets my eyes. "You're not the only one who thinks about the end, Clover," she says.

I look at her thoughtfully, then avert my eyes. Rayen didn't need to be told why I slept with a gun. The others probably thought that it was for protection. I had only told the truth to Violet.

But Rayen knows. There's some sadness in her eyes, but she's survived, too. It gives me hope. Maybe we'll keep surviving together.

"You think it's dead?" I ask.

"As dead as it can get."

Andy mumbles something from the floor, and we turn toward her. As I approach her, my alien gun beeps.

Andy opens her eyes and looks at it. It beeps again. And then it keeps beeping, faster and faster, as if it wants me to recognize something. Andy widens her eyes, and suddenly, I know how all the pieces of the puzzle fit.

I crack the gun against Andy's skull and she slumps down, unconscious.

CHAPTER 39

The first thing that Andy does when she comes to is fight against her shackles. Rayen and I watch her desperation as she rattles them incessantly. It's no use. Her hands are chained to the table, and the table and chair are firmly bolted to the ground.

"Okay. Who's the bad cop and who's the good cop?" Andy asks. There's something different about her face. She's not scared or wincing, like usual. She's defiant, like we're the bad guys in all this. I'm not sure if the change comes from being found out, or if she's just trying to be brave.

"You're out of luck," Rayen says dryly. "Neither of us is feeling very nice right now."

Rayen leans against a wall, her pistol in her hands. I sit down in front of Andy, who sets her jaw in anger.

"You think this is fair?" She looks up at Rayen, then furrows her eyebrows. "Let me go."

Rayen doesn't move.

"Please. You don't realize what you're doing."

She could almost convince me that she's human, if it weren't for the glint in her eyes, that multicolored shine. It's exactly like the spaceship in the bunker, and it makes my arms tingle with goose bumps. The hidden spaceship, the fact that they hunt at night, the reason why Andy is so afraid of them. It all makes sense now.

"I haven't done anything," she says.

"I know what you are, Andrea," I reply. "Or is that even your real name?"

Andy looks up. Her eyes are pink, shining like a dying star. It would almost be beautiful to watch, if I didn't know what she was.

Outsider.

Alien.

"You know nothing," she says, her voice becoming stronger. It's like the Andy we knew was just an act. She sits up, and her posture is straight for the first time since I met her. Without her huge glasses, I can see her properly. "Let. Me. Go."

I pull out my gun and lay it on the table, just out of her reach.

"It's your choice," I tell her. "Either you start talking, or I start shooting."

"You can't shoot me," she says.

I pick up the gun, click the safety off, and shoot her in the foot. Andy screams. She looks at me incredulously, like I'm some kind of monster.

Rayen doesn't even blink.

"So that's the kind of thing humans do?" She almost spits. "I was right to hide."

"No," I say. "That's the kind of thing we're driven to do when freaking aliens come knocking on our door and bring total destruction with them."

The hole in her foot has already disappeared. I look up at her again, and she's smiling.

"You can't kill me."

"Well, it still hurts, doesn't it?" I sit back in my chair again, gun in hand. "I've got plenty of bullets."

"I never took you for a torturer."

"You didn't take me for a lot of things, Andy," I say, eyeing her. "You killed Adam. Doesn't that make you a murderer?"

She looks away. Her cheeks burn a bright red. "I didn't kill him."

"You knew what would happen. You knew what they were after. You had information that could have *saved* him."

"Violet is going to get me out of this."

"She'll be a little angry, yes. But she won't be back until tonight. That gives us plenty of time."

Andy doesn't move.

"I'm not letting you out until you tell me what the hell you are."

"I owe you nothing."

"I hope you enjoy staying locked up here. Because until we have answers, I'm not moving. You lied to us, Andy."

She looks away.

"You lied to us, and you manipulated us," I tell her. "You were the one who messed with the blood-analysis machine so your alien blood wouldn't show. You were the one manipulating Violet so she wouldn't send us out there. So you wouldn't have to fight."

She refuses to look at me and Rayen. Beneath her skin, I see the tainted glint of blue and pink, and her eyes burn bright like a supernova. Andy's never looked more beautiful, but she's also never looked more distant. She was never one of us.

"The blackout. That was you, too, wasn't it? Twenty years ago. You arrived on a spaceship. The one hidden in the bunker."

At that, she looks up again, eyes wide. "In the bunker?"

I smile. "Yeah. You blacked out the information from your arrival and hid the ship so nobody would know. But I found out, and all the pieces fit."

"It's in the bunker?" she asks again.

I narrow my eyes and, of course, now I see. If Andy knew that the spaceship was there, she wouldn't be acting like this.

She didn't know.

"Yes," I say, annoyed that I've given away this piece of information. I still don't know Andy's abilities. "So, do you want to tell me how you ended up here?"

Rayen crosses her arms, her jaw set. Just observing.

266

"Or would you prefer to tell me why the aliens are here?"

Andy stays silent. I see her anger growing like a burning ember in the fire, her expression fierce. But there are also tears in her eyes, and I'm not sure which to trust.

But I know that I can't trust her at all.

"They came for me," she finally says. "Me and my species—we're what they've been looking for. We fled our planet," she says, her voice distant. She doesn't look at me. "We found refuge on Earth, where we could hide among a species that looked like us. But they came, too."

That explains why they chose to kill humans one by one. That way, they could figure out who was human and who was alien. Dropping bombs would risk killing one of Andy's species. They were needles in a haystack—almost impossible to find.

And the easiest way to find a needle is to burn the whole haystack.

It all fits, why the spaceships had come and why the aliens had wiped us out. They destroyed our planet, but it had never been about Earth at all.

"Do you even realize what you've taken from us?" I ask her. I'm exhausted. Killing Andy won't bring justice. It won't bring back my family. That's what hurts the most. "Do you?"

There's no repairing this. There is no changing the past.

"Are we in danger?" I ask her. "Do you think that they had time to recognize you? That they'll come back for you?"

For a minute, she looks panicked, like she hadn't thought about that possibility. "You can't..." she starts. "I don't think so."

"We can't what?" Rayen looks up and stares at Andy. There's something unwavering about Rayen's look. It scares the hell out of the girl sitting across from me. "We can't give you to them?"

"They will kill you."

"What does it matter anyway? We're all dead. Our planet is finished. There's nothing left to lose."

"They won't leave Earth. And they will kill the rest of you. You can't exchange me like a war prisoner. They have no mercy."

"And neither do you."

Andy doesn't have an answer to that. We're not going to try to exchange her for anything—we're not that crazy. I hate those aliens as much as I hate Andy.

"Let's start again," I say. "This time, from the beginning."

"And God help us, if you leave anything out…" says Rayen. She means that seriously, and I can't help but think that no one is ever going to say "Holy Mother of Sweetened Peas" again.

Andy looks at us, and I can see the change in her eyes.

"We are not your friends," I say, my voice beginning to show the rage that I feel climbing up my throat. "You destroyed our home."

"And you're willing to hurt someone who's innocent," Andy fires back.

"Innocent of what?" Rayen spits. "What are you so innocent of, Andy? Tell me. Enlighten me, please! Innocent because you did nothing to prevent the destruction of an entire planet? Of an entire race, who had nothing to do with this fight?"

Andy is quiet for a minute, then she asks, "If I tell you everything, you'll release me?"

"We'll think about it," I say evenly, but I have no intention of doing so. Not now, not ever. "When did you arrive on Earth?"

Andy sighs. "Twenty years ago," she starts. "I was very small. I barely remember the crossing. We arrived the first week of June. There were twenty-three of us."

"How many are left?"

"Only me."

"And why did you destroy the records?"

"We couldn't let anybody know about us. We had to hide the ship," Andy says. "I didn't know what had happened to it. The only person whose memories we didn't wipe was Violet's mom. She was in charge of the project."

"And how do you know that the other ones are dead?" Rayen asks.

"I felt it," she says quietly, looking at me in the eye. "I know that I'm the last one."

Her tone is something like a plea, but it's Rayen who answers it. "Do you want us to pity you? That you're the last one?"

Andy's lower lip quivers. She looks at Rayen, tears forming in her eyes. "I am the last of them *all*," she repeats, almost whispering. "The last."

"And so are we," Rayen says, her tone harsh. "Thanks to you."

"You knew that they were going to come after you," I say

angrily. I couldn't care less about her species. They had killed mine. "How did this happen? When did it all start?"

Andy tries to wipe her tears away, but her hands are shackled to the table.

"Thousands of years ago," she says. "Millions, maybe. Our species prospered in our system. We were known for our knowledge, which we passed down to all species. We were the most powerful beings in the universe."

"You don't look so powerful now," Rayen points out.

Andy doesn't respond.

"Why the war here?" I ask. "What do you have that made them willing to decimate an entire planet to get to you?"

Andy breathes deeply, taking her time. "It's a power, inherent in my species. We can…change things."

"Change things?" Rayen asks. "Be specific."

"Change things in time," Andy says, looking me in the eye. "Wipe out the past. Rewrite the events of the universe."

I am stunned into silence. I don't need to ask Rayen what she's thinking, because I know that we're both focusing on the same idea—maybe we could rewrite Earth. Bring everyone back.

"That's not how it works," Andy says, as if she can read my thoughts. "Most of us can't access that kind of power under normal circumstances. And the death of billions of people is too much for me to change."

"So they came after you."

Andy nods. "Years and years ago. They destroyed our planet, made us slaves. The ones who couldn't be enslaved were killed."

270

"Why didn't you fight back?"

"We're pacifists."

Rayen scoffs. "There is no pacifism when it comes to war. You either fight or you die."

"Perishing was the honorable thing to do," says Andy, and a part of her is proud. "We chose not to fight, and we chose not to give them the answers they wanted. The ones who got away from the massacre fled."

"So they followed you to Earth."

"The Hostemn are exterminators," she says, with a deeper anger than I've ever seen from her. It burns inside her, lighting up in flashes in her retinas and beneath her skin. "They conquer planets and enslave species. Take the best of them and leave the rest to rot."

Hostemn. So that's what our enemy is called.

"And they build themselves in the process," Rayen says quietly. "The human faces?"

Andy doesn't need to answer. What are humans compared to beings who can bend the laws of the universe? They wanted to look like her species, not ours. We were just a small coincidence.

"So you left us to die. Better for them to kill off the entire human race than for you to get hurt." Rayen's words are daggers.

"Do you know their weaknesses?" I ask.

Andy shakes her head, and I don't think that she's lying. "I don't have the knowledge."

"How's that?" I ask. "Wasn't your species the wisest in the universe?"

Andy doesn't answer. There's something that she's not telling us. Even if she is what she says she is, it's not possible that this Andy doesn't know anything about the universe at all.

"You have to let me go," she says again. "Please. They'll hunt me."

"Why do they want you?"

"Because I'm the last," she says. "Because they killed all the others. They know that I can't resist, that I'll give them the knowledge that they seek."

"And what knowledge is that?"

"Everything."

Rayen and I exchange a look. I'm not convinced. I don't really believe in this kind of thing in the first place. An alien species that knows the answers to everything in this universe sounds like a fairy tale.

"You mean the answer to life, the universe, and everything?" I ask.

Andy blinks, and a corner of her mouth turns up in a half smile. "I know the answer. Do you want to know the question?"

Rayen rolls her eyes so hard that I think they might get stuck to the inside of her brain.

Andy has given us all the answers we wanted, the answers to the questions that we wrote on that whiteboard two weeks ago. It seems so long ago now.

Humans were nothing at all to the universe. Only a speck, an instant.

"One more question, Andy," I say. "If Violet's mom knew

about all of this, if she knew that another alien race might come and invade our planet, then why didn't she do anything to stop it? Why didn't she do anything to prevent an invasion?"

Andy stares ahead in silence.

"Wasn't there anything that could've been done?" Rayen asks. She's frowning deeply, because this is the only thing in this story that doesn't make any sense. "You may not have wanted to fight, but we all know that humans aren't pacifists. That's bullshit."

"There was a project," Andy says. "'Insider.' At least, that's what it was named before everything was called off."

"Why was it called off?"

"Because it didn't work," she replies, her voice cold. "Most of the subjects died during the experiments. There was nothing that could be done."

"Human experiments?" My eyebrows shoot up.

Andy nods. "Yes. That was the only option. Earth didn't have the right resources to combat them. And we would not give our knowledge away for free."

"So you'd rather let us die than defend ourselves."

"There was no defense!" Andy's voice rises and tears burn in her eyes. "There was nothing that could be done! Don't you understand? We fled in desperation! They took our families and our planet and all they wanted was to learn what we know. And if humans had been allowed to see our knowledge, there's no doubt that they would've followed the same path."

She sits back against the chair, huffing from the sudden

outburst of anger. Her cheeks are reddened and her eyes burst into a hundred different colors—green, red, purple, pink, orange, blue, and yellow, shifting like stars. It's beautiful.

"What was the project?" Rayen asks, pressing for more information.

"They were trying to breed special soldiers," Andy mutters. "Stronger than humans, blended with a little bit of our genetic code. Enough for them to stand a chance."

"What happened?" I ask.

"As I said, they died."

"You said most of them died."

Andy shakes her head.

"How many survived?"

She says nothing.

"How many, Andy?"

"Six."

She looks up and meets my eyes, and I understand. I know the truth.

But Rayen doesn't. "And where are they now, these super soldiers?" she asks.

Andy looks straight at her.

"Two of them are standing right in front of me."

CHAPTER 40

Rayen runs from the room. The door bangs behind her, and I have no idea where she's going or what she's looking for.

"When did you find out?" Andy asks quietly.

I look back at her. "I tested the blood-analysis machine again. Put in my blood and Flint's."

Andy nods, understanding. "I never meant for this to happen."

"That's a half-ass apology and you fucking know it," I tell her. "None of us meant for any of this to happen."

She stays quiet, regarding me with her multicolored eyes. When we put Andy in these restraints, another person emerged. It's like she cracked a shell and let her true self out.

The thought creeps me out. I'm done with aliens in shells.

"I know," Andy says. "And I'm sorry that I can't change what happened. I'm sorry for what has been done to you. Most of us were against the experiments."

"What exactly is wrong with us?" I ask.

Andy shakes her head. "There's nothing wrong with you, Clover."

"I'm not human."

"You survived because of that," Andy says quietly. "Do you really think you could have survived all those car wrecks and plane crashes if you weren't genetically engineered to withstand the odds?"

Anger burns in my throat. There are no miracles in this world. It wasn't luck that helped me survive. I was conditioned, like a lab rat.

"It's in your genes," Andy continues, her voice even. "Your piloting skills, Avani's ability to stitch everyone up. You're smart. You're strong. You're *better*."

My hands ball into fists. "I know how to fly because of my abuelo. He taught me. Because that's what our family does." My throat catches, my voice breaking. "We fly."

"You piloted a Blackbird by yourself. It's in your blood, yes, but what our genes do is improve yours. The project was supposed to take your talents and enhance them, to achieve one hundred percent of your potential. To make you the best. To make you survive, no matter what."

Part of me doesn't want to hear any more of this, but I force myself to keep asking questions.

"How did you choose the subjects?"

"Most of them were voluntary," Andy says. "We told people that the government would provide for their children."

Had my mother volunteered me? What did she think she would get out of it?

"What happened?" I ask.

"The experiments started going wrong. We returned the children to their parents and kept track of those who survived. But we weren't sure how many experiments had actually worked."

"The six of us," I say. Five of us who are still here, and Adam.

Oh, Adam. The only one who didn't have to see this mess. In a way, I envy him.

"The six of you."

"Was Violet ever a part of it?" I ask, eyeing her. "Was she ever part of the experiment?"

Andy shakes her head. Violet's mom wouldn't volunteer her. I wonder how many kids lost their lives before this war even began.

Rayen barges in again, this time carrying an enormous folder with her. She drops it on the table, and I recognize it from Melinda Deveraux's archives. She must have searched them quickly to get back here so fast.

She opens up the folder and spreads its contents on the table. It's thick with files, photocopied birth certificates, and Polaroid photos of hundreds of kids. On file after file, I see the word "Deceased." My stomach churns at the thought.

Rayen flips through the pages and pulls out the six birth

certificates that we know we should find among them. The only experiments that worked, the only ones who made it through the final phase of the project. She stacks them up, leaving countless others in the folder. I look at the detailed biological processes that were done to us to alter our genetics. We're man-made, a product of science. We were made for the purpose of stopping this invasion.

It looks like we failed.

Rayen closes the folder and looks up.

Our names are lined up on the table: Adam Foster, Avani Sharma, Brooklyn Spencer, Clover Martinez, Flint Rogers, and Rayen Kindelay.

"Why us?" she asks, turning to Andy.

"I told Clover. It was voluntary," she repeats. "We didn't tell the families what we were doing, but we offered them government aid."

Rayen nods, slowly. She doesn't look all that surprised. "Why didn't you bother to check whether the experiments had worked or not?"

"The program's funding got cut off before we could contact all the survivors," Andy says, patiently. "We tried to keep tabs on them, but we couldn't contact them further. How do you think everyone would've reacted if we'd told them that they'd all been part of a government experiment?"

Rayen has no answer to that. I know what would've happened—Abuelo would've kicked the government off our farm before they could even say "alien invasion." There's no way we would've believed this, unless the world had turned upside down. And in the end, it had.

"You were conditioned to return to Area 51 in times of extreme stress," Andy explains. "That's why you all made it back here."

"How different is it?" Rayen asks. "Our DNA. How much of it is yours?"

"Your DNA differs from regular humans' by about three percent," Andy states. "For monkeys, it's about four percent, so you have an idea. You're a completely new species."

But Rayen seems to be driving at something else, something that I hadn't even considered yet. The aliens can detect humans, and they can obviously detect Andy's species.

But they can't recognize us.

"Andy, how much of that three percent is your species' DNA?" I ask.

"About two percent."

The question hangs in the air, and I'm too afraid to ask it.

Rayen does it for me. "What's the other one percent?"

Andy's lips tremble before she gets the answer out.

"It's theirs."

CHAPTER 41

We have their DNA.

I barely have time to wrap my mind around this as Rayen and I leave the room, only to find that Violet, Brooklyn, and Flint are back. Rayen goes back to call Avani in the lab, since we have told her nothing. We call an emergency meeting in the war room, trying to keep it together.

When we're all gathered, Violet frowns. "Where's Andy?"

"She's indisposed," Rayen says, before I can answer. "We need to talk to you."

"You'll talk to me after you tell me where Andy is," Violet snaps.

"Violet, please, let us explain," I say.

Rayen and I exchange a look. She hands Violet the project

folder. It's better for her to see it for herself, rather than hearing it from us. Our story sounds like madness even to our own ears. It's easier to back it up with proof.

Violet opens the folder, eyebrows raised, until she actually sees what she's looking at. She takes her time, reading through the information and turning over pieces of paper. I watch her so carefully that I can see when her breath hitches.

"What is this?" she asks calmly, but her voice is an octave higher than normal.

"The truth," I say with a sigh. "I put the pieces together, Violet. We know why the aliens are here."

She stares at the documents, still turning pages, open-mouthed.

"I need to talk to Andy," she says. But she doesn't move.

"What the fuck is going on?" Brooklyn asks, unable to hold it in any longer.

Rayen and I wait as Violet continues reading in silence.

"We leave for one day and you turn the place upside down," Brooklyn complains. "It's not like—"

"Brooklyn, shut up," Violet says. Breathing hard, she runs her fingers through her blond hair, tangling it. She breathes deeply, once, and regains control. "Okay," she finally says. "But these files mean nothing. I need proof."

"This *is* proof," Rayen says. "Besides, Clover already shot her, and she's fine."

"What in hell?" Flint asks, and he looks even more confused than Brooklyn.

All eyes turn to me. I blush. Rayen gives Violet a pointed look. The answers are all in that folder, and she knows it.

"Are you sure of what you're saying?" Violet asks.

"Yes," we say in unison.

"Excuse me, but again, what the fuck is going on?" Brooklyn asks.

"Andy—" Rayen starts.

"Has lied to all of us," Violet cuts her off, her tone harsh.

"What the hell?" Brooklyn says. "None of you are making any sense."

"Andy is an alien," I finally say. "She's been hiding here because they're after her."

The silence in the room is deafening.

"There's more," Violet says calmly. She hands the folder over. "This is why all of you survived."

Brooklyn, Avani, and Flint huddle together to read the folder. Brooklyn flips the pages quickly.

I wait, still tense.

After a while, Brooklyn closes the folder, leaving all the papers inside. Tears are welling up in her eyes, and she's clearly struggling. "What do you..." She doesn't manage to complete the sentence, choking halfway through. "What do you mean? Not human?"

They all look up at Violet. As if she can offer an explanation. As if she can offer an apology.

She can't, of course. Something is deeply wrong here, something that we'll never be able to overcome. Boundaries were broken, and we can't be defined anymore by our losses or our families or what we used to be, simply because we're not the same as we were before.

We are not human.

"I didn't know about the experiments," says Violet. "I knew that they had worked on some sort of countermeasure, in case of an alien invasion. I just never guessed…"

"*Never guessed?*" Brooklyn suddenly shouts. "You never fucking guessed? What is this?"

She turns to me, turns to Rayen, her breathing hard. Avani murmurs under her breath, quickly scanning the files, taking in whatever information they can offer. The information that was stolen from us. Something that we should never have known.

"Don't tell me that you really think—" Brooklyn says.

"It's true," I tell her. My voice isn't harsh. It isn't soft, either. "Everything that is written in there is true. Andy confirmed it when we interrogated her."

"You interrogated that thing?"

Suddenly, just like that, it shifts. Andy is not a friend. She is a thing. She is the enemy.

"Yes, we did. But we can't lose ourselves—"

"*We can't lose ourselves?* What the fuck, Clover? We just did! We are not human, or haven't you read the folder?"

"You were made to fight this," Violet says. "That's what you were meant to do."

"Well," Brooklyn says, "then it looks like we fucking failed, didn't we?"

She gets up from the table and storms out of the room. Avani follows her out.

Brooklyn's words still echo, resonating with each of us. I can understand her desperation, her fear, her anger, because everything that's been taken from her has been taken from me, too. We have nothing left to identify with. Our whole lives have been a lie. And the only people who could help us understand are dead.

We have nothing.

Nothing.

CHAPTER 42

We all scatter to different places in the facility. Brooklyn and Avani huddle together in a corner and share a moment so private that I turn away. I go back to check the door of the room where Andy is being held, but it's secure. I can see her on a surveillance monitor.

Sputnik follows me, ever silent, a loyal companion who I don't deserve.

I roam around the compound, my feet aching for exercise even though they hurt. I check all the rooms out of habit. Sputnik goes in and out of them, circling around, but even she can't cheer me up. I just keep walking, as if it will take the weight off my mind.

Adam died for nothing.

Somehow, I wind up near Violet's quarters, outside her

office. I can hear a sniffling noise, so I push the door open. Violet is sitting in her mother's chair, her eyes red, a bottle of whiskey on top of the desk. I slip past the door and walk forward, my shoulders slumped, unsure if I should even be here.

Violet looks up. Her blond hair is a mess, and she stifles another sob. Her whole demeanor is undone. She glares when she sees me.

"What are you doing in here?" she asks.

"Are you okay?"

"What the hell do you think?"

She takes a swig from the bottle. She coughs and sputters a little but doesn't stop crying. Her sobs shake her body, and I want to do something, reach out, help her, but I'm frozen in place. Because I've never done it before. Because I never cared enough before.

"I just..." She sniffles, grabbing a tissue from the desk and blowing her nose into it. There's a folder lying open on the desk. "I was supposed to protect her. When the shells landed, she was so scared. I didn't realize that it was because they came here for her."

She looks up at me. I sit down at the desk, across from her.

"How could she do this to me, Clover? She's my best friend."

I feel bad that she's drinking alone, so I take a swig of whiskey, too. It burns my throat and my stomach, making me cough. Violet slumps in her chair.

"She was never..." She pauses. "Andy is the only one I have left. She's the only one who never questioned why I am the way I am, why I do things the way I do." She shakes her head. "You know what it's like. Always thinking. No feelings."

It's easy to put it like that. But I understand Violet. We think alike, always weighing the sacrifices, weighing things logically. Keeping our hearts out of it. Abuela taught me to love and be strong, and Abuelo taught me to shoot and look people straight in the eye. The rest, it all came from inside me. From who I am.

But it's hard being like that. Not everyone understands it.

Violet shakes her head again. "I love her. But now this."

She shoves the folder in my direction, and the papers go flying. I catch them before everything falls to the ground and gather them in a pile. The folder is stuffed full of papers, and I realize that it's Andy's file.

I glance through pages and pages of information, drawings of her species and their original planet. These aliens look nothing like Andy. They're well-built and muscular, glowing with the power of the galaxies behind them. Sorting through the files, something catches my eye: the Burst, a self-defense mechanism that supposedly wipes out all existence around them.

The folder doesn't mention anything about what the Hostemn are actually after—Andy's knowledge and her power to change the universe.

I close the folder and put it back on the desk. Sputnik approaches Violet, putting her head in her lap. Violet manages a small smile through her tears, reaching out to pet the dog.

"How could she?" she asks me. "Why didn't she tell me?"

"Would you have believed her?" I keep my voice even and logical.

"It doesn't matter!" she half shouts, her hands trembling.

"She should've… I'm the last one," she says, her voice falling to a whisper. "What if there aren't any others out there? What if it really is just us?" She grabs the whiskey again and drinks deeply. Just when I think that she's going to drain the bottle, she puts it down and wipes her mouth. "I don't want that responsibility."

"I don't think any of us want it, Violet."

"I can't do this," she says, shaking her head. "I don't think I can save anyone anymore. I'm not a hero." She breaks down crying again.

"I'm not a hero, either," I say softly. She looks up, her blue eyes wide and sincere. "We're just here, Violet. And we have to deal with what we got."

She nods, biting her lower lip. And I find enough courage to get up and put my arm around her. Violet embraces me back, her tears wetting my T-shirt as I stand there, numb, in a three-way hug between two girls and one big dog. I can't bring myself to say anything else to this girl who never breaks.

"I love her," she says quietly, into my shirt. "How can I, after all this? But it hasn't stopped. She's still my best friend."

"Love doesn't just go away. No matter what."

She holds me, and I hold her. Like Abuela used to do. I try to be the person who she can lean on, when she can't hold herself up. And after all, I can do this. This small moment of redemption.

And we stay like that, together, even though we're different and rough with each other. Because in this moment, none of that matters. We're the last ones left, and our grief unites us all.

CHAPTER 43

The next day, everyone meets outside Andy's prison. None of us really feel like talking. Brooklyn's eyeliner is smudged, and her all-black outfit is rumpled. She looks she hasn't slept at all.

"Where's Violet?" Rayen asks.

I shrug. I helped her to her bed last night to lie down and rest, but I haven't seen her since.

"Look, I don't want to be the spoilsport, but isn't it a bad idea to keep Andy here?" Flint asks, his hands stuck in his pockets. "These aliens don't exactly seem to give up."

"We thought about that, too," I answer, sighing. "But moving her seems pointless. They might track us here, but…"

I shut up. Right now, it's hard to think about anything other than the fact that this is totally pointless.

It's all meaningless, fighting back, the idea that I could do something to make a difference. The idea that I could honor Abuelo's legacy. It feels stupid. It falls short. A small part of my brain keeps repeating that it would have been easier if I had just shot myself all those months ago.

Violet shows up a few minutes later, and without saying a word to any of us, she storms past us and locks herself inside the room with Andy. We all wait outside—Avani and Brooklyn on a bench, Flint sitting cross-legged on the floor biting his nails, Sputnik trying to sit on his lap but failing miserably, since she's too big for it. This could almost be like a regular day around here, except that it's nothing like it.

Brooklyn is pressing her hands against her head, not daring to look up. Her breathing comes in short spurts, her chest rising and falling. Rayen and I lean against the wall, exchanging looks from time to time. We have no idea what to do next.

Violet comes out a while later, and we stay silent. She closes the door behind her quickly, not letting us catch a glimpse of Andy. She looks exhausted, like she's aged ten years in the last hour. She doesn't acknowledge me or what happened last night.

"So?" Brooklyn asks.

"It's all very true, unfortunately."

Brooklyn sighs, the sigh of the defeated and the hopeless.

"What are we going to do?" Flint asks.

We've been used as pawns, then discarded. All that's left is the terrible, aching emptiness that we feel inside.

Violet peers at him, shaking her head with a slight movement. "I don't know, Flint."

She looks to me, but I don't have the answers. I was the one who had insisted on fighting back, who had insisted that we should try to push ahead. That the aliens could be defeated and we could take back our planet.

"We should keep going," I say, and everyone turns to me.

I can't let something from my past determine my future. I can't let it shape me and mold me into something that I'm not.

"What?" Brooklyn asks, perking up. "Didn't you just tell us that we've all been lied to since birth? That those awful aliens are in our DNA?"

Maybe there is a tiny part of my DNA that comes from the Hostemn, the merciless creatures who destroyed my home. But there's another part of me that didn't come from outer space—97 percent of me still belongs with my grandparents on our farm, still wants to go to Mars, to fly high, to belong in the sky again.

"My DNA doesn't define me," I say. "It doesn't matter. Don't you see? It doesn't matter what's in it."

No one speaks.

"What Andy said about us doesn't matter," I repeat, and every second my voice gets stronger. Because I know now that it's true. I understand. "This is not something that's going to define me."

I look around, hoping for some kind of support, but all I see are faces that don't understand, faces of people who have been crushed and left standing alone. But they're all warriors in their own right.

"This doesn't change who I am. And it doesn't change any of you," I assert. "Avani, you're the smartest girl I've ever met and your projects are wonderful. You are absolutely brilliant and you always will be."

Avani looks at me, a light shining in her dark eyes. And even though I'm just another lost girl—I'm not Violet, I'm not the leader—I know what to say. Violet can't understand this, because she's human. But I know what to do.

"Flint, you're the greatest guy on the planet. And I'm not just saying that because you're the only one." He breaks into a smile. "Rayen, you're brave and badass. When aliens have nightmares, they dream of you." The corners of her mouth turn up. "Brooklyn, you're the weirdest and funniest person I know. I can't believe that you haven't even cracked an alien joke yet."

Somehow, Brooklyn manages to smile, too.

No words will ever be able to translate what we're feeling right now, but maybe there's a part of our DNA that connects our minds to each other, and I'd like to believe that they all know how I feel.

"My DNA has been the same since I was born. I just didn't know what it was made of. But it doesn't matter. I'm Clover, someone who survived the impossible and struggles with suicidal thoughts. I'm a pilot. I'm a Martinez." I take a deep breath. "And they will never, ever take that away from me."

And when I look around at them, I can see that they

understand. It doesn't matter what's in our blood or where we come from. There are things that only you can change for yourself. And I'm not going to let anyone else tell me who I am.

"I was born on Earth," I say. "I *belong* to Earth. Fuck those aliens who think they can come here and destroy my home."

Wild cheers break out all around me. Suddenly Rayen wraps me in a hug, and Flint, Avani, Brooklyn, and Violet join us, laughing, in a weird, six-way group hug. And for the first time, all our hearts beat in unison. Sputnik barks, trying to weave her way in between our legs, and somehow, this makes us laugh harder. It fills the room, this strange, hesitant laughter. The laughter of people who have been desperate and hopeless, but have found hope again. Not within the universe. But within ourselves.

I close my eyes for a minute, letting it all sink in. I know who they are. They know who I am. And somehow, despite our mistakes, despite our flaws, despite whatever we've done to get here, we forgive ourselves.

"So," says Violet. "I guess we need a new plan."

CHAPTER 44

Rayen, Violet, and I enter the room where Andy is sitting. She has a split lip now. I wonder if she can choose whether or not to heal a wound, and if she chose not to heal this one because it was from Violet. I hadn't heard them screaming or crying, and I didn't want to, but I doubt that their relationship will ever be the same again.

"Are these visits going to become frequent?" Andy asks, perking up, her eyes shining a deep blue. "Look, I've already answered all of your questions."

"Yes, we know that," I tell her.

I pass the keys to Violet, who starts unlocking Andy's shackles. Andy's eyes widen, looking at her freed hands in confusion.

"Is this some kind of trick?" she asks.

"No," Rayen answers. "But if you run, I *will* shoot you."

Andy seems to take this threat seriously and doesn't move. Violet undoes the rest of her chains, releasing her feet, but she doesn't get up.

"What do you want?" Andy eyes us. She doesn't trust us, and we don't trust her, but we really have no choice in the matter. "I told you what I know."

"Yes, Andy, but now we have a proposal for you," Violet replies.

She narrows her eyes, an expression that is so human that it makes the hair on the back of my neck stand up. But if we haven't changed, then neither has Andy.

"I'm listening."

"You're the last of your species," says Violet. "So are we. Now you have a decision to make. Are you going to help us fight the aliens who destroyed your planet or not?"

She doesn't answer for a couple of seconds. "I told you, I'm a pacifist."

"No one can afford to be a pacifist in a time of war," Rayen says. "That's just being apathetic. You can't say 'I won't use a gun' when other people are shooting at you."

Andy is focused on Violet, who avoids looking in her direction.

"It's not that I don't want to help," Andy finally says, with a small sigh. "It's that I can't help."

"Why the hell not?" demands Rayen.

"I don't have enough power or knowledge," she says,

pointing to her body, as if we're supposed to know what that means. "Remember what I said about being the most powerful beings in the universe? Well, that only happens once you've gone through some deep emotional happening."

Rayen groans by my side. "And being the last of your species isn't emotional enough for you?" she asks, frowning.

Andy shrugs.

"What about the ship?" I ask.

"The ship?" Andy replies.

"Yes, your freaking spaceship. The one we found in the bunker."

The ship had recognized Andy's fingerprints or DNA or whatever was in that pair of gloves that she'd lent me, so there's a chance that it could help us.

"We need that knowledge, Andy," Rayen says. "And we're gonna find a way to get it."

Rayen keeps her gun pointed at Andy while we head down to the bunker.

When Andy sees the beautiful spacecraft, the chromed silver shining like nothing this planet has ever seen before, her eyes water. She skips toward it, and for a minute, it's like we're not even there—like it's just Andy and the spaceship, her last connection to her people and the place she came from. Rayen, Violet, and I follow her as she climbs up the ramp. Sputnik, refusing as usual to be left behind, follows me.

As we enter, the computer screen lights up, displaying a hologram of the universe.

"Scanning complete," says the pleasant female voice. "Welcome Andromeda, last of the Universals."

Just like last time, I comprehend that the voice isn't speaking English, but I can still understand it. A deep chill runs through me. Rayen glances at me, and I know that she can understand it, too. It's like this language was etched deeply into our bones and our memories, but so long ago that we had forgotten it.

"And welcome Rayen and Clover," the voice continues. "The Protectors."

Rayen and I exchange another look. Violet steps forward, close to Andy, frowning. The computer screen, seeming to recognize her, changes to a deep tone of blue, like the ocean, and a round blue planet appears, spinning on the screen.

"Violet Deveraux, human," says the voice.

Violet sets her jaw, like she's determined to keep alive whatever legacy has been left for her. She watches the little blue planet turning and turning on the screen, like she can't get enough of it. Then, with a conscious effort, she steps back.

"What exactly is this?" Rayen asks.

"The Arc," Andy says, awe in her face. She presses her fingers against the spaceship, as if she's trying to absorb a feeling. "This is the ship that we used to make the crossing to Earth. It's thousands of years old."

Andy reaches for the screen. "Computer, please tell me the status of the Universals."

"One moment," the voice says, as the computer gathers data.

"What language is that?" Rayen asks, confused.

"It's the universal language of creation," the computer's voice responds. "Every being is able to understand it. It's built into the genetic code of life."

Sputnik sniffs, unimpressed. She walks through the spaceship, nose to the ground, making sure that she sees everything.

Rayen narrows her eyes at me, trying to communicate in the silence. She seems to find it atrocious that, in the end, she wound up in a scenario that really does resemble something out of *Interstellar*.

"The Protectors are wary," the computer states. "I can assure you that I mean no harm."

Sputnik barks.

"Then shut up and do your job," Rayen says.

"Rayen, don't abuse the computer," Andy scolds her, and I can't believe that this is a conversation that we're actually having. "Computer, please assemble all the data left behind by my species."

"The data is locked."

Andy cracks her knuckles. "Computer, find the data."

"The data is locked," it repeats stubbornly.

"Are you sure that your ancestors built this thing to work?" Rayen mutters.

"This is the most powerful computer in the universe, designed to contain the knowledge of all species." Andy glares at her. "Of course it works."

"Well, it doesn't want to cooperate."

I sigh heavily, moving forward to the screen, and say, "Computer, tell us *why* the data is locked."

"The data can only be accessed by a Universal at their full power," it says. Sputnik follows me and puts her head over the screen, sniffing it. "Please remove that object from the panel."

I look at Sputnik. She seems slightly offended that she's been called an object. She keeps her paws on the panel, in complete defiance of the computer.

Violet turns to Andy. "So when exactly does your 'full power' happen?"

Andy sighs. "It's complicated. As I said, it involves a deeper calling, something that makes you understand the nature of the universe. Something happens between you and the world."

"That sounds amazingly vague and unhelpful," Rayen offers.

"Andromeda is correct," the computer says. "An emotional bond must be formed between the Universal and the cosmos itself, resulting in comprehension of the fleeting nature of existence."

"Could you say something that actually make sense?" I ask.

"The data is locked," the computer says. "The only alternative is data reproduction, although the process is long and may take thousands of years."

"I don't have thousands of years!" Andy exclaims.

I turn to her. "Andy, you're the hacker," I say. "You're the computer nerd. And you understand whatever is going on here. If there is one person who can do this, it's you."

Andy hesitates. "I don't know if I can," she says quietly, looking at each of us. "It's just not that simple."

"You can," Violet says firmly. But it's not the voice of authority. It's something else. For the first time, she faces Andy and looks her straight in the eye. "I've seen you do amazing things," Violet says. "I know how great you are. It doesn't matter whether or not you have supernatural powers. I know that you can get this information."

"I don't—"

"Yeah, you do," Violet says. "I know you better than anyone else. Even if you did lie to me."

I feel like I'm intruding on this moment between two girls who grew up together, who have always been best friends, almost like sisters—inseparable, except for the fact that they come from two completely different species.

"I know that it wasn't right," Andy says, her voice pained. "I should have told you. But I thought you might have kicked me out."

"Kicked you out?" Violet scoffs. "Friends don't do that, Andy. Even if they are from another planet."

Andy winces, shrinking again. "Listen, I—"

"No, *you* listen!" Violet commands. She looks tired but beautiful, and there's a warmth that spreads around her. If Violet does represent the last of the humans, it's enough. "You lied to me," she says. "You lied to everyone, and you kept trying to convince me not to fight. Trust is something that you have taken from me, and I might never forgive you for it."

Violet breathes once, hard, her hands on her hips. "But you *are* my friend," she continues, "and you will always be the girl I grew up with. My best friend. The one who came with me to the end of the world, who protected and defended me when I couldn't do it. You came to this planet seeking refuge, and even if you've learned nothing from this, I still hope that you've found the meaning of friendship." Violet sighs and looks deeply into Andy's eyes. "Even if I had to do this all over again, I would. If it meant that you would still be my friend."

Andy starts to cry. Tears that she hasn't shed before, that she has been avoiding, come flooding out like she's crying the light of galaxies. Andy comes forward and embraces Violet, and Violet wraps her arms around her.

"Thank you," she whispers quietly to Violet. "Thank you."

I don't know if aliens have this concept called friendship, but I know that it's the one thing that planet Earth had to offer. Friends are the family you choose, the one you fight for. And it's a pity that it took me so long to see it.

The only thing I see now is Andy and Violet, and for a few seconds, I can believe that the universe is actually in the right place.

"Right," Andy says, wiping her nose. "Let's do this."

CHAPTER 45

It feels strange to be back in the war room the next morning, planning our attack. It's only been two weeks since the last time we did this. Adam's scribbling is still on the whiteboard, and no one has the courage to erase it. This is our last chance, and we have to be ready.

We sit in the same positions as before, as if nothing has changed, but of course, everything has. Everyone's gaze occasionally shifts to Andy, who now has just a bit more color in her cheeks and eyes, like she isn't afraid to show herself anymore.

"All right," Violet says. "Now is the time to make our move, before they can come after us again. We have to be the first to strike—in their territory."

"And how are we going to do that?" Avani asks.

Violet turns to Andy. "Your turn."

Andy clears her throat and spins in her chair. "Okay," she begins. "You know how we've arrived at the conclusion that they're a hive mind?"

Flint nods. "Get on with it."

"It's an easy target," says Andy. "They might not all be able to see what every single one of them can see, but they work together toward a certain purpose. They need orders to do that."

"So what are you saying?" Brooklyn raises an eyebrow.

"Their orders have to come from somewhere," I cut in. "They're a hive. They must have some sort of queen."

Andy tries to look like I haven't just ruined her big moment.

Rayen nods by Violet's side. "Makes sense. But the problem is, we don't know where she is."

"Actually, we kind of do," Andy says, opening up her laptop. Beneath its translucent cover, I catch a glimpse of the Milky Way and the stars. On the screen, a globe appears. A million dots cover the world, all shining bright red.

"Those dots are the signals that the spaceships have been sending out," she says. "All the shells that landed on our planet."

Then, above Earth, another bright dot appears, except that it's not a dot. It's a spaceship so big that it must be the size of a continent, rotating in our orbit, just above us.

"Excuse me, but what the hell is that?" exclaims Brooklyn in surprise.

"Their mother ship and base," Andy answers. "Above Earth's atmosphere."

"Wouldn't a thing like that be visible in the sky?" Avani asks. "It seems strange that we haven't seen it before. It's big enough to cause an eclipse."

"It might," Andy concedes. "But it's been staying far enough away that no one would necessarily consider it a threat. Especially now that humans have been eliminated."

"So what are you suggesting? That we go up there?" Brooklyn asks.

"Yeah. With a spaceship."

Brooklyn refrains from rolling her eyes. "So what do you expect us to do? Wave a towel and hope that they pick up hitchhikers?"

No one dignifies that comment with an answer.

"They'll notice a spaceship coming," I say to Violet. "It's impossible to sneak up from that kind of distance."

"Unless we have some cover," Andy says.

I frown, not understanding.

"We recall all of the shells to the base and use them for cover," she continues. "There are about a million shells on Earth. We can go unnoticed."

"But how do we get them to recall their shells?" I ask.

"It'll be a peace offering," Andy says. "I'll go up in one of them. The only thing they're looking for here on Earth is me. If I come to them, they'll have no reason to leave their shells here."

It doesn't sound like a particularly good plan.

"And then what?" Flint asks.

Violet sighs. "We can't kill the queen. It'd be too dangerous, and we'd be facing a lot of security. But Andy says that, like us, the Hostemn can't survive if exposed to outer space."

"Meaning that we have to break their ship," Flint says. "So we blow it up."

Violet nods. "We'll need to create a diversion. Something to draw them away from where we intend to attack. That's where you come in, Clover."

"Me?" I raise an eyebrow.

"You steal a ship," Andy explains. "Meanwhile, another team plants a bomb in the core of the mother ship. The bomb disables the whole system, and the ship goes down."

"A bomb?" Rayen asks, suddenly paying attention.

"I can make one," Violet says. "We have plenty of firepower here, of the nuclear kind. I know the protocols to set it up."

"That's reassuring," Brooklyn mutters. "Nuclear weapons in the hands of teenagers."

We all ignore her.

"My arrival will keep them busy for a while," Andy says. "With a million shells coming back at the same time, they could spend hours looking for the one with me in it. I can buy you time to get to the core and plant the bomb."

"Then we get Andy," Violet says. "And we get the hell out of there."

"And when we blow up that ship, we end the Hostemn once and for all," Andy finishes.

It sounds nuts. It sounds impossible.

"That's a plan, but how can we be certain that everything

will work? That we're not going to be running right into some kind of trap?" Flint wonders.

"Oh, it's a trap," says Avani. "We'll be going right into our enemy's lair, like complete idiots. How are we supposed to do this?"

"Take over the ship's controls," says Brooklyn, and we all turn to her. "It's probably a computer, right?"

She looks at Andy, who nods slightly.

"So we take it over," Brooklyn says, like it's the easiest thing in the world. "Disable the shields and the weapons system, so they can't fire at us. Then all that's left to worry about is the aliens. And then, like Violet says, we plant the bomb and get the hell out."

It's a damn good idea. Losing control of the ship would throw the aliens into chaos, at least for a while. We might actually have a chance.

Three teams. One to disable the controls and one to plant the bomb. A third to go get Andy.

These aliens aren't counting on us. It's going to be one hell of a surprise when they open up their hatch and find us there. But by then, it'll be too late. We've got nothing else to lose, and luck is on our side. And even if we can't exactly save Earth, we'll at least avenge it.

I guess that's the only thing left for us to do.

A light feeling spreads over me, and I realize that it's hope. It feels strange to have it again, even if it means that we might all be dead by the end of the week. But as I look at all my friends around the table, I have faith. We'll get by. We'll find a way.

And we'll make our plan work.

CHAPTER 46

This might be my last night on Earth. Tomorrow, I officially leave my planet for the first time. I wonder what it'll feel like, bursting out of the atmosphere, seeing the stars. Flying in outer space, like I'd dreamed of doing before the aliens came. I'm ready to fly through galaxies.

In true human fashion, Brooklyn decides that it's time to throw a party. A goodbye party. A party to rock the end of the world.

Music is blasting in the messroom so loudly that my ears are barely functioning. Brooklyn decided to look through some of the old quarters for new clothes to wear, and now even Rayen is wearing a dress, which flatters her figure incredibly, showing off all her curves and tattoos. She raises an eyebrow when she catches me looking, and I roll my eyes. Flint is wearing a nice shirt that actually looks clean for once, and I let Brooklyn dress me up in a loose black tank top. Even Sputnik gets a new outfit, a ridiculous pink bow tie that she proudly struts around in.

Brooklyn also produced an impressive stock of alcoholic beverages, to Violet's utter disapproval. Violet had complained that no one could afford to have a hangover tomorrow, but Avani had countered that with the fact that we have more than enough medicine for that. Violet didn't argue, and now I see her across the room, sipping vodka from a plastic cup.

Flint, Avani, Andy, and Brooklyn are together on an improvised dance floor, shouting song lyrics at the top of their lungs, acting like regular teenagers for once. Sputnik roams between them, and Brooklyn picks her up by the paws and waltzes from side to side as if they're dance partners. Even Rayen is swaying. I stand in the corner and sip my drink, watching them.

"Not going to join in?" Violet asks as she steps by my side.

"Never been one for dancing."

Violet watches them carefully. She still looks like she's set apart from the others. Now, more than ever, we know that she's different. It's only 3 percent of our DNA, but I guess it's enough. Enough to change things forever.

"Excited for tomorrow?" I ask.

It takes a minute for her to notice that I'm talking to her. "Nervous, more like," she answers.

"I thought you didn't get nervous."

Violet snorts, a half-smile playing on her rose-colored lips.

With her bright blue dress, it's easy to picture her shining on a runway, had things been different. "You're not the only one who pretends."

We exchange a look, remembering the other night, in her office.

"I don't pretend."

She laughs again, and I think it's the first time that I've ever seen her truly smile. For a moment, she manages to let go of everything else. Watching everyone, I wish that this night could last forever. There's nothing like a party at the end of the world.

"Do you think we can succeed?" I ask.

"You tell me. I know you're good at running numbers."

"Running the numbers won't help," I tell her truthfully. "The odds are crazy. And definitely not in our favor."

"Not looking so good, then, huh?" she says lightly.

Violet has an unwavering strength, the kind that very few people possess. She's not scared of the truth. She knows her own worth, and I wish that I was half as confident as her that we can do this. I want to believe it more than anything. She'll sacrifice everything to make this work. And so will I.

"Look on the bright side," I say. "The odds of aliens invading our planet twenty years ago were also pretty low."

Violet smiles at me affectionately, patting my shoulder lightly. "Let's go dance, Clover."

"Are you inviting me?"

Violet grins and moves toward the dance floor. Brooklyn

sees us coming and howls, then turns up the music even louder. We dance, sing, spin around the room, and drink and eat like it's our last night on Earth, because it might well be. Brooklyn changes songs, putting on our favorites, making us sing out loud to stuff that we used to sing as kids and choreograph it perfectly in time with the music. Sputnik dances with us, her paws heavy on the dance floor as she jumps and barks. I can't remember the last time I laughed so hard.

By the end of the playlist, we're all sweaty and dizzy and falling down laughing. My breath comes out in gasps, and my head swirls from all the drinks I've had. We sit down, one next to the other, interconnected by the touch of our shoulders. Sputnik sprawls on the floor at our feet, her tongue hanging out.

"Okay," announces Brooklyn. "Last night on Earth. What do you wish you could've done?"

We all hold our breaths. It's a sincere question, not just a joke, so we have to make our answers count.

"I'll go," says Flint. "See England one more time and eat fish and chips by Big Ben. The place where Mum and Dad first met."

Brooklyn boos him, but we're all smiling. Small things, easy things matter now. We know that we can't long for the big stuff anymore. And it's the little stuff that we'll miss the most.

"Take my brother to school every day, even though I used to hate doing it," says Rayen. Then, as an afterthought, she adds, "Star in a movie with Jet Li."

"Beat *Dark Souls*," Andy says with a tired sigh, like this is the last challenge she'll ever have to go through. Violet pats her back.

"Go to the amusement park," Avani answers. "It was by my place. I wish I could go one more time."

"Go on a date." Violet surprises us all and then bursts into a fit of giggles. Her smile spreads across her lips and her eyes shine an impossible blue.

"You've never been on a date?" Rayen asks incredulously.

"No," says Violet. "It sounds clichéd, I know. But I'd like to go on one."

"I'll take you," Rayen says firmly, and Violet giggles even more.

"Oh, it figures," Flint says. "Every single person left on the planet is gay."

All of us start laughing at the irony. Then everyone turns to face me. I look at the ceiling. I don't know what to say. I want my answer to be true and from my heart. But I don't know what I would've done differently. Or what I would change, if I could. Everything that's happened has made me who I am, has changed and shaped me. But there's one thing that doesn't feel like too much to ask for.

"I guess I want to belong in the sky again," I answer quietly. "Just to fly, without anybody coming after me."

They all smile, secretly, the kind of smile that you give to your friends when you know what they mean, even if they can't fully understand it themselves. And then it's Brooklyn's turn, and she gets up.

"There's something that I've been meaning to do," she says. "I guess I'm fully drunk, to have enough courage, and besides,

311

what the hell? Last night on Earth and all that." She breathes once. And then she leans down and kisses Avani on the lips.

We all watch, surprised, and Flint cheers in the background. Avani blushes a deep crimson. Her mouth is open, and she stares at Brooklyn.

"Will you be my girlfriend for as long as we live?" Brooklyn asks dramatically, and Avani frowns, giving her that deep, Avani-like expression that she reserves only for Brooklyn. "Bear in mind, that might only be for the next twenty-four hours."

"Oh Lord."

Brooklyn grins. "I knew you'd say yes."

And then they're kissing again. We all roll our eyes, but there's a bubble of happiness growing inside me, and it doesn't matter how long it will last, because at least for tonight, it exists.

And that's all that matters.

CHAPTER 47

The next day, Andy is already seated in the spaceship when I climb up the ramp. She doesn't look up when I enter but keeps typing away.

"Ready to go?" I ask.

Andy sits at one of side stations, leaving the main command chair in the center empty. She gives me a tight-lipped smile as I eye the chair.

"That's yours, you know," she says, as if sensing my doubt. My unwillingness to step up and take my place.

But it's not unwillingness. It's the fear of not being able to fulfill what I've always wanted to do, the fear of reaching out and letting it slip through my fingers one last time.

Breathe.

I do, firmly, a couple of times, before I'm steady again. Andy watches as I square my shoulders, set my jaw, and cross the room with sure steps. This is my mission. This is what I want to do. No one can take this from me, and no one can do the job like I can. It's simple and it's essential—I'm needed, and I have to complete the mission and fly this ship out of the atmosphere, straight and true. I'm the only one who can do it.

I sit down and place my hands on the controls. The computer screen comes to life, and the calm female voice asks if I want to turn on the automatic pilot, but I shut it down. I familiarize myself with the controls and get a feel for the size of the ship around me, which is a lot bigger than anything I've flown before. I wish we could do a test flight, but there's no going back now.

"You okay?" Andy asks.

I turn my head to face her and see that her eyes are following my every movement. I nod my head, slowly, trying to comprehend what I'm about to do.

"Excited?"

"Afraid," I answer her sincerely. "I don't know what it's going to be like up there."

Andy looks up in the direction of the sky, as if she can see through the roof of the spaceship and the compound and far beyond that. She seems to lose herself for a moment, only to come back with a small smile. She looks at me again.

"It's going to be exactly like you dreamed it would."

And I believe her.

Andy locates the nearest landing shell. It's a forty-minute drive in the truck, which means that they must've known somehow that people were nearby. Even in Area 51, we weren't going to be safe for long.

When we arrive, Andy gets out first, standing in front of the shell.

"You sure you know how to open it?" Brooklyn asks, looking at her.

She nods. She walks forward and puts her hand on it. It takes a few seconds, but the ship responds. Its reflective surface gets darker and darker, and suddenly, an entire hole opens up for Andy to crawl through.

"How the hell did you do that?"

"It's sensitive to space matter," Andy says. She looks back at us, and we all face her in silence. "All right," she says. "This is goodbye, then."

"Don't be so dramatic," Avani snaps. "We'll see you up there."

Andy nods. She takes her laptop into the ship, ready to initiate the recall of the shells. We synchronize our watches. We've got one hour to get back to Area 51 and into the ship.

And then we'll be ready to take to the sky.

The control room is finally full as everyone settles into their chairs, holding weapons and provisions. Violet sits by my side, lighting up the computer's controls as she taps them incessantly, one after the other, biting her lip hard.

The spaceship is enormous. It has a kitchen, labs, sleeping quarters, and everything else we might need. It's like a motor home, but destined for outer space. Sputnik is aboard, too. It feels strange, but I can't bear the thought of leaving her behind. I put her in one of the spare rooms, tied by a leash, and hug her fur one last time.

She's a good reminder that we must survive this.

"Seat belts on," I say. I breathe deeply, letting my heart calm itself.

People start strapping on their seat belts, chatting as they do. I'm not sure how well everyone will tolerate blasting into space.

I slide the button that turns on the engine, which starts humming beneath my feet. I can feel the ship echoing my own heartbeat as the whole thing comes to life. It isn't as loud as the airplanes that I've flown, but still, it's like the spaceship can feel my anxiety, and it's trying to calm me down.

"Open sky hatch," I say, and Violet taps the command.

The hinges of the hatch creak as it slowly opens, giving way to the sky. I put my hands on the steering wheel, which is designed like an old maritime wheel from an eighteenth-century ship, and try to calm myself. This is something that I've done a thousand times before.

Just not with spaceships. And I wasn't flying directly into outer space.

"Is it time?" I ask Violet.

"Countdown initiated," she confirms, her voice steady. "Five. Four. Three."

I breathe again, gripping the wheel hard, sliding back in my seat. I can do this.

"Two. One." She lets out a sigh. "Shells are retreating."

I speed up and fly out of the sky hatch, and suddenly we're roaring into the sky, faster than anything I've ever piloted before, like a silver comet crossing the atmosphere.

But I'm not the only one up here. As if in a coordinated dance, thousands and thousands of shells start rising in the distance, each one a silver shell called back home, like angels ascending to the heavens. As one, we all rise toward the endless universe.

There's a buzzing sound, and our comm units are affected. Andy's face appears inside a shell. She's managed to transmit her recording throughout the entire system of spaceships, and she's the only one commanding their route. She's taken over their controls.

She delivers her message.

"I am Andromeda, the last of the Universals," she breathes, and her eyes flash bright orange on the screen. "This is a message of surrender. I am coming up in one of your shells to meet you. This is a negotiation for peace on Earth."

The message ends.

They can't track Andy in her shell, but she's right—there's no need for the shells to stay on Earth if she's coming to them.

We'll be able to hide in plain sight. Our ship may be much larger, but we're counting on getting lost among the volume of a million shells.

And then, we'll emerge from the shadows and attack.

"Direction steady, moving upward," I say, and my heart pounds as the spaceship is turned ninety degrees and flies up and up toward the sky, toward the sun, toward the end of the universe. "Time to destination: one hour and twenty minutes."

My heart races, but it's from excitement. The ship roars beneath me and I control it completely, like I was born to fly it. It responds to my every command. I speed up, preparing to cross the atmosphere so we can face the spaceship that we know is hovering near our planet. So that we may end all of this.

"According to Andy's schematics, the shells will dock on the forward side of the mother ship," Violet says. "While they head there, we'll slip past their defenses and dock on the rear side, allowing us to enter the ship undetected."

We all nod in agreement.

"Andy gets captured," Violet says steadily. "Then Avani and Brooklyn go disable the shields and the weapons system, so Clover and Rayen can steal one of their ships and plant the bomb. Then Flint and I go get Andy so we can get the hell out of here."

It sounds so simple. But there are so many flaws.

"We do not, under any circumstance, engage with the enemy," Violet orders. "We are here to plant a bomb, not to go after individuals by ourselves. We go in, Clover creates a diversion, we get out. Understood?"

We all nod again. It isn't particularly strategic, and we don't have a backup. This is the plan of desperate people at the end of the world. We're doing it because it's the only way.

"Exiting Earth's atmosphere now," I say, and everyone goes silent.

We sit in awe as the ship crackles, hitting the last atmospheric barrier, and we feel the impact as we break free from the last restraints of Earth. I accelerate, and I don't need to worry—it's as if I've done this a thousand times, as if my own body is responding easily to something that is second nature, ready to leave everything else behind me.

And then we're out of the blue, out of Earth, and into space.

The sight astonishes me. Out here, I can see countless stars, the blackness of the void covering them like a mantle. I look back and see Earth getting smaller and smaller as we leave it behind, the little blue planet spinning in space, oblivious to everything.

It's beautiful, stunning, a sight so great that it takes my breath away. And although it's space that should awe me, it's that one little blue planet that's mesmerizing. It's glorious and small, almost insignificant compared to the other forces of the universe, but still it stands, like nothing ever happened. It remains there, a force to be reckoned with.

A single tear escapes my eye and I wipe it away, not wanting to lose the experience of looking at Earth from up here for the first time. This is the one thing that I want to keep with me when I go. And I know that if I die, this is the one thing that I'll remember. Earth, spinning in space, resilient. Beautiful, strong, and a little ruined. But from up here, it looks perfect.

I'm on top of the whole wide world.

The silence in the spaceship is overwhelming. We know that we might be the last people of Earth to make it out here. This is what I'm taking my revenge for. If I'm going to be the last, I'll also be a force to be reckoned with. I'll be my own strength.

Just as I'm thinking this, the most gigantic spaceship that I've ever seen appears, almost like an entire planet of its own. It's dark and foreboding, like the Death Star looming on the horizon. I tighten my hands on the steering wheel, forcing myself to maintain a steady speed as I move along with the shells returning to their base. They cross the universe and the vacuum of space like silent comets, silver slivers of destruction heading toward their home.

"Entering mother ship's gravity," I say as I feel its pull and the controls light up. I control the ship carefully, forgetting everything else around me.

I keep my mind blank, and I breathe deeply, focusing. This is my last mission, and I might never fly a plane again. But this is also my first time flying a spaceship, and I can't help but think about how proud Abuelo would be.

The ship gets pulled along with the others. The cabin has pressurized itself for humans, so there's oxygen and simulated gravity. And that's how I ground myself—I've done this many, many times before. And I can do it again.

We approach the mother ship, a dark mass of metal, moving

toward one of its entrances. As the shells begin docking, I accelerate, just enough to break out of the ship's gravity and fly, as stealthily as possible, toward the opposite end of the ship. I locate the rear bay.

"Approaching."

I enter the docking area. It's empty, as far as I can tell, but that brings me no relief. The hardest part starts now. We've only got one shot, and we have to make it count. This is our last chance.

I dock the spaceship carefully on one of the platforms, landing it with perfection. There's no noise as the main engine shuts down. Everyone grabs a mask and suits up in a special spacesuit designed by Andy's people.

I stay silent as we dress and, with a last nod of my head, wish the others good luck. Flint and Violet exit down the ramp, their figures disappearing from sight. We wait five beats, and the next team leaves.

I look at Rayen. It's only the two of us left.

"Ready?" she asks.

I nod. "Let's go steal a spaceship."

CHAPTER 48

Rayen follows behind me as we sneak around the spaceship. We pass several docks with shells, but we don't need one of those. We need a fully equipped fighter, with enough firepower to cause a big distraction.

I turn around, listening and looking for any sign of movement. Between the two of us, we only have one useful gun, and Rayen keeps it raised. We stumble upon a divide, and I wait to see if anything is coming, but the whole place seems empty, devoid of alien life.

"Anything yet?" I murmur.

"According to Andy's map, the ships should be on our left side, if we follow this corridor."

I move forward, taking lefts each time the seemingly endless corridor splits, my feet padding against the white floor of the ship. It's surprisingly clean and sterile, as if the creatures prefer a hospital-like aesthetic. We've been walking for ten minutes when we turn a corner and I almost slam Rayen against the wall. She holds the case with the bomb close to her chest, glaring at me.

"Shit," I say. "There must be dozens of them in there."

Rayen sneaks a glance at the open dock. It's enormous, and if they only send half of their spaceships after me, we're doomed.

I slam Rayen against the wall again, holding my breath as one of them passes by. Our invisibility factor still stands, and I breathe a sigh of relief as it marches forward, ignoring us.

The dock area is crawling with more than thirty aliens. I take one deep breath, calming myself. One slight noise, and they'll start shooting. As long as we remain silent, we're safe.

I walk forward, taking slow, careful steps, observing the movements of the Hostemn. They move back and forth across the bay, patrolling it. I can't figure out whether or not they can communicate verbally, and the only thing I hear is an alarm blaring in the distance.

I spot the ship I want. It's a fighter, and it isn't too big. I need it to be quick and maneuverable. I point it out to Rayen, who nods. To my shock, the ramp is open.

I run across the dock, forgetting everything else, charging up the ramp and heading straight to the cockpit. The seats are strange and uncomfortable, but I can't be picky. Rayen sits down next to me, panting, and I look over the controls.

"Clover?" Avani calls over the comm unit. "Are you there yet? The aliens are heading toward the system room."

"I'm here," I say breathlessly.

There are too many buttons. I press one of the iron buttons on the panel before me, and the engines roar beneath me. I grin wildly as I pull a lever and the ship rises unevenly out of the bay.

"They see you!" Avani warns me, but I ignore her panic. I have to familiarize myself with the controls.

"Ramp's still open," Rayen yells, pointing to the bomb on the floor, and I press another button.

I hear the ramp start to close, and I grip the joystick. In a second, I'm zooming past the other ships, ready to take control. I pull the trigger on the joystick and start shooting.

The laser blasters fire off aimlessly as I spin the ship toward the exit of the dock, without looking where I'm shooting. One blast hits a destroyer so hard that it smashes against another spaceship, slamming up against a wall. Rayen screams gleefully by my side and I accelerate, making my way back out to space. The darkness welcomes me.

"We're up," I confirm. "Instructions please."

"Okay, here we go," Brooklyn says. "They're chasing after you. Thirty or so ships."

"Fuck." I sigh and maneuver the ship as blasts start shooting in my direction. Some of them hit, and pieces of metal go flying into space, but I don't see any signs of serious damage. "Let them come. You done with the shields?"

"Hold on," Avani says, and if I concentrate, I can just make out the sound of her typing away. "The shields are going to take about twenty minutes. But I think…"

Her voice fades, and a blue button starts blinking on the panel. I press it and a hologram pops up showing the design of the whole ship. But it isn't really a spaceship—it's more like a planet, a gigantic space station with the capacity to hold the population of an entire species. And it's completely covered with shields.

"Damn," I hear Rayen say by my side. "How are we going to destroy this thing?"

"Weak points," I say, pointing out several channels in the design. "Air ducts and machinery. We'll set off a bomb in the middle and the whole thing will implode. That is, if we can take the shields down."

"Hey, we're working on it," Brooklyn complains. "Just keep firing at their ships so they won't notice that we're taking down the shields."

"Got it," I mutter.

A warning comes up on the screen and I barely twist away from a blast before another one sends us spinning through space. Dodging shots is more difficult in space, without the familiar sounds of battle to go by. I'm going to have to be smarter than them.

"Raise shields," I say, as I press another command and push forward. "Rayen, there's another blaster on the other end of the ship."

"I was waiting for you to say so."

Rayen leaves the cockpit and heads back to the blaster, grabbing onto it. Soon enough, I can hear her cursing. Blasts keep coming from behind me, and I can see spaceships trying to lock onto me. I fire shots into the blackness and hit them almost immediately. Our advantage is that the area is full of their ships, and we're only one target. My aim doesn't have to be perfect. Theirs does.

"Clover, we've been hit," Rayen warns me.

"Shit. Are the shields down yet?"

"Working on it," Avani repeats. Then, a moment later, she says, "Done!"

That's all I need to hear. I descend until I'm so close to the mother ship that a couple more feet and I'd hit it. I'm firing the whole way, now that the shields are down. So when they try to hit me, they hit their base instead. It's a perfect, if completely insane, plan.

"Got it!" I say. "They're still firing at me!"

"Sorry!" Brooklyn says desperately.

The blasts hit the ship behind me as I spin again, narrowly avoiding them.

"I'm heading in. Just get those damn things off my tail!"

A blast hits one of my wings full on, and the ship turns, almost slamming into the base. I scream and grab the wheel, pulling the ship up so it doesn't hit.

"Shields are failing!" Rayen screams.

"Tell me about it!"

The case with the bomb slides toward me, and I hold it down with my foot, my whole body cold.

Another blast hits and I know that I don't have long. I loop the ship around, making a turn. Two enemy ships collide, bursting into pieces. It's strange to see a collision like that in space—there's no fire and no explosion, with no oxygen to make it burn. The ships are destroyed on impact, their pieces floating in zero gravity.

I zoom past the debris, and I can see an opening in the ship. I have to go for it. Another blast shoots past me, striking near the opening.

"*Shut down their weapons, for fuck's sake!*" I shout.

"*We're trying!*" they shout back.

There's another blast, this one hitting the left wing. It sends my ship hurling toward the opening. And then I'm through. But enemy ships follow me, and there's nowhere for me to go as they shoot in my direction again, tearing off part of their own base in the process.

A string of curses escapes my mouth. "If this keeps up, there isn't going to be anything left of this ship for us to blow up!"

"Got it! They're down!" Avani confirms. The alarms on my panel are still blaring, warning me about my damaged wings, but I can still fly the ship, and now their whole weapons system is finally down.

I accelerate through the hole, and Rayen comes back to my side.

"How much time have we got?"

I shake my head. "I don't know. We still need to set the bomb to self-destruct."

She nods and looks over her shoulder. "They're retreating."

"Thank God," I murmur, slamming on the accelerator until the ship is going flat out. "You guys ready?"

There's silence over the comm unit.

"Guys? Where are you? Come in."

More silence.

"What do we do?" I ask.

"Stick to the plan. They might have been captured."

"That's not good."

"No, but we're almost done."

Prioritize, my brain screams inside my head. I've got everything I need to blow this ship to smithereens now that the shields and weapons are down. And if Brooklyn and Avani have been captured... The aliens will be too distracted by them to worry about my bomb. It's an advantage.

My hands sweat on the wheel as I pull my ship inside to dock on one of the main pillars of the mother ship, just as we planned. Our bomb isn't powerful enough to blow the whole ship apart, of course. The aliens aren't dumb enough to not notice a bomb that big. But if a main pillar blows, and they can't stabilize the ship in time, they're done for.

If Brooklyn finished what she promised to do, then all their systems are blocked, and they won't be able to do anything about it.

They won't be able to save themselves.

I slow the ship down and bring it to a complete stop, breathing hard until I'm back in control. Rayen and I look down at the case that holds the bomb that's going to set everything off. The last thing we need to end this.

Violet told us how it works and made sure that we knew how to set it. We take it out of the case, and my hands are steady, even though I'm holding a uranium rod that has the capacity to blow a small city to dust. We place it on the pillar and turn it on. The timer appears, and I set it for two hours from now. That should give us enough time.

I nod at Rayen, and we watch the countdown begin. One hour and fifty-nine minutes till it explodes.

"Brooklyn?" I say again into the comm unit.

There's nothing but static.

CHAPTER 49

"Flint? Violet?" I ask. "Come in please. We've got the timer set."

There's no answer.

I start getting nervous, my heart not reacting well to the threat. No one is responding, and the bomb is ticking in the background.

"Let's go back to the Arc," Rayen says, looking me straight in the eye. "That's the plan—we're all supposed to meet up at our ship. If the others aren't there, then we'll decide what to do."

I lead the way into a corridor, my heart pounding in my eardrums, adrenaline pulsing and rushing through my veins as I hold my stunner rifle up to my shoulder, not daring to lower it.

The base is not as dark as I imagined it would be. It looks more like a hospital than a spaceship. It's white and silver, almost tasteful in its colors. Andy's map is imprinted in my brain, and I try not to make a sound as I turn a corner, but I don't meet any aliens.

The silence creeps me out. Every single cell in my body is warning me against going any farther. I don't know whether it's my genetics or something else that's warning me of danger ahead.

We climb, uneasiness crawling under my skin, and there's still no answer on the comm unit. We're almost to our ship when Rayen stops me.

"Did you hear that?" she asks.

I didn't hear anything, but I pause and listen.

"What if this is a trap?"

I wait, licking my lips. It could be. But with no way to contact the others, the only safe place to go is back to our ship.

Those aliens better not have touched Sputnik.

Rayen and I follow each other through the corridors, not running but not tiptoeing, either, until we reach the docking bay where we left the Arc.

The instant we enter the bay, a piercing noise blasts out.

The noise in my head is too much, and I fall to my knees. Rayen doubles over behind me.

The alarm goes on and on, and it's too painful. My vision goes blurry. I try to fight it, but it's a relentless, piercing sound, and I feel something wet and warm seeping from my ear. I touch it, and my fingers come up red.

My eyes are full of tears, and I'm begging for the pain to stop. Eventually, the world goes black.

When I come to, there are two metal guns pressed to the sides of my head, and my hands are tied behind my back. I'm on the cold spaceship floor, and as I sneak a glance to the side, I can see four other people down here with me. Not all of them are conscious yet.

Aliens hold the metal guns. I see eight of them in the room, guarding five of us. Rayen is also awake. I try to catch her eye, but there's not much I can do in my current position. They've taken our weapons, with the exception of Abuelo's gun, which I still feel pressed to my back. They must have missed it.

But Abuelo's gun isn't going to help us now.

"Ah, they're awake," says a strange, slithering voice, and I realize that it's a sound I can only hear in my head.

I look up to the front of the room and see what looks like a huge insect, double the size of the other aliens, sitting in a white chair. Her face is an imitation of human—her eyebrows are angled and cruel, and her four blue eyes stare right at me. I know that her form is just covering what she truly is inside, but it's still unsettling.

She's their queen.

"Are you listening?" she asks, and then I hear that piercing noise in my head that makes me want to scream, to beg for her to stop.

The alien behind me pulls me up by the hair, forcing me up on my knees to look at the queen.

I nod my head, and my friends do the same. They're all

awake now and struggling with the pain. We're tied down and badly hurt. Avani's ears are bleeding onto her green shirt, forming a puddle of blood on her shoulder. None of us try to move.

"Good," the queen says, her voice echoing inside my head. "So you have the ability to comprehend. Do you understand me?"

I nod my head again, so that she won't come back at us with that piercing noise. I wonder if that's how she controls the other aliens. However she does it, she's got them all in perfect file. And somehow, I know that she can see us.

"Of course I see you," she says, as if she's reading my thoughts. "I am, after all, your queen."

The terrible noise starts up again, and I bend over toward the floor. When the noise stops, I try to straighten up, but I still feel it lingering in the background, as if it could start again any second. The queen holds her chin up.

"You are indeed monstrous creatures," she says.

"Look who's talking," Brooklyn manages with a gasp, then she doubles up in pain. The queen seems to be able to hurt her just by looking at her, and then the piercing noise starts all over again.

I try to clear my thoughts. I don't think that the queen can really control us the same way that she can control them. We are not part of her hive.

And that's what makes us strong.

But two people are missing from this equation—Andy and Violet. Where the hell are they? They're the ones who were supposed to end this.

"Where is she?" the queen asks. "The last one."

We don't have to be geniuses to know that she's referring to Andy.

"She surrendered," Brooklyn says. "Or didn't you find her in one of your ships?"

The queen snarls and moves forward to stand in front of Brooklyn. Her legs are powerful, made of sharp metal that glints like blades.

"She will not be able to hide for long," the queen hisses. "There is no way out of my ship. And if she ever wants to see you again, she will come."

The queen snarls again and returns to her throne. Another wave of pain hits, squeezing my lungs and my brain, so that my whole body is on fire.

I cry out, tears in my eyes, and then I see Andy enter the room.

Facing the queen, she looks so small. Human, even. There's nothing that distinguishes her from us.

"Let them go," Andy says firmly. "We've disabled all your ship's systems. This whole thing will explode in one hour."

Andy risks a glance at me. I give her the smallest of nods.

"I thought you'd run," the queen says, not moving one inch in her throne.

She clicks a leg against the floor, and three aliens immediately surround Andy. They face her, guns at the ready, but they don't dare touch her.

"Well, well," the queen says. "I did not expect you to look

so pathetic." She doesn't move a muscle, and neither do the aliens holding us hostage.

"What do you want?" Andy asks.

"You know what we want," the queen replies, her voice calm. "We have come a long way for you, Andromeda."

"Let my people go."

The queen scoffs, or at least that's what it sounds like, a choking noise made by an insect. "These are not your people. They have Hostemn DNA. They belong to me."

"They belong to no one," Andy says firmly. "Let them go and abandon planet Earth. Then we won't kill you."

The queen laughs. "Kill me? All that your ancestors have done for eons is run. You can't destroy an army as powerful as ours." She laughs again, her face distorted. "And what makes you think that we cannot deactivate the destruction of our very own ship?"

Andy doesn't look at us directly. Just to prove her point, the queen screeches again, and we writhe in pain.

We have been rendered useless by our DNA. The one weapon that we had has been taken from us.

"Let them go," Andy repeats, "and we will talk."

The alien behind me clicks its gun, readying it to fire.

"Let them go, or I will use the Burst."

The queen turns to Andy again, evaluating her from head to toe. Then she laughs. "You?" she says. "You're not even grown. You're much too small. Too fragile. You look human. One swipe from my leg and I would kill you." She pauses. "Seize her."

The aliens approach Andy, but she opens her arms.

"I'm not afraid," she says.

"You wouldn't dare."

"You don't know me."

"I know your ancestors," the queen spits. "A bunch of spineless cowards who would let us die rather than share their knowledge of how to save our planet."

"You destroyed your planet on your own," Andy counters. "Why should they have helped you, when—even after you had destroyed everything—you still would not negotiate peace?"

"There is no peace to Us. There is only Us. And those who will not become a part of Us must perish."

Andy takes a step back, breathing hard. Suddenly, she starts glowing, and the queen stands up, alarmed. Instead of looking powerful, Andy looks like she's in pain, trying hard to concentrate on whatever it is that she's doing.

"You wouldn't dare," the queen says. "You will kill them. You will kill your friends. You will kill everything that is not your species."

The queen advances until she's standing face-to-face with Andy. She reaches out a hand, touching Andy's face, and the girl recoils.

"Leave Earth behind, and I will do nothing to harm you," Andy says, her hands balled into fists. "Go and leave us in peace."

"But we need you," the queen replies, raising her eyebrows. "Why not strike a deal, Andromeda, last of the Universals? We all know that your species doesn't fight, even though you have the power to. Stay on our ship. Provide Us with answers. Give Us the power of the universe, and we will let your friends go."

Rayen tries to move, but the queen turns to her, and she starts seizing on the floor.

"Andy, don't," Avani says, but the queen silences her.

Andy looks at us and then back at the queen.

"Stay, and they live," the queen repeats.

It's an offer that, before, Andy might have accepted. She might still accept it. I don't know.

There is nothing that we can do.

"Your weapons are powerless against Us," the queen says, and I can hear her voice everywhere, everywhere, everywhere. "You made a mistake, thinking that you could fight Us. No one can fight Us."

And she's right. We made a dumb mistake, thinking that we could get through their defenses, that we could defeat their queen. Not realizing that our DNA might give her power over us. Not thinking about anything other than getting our home back.

I try to lift myself up, to take deep breaths. Flint is unconscious by my side, and I pray silently that she'll kill us quickly, so that no one will feel a thing.

Just end this.

End this.

And then the door blasts open, and everyone turns to look as the last human girl on Earth steps through it.

CHAPTER 50

Violet walks into the room holding a stolen alien gun and approaches the queen, holding the barrel close to her stomach, where we know their weak point is. She doesn't hesitate. There is no mercy in Violet's eyes, and instead of trembling, she's firm and steady.

"What have we here?" the queen asks.

Violet clicks the gun, ensuring that the slightest shift of her finger will blow the queen's cover right off of her. "Don't move," she hisses.

The queen closes her eyes, but the piercing noise doesn't reach us this time, and it obviously doesn't affect Violet. The queen opens her eyes again, and I swear I see a flash of surprise in them.

"Human," she spits. "How dare you defy us?"

"How dare you invade my home?" Violet's reply is fierce, full of fire. This isn't about rescuing us—it's about striking back at them for everything that has happened. This is about getting revenge for Earth.

Violet keeps her gun pressed to the queen. Nobody in the room dares to move.

Violet meets my eyes, and I try to give her the slightest of nods. My ears are bleeding and my brain feels like mush, but I trust my own instincts. Whatever DNA is inside my body, I know that it will heal any injuries that I take here. I just need to find the right time.

If Violet makes a move against the queen, the aliens will shoot us. That's what she's trying to avoid, but we could get shot anyway. If she doesn't kill the queen, then we're all as good as dead. I doubt that any bargain we can offer is good enough.

Everything hangs in the balance.

"Let's make a trade," the queen suggests. "You take all these hybrids. They may live on your planet, if their lives are worth so much to you. But the Universal shall stay here."

"She'll do no such thing," Violet says, looking up at Andy. In the blink of an eye, she shoots.

The queen's cover skin explodes into dust, dissolving in the thin air of the spaceship, exposing the metal skeleton that these aliens have built for themselves.

But to my horror, instead of the pulsating green organ that gives them life, I see nothing but metal. The queen has a tight, protective cage all around her body.

She's impervious.

The queen smiles, and Violet stumbles, shooting the gun again as she falls on her back. She doesn't stop shooting. Each shot hits the queen, but nothing comes close to hurting her, and the blasts simply vanish into nothingness. She raises herself up on her six enormous, razor-sharp legs, ready to strike.

Andy rushes toward them, putting herself between Violet and the queen.

"Stop!" Andy screams. "I will do it."

The queen snarls and lunges for Andy, who stumbles away, not ready for a fight. But she provides a distraction, and for a second, the queen's grip on our minds loosens. Then the whole room goes to hell as Rayen rises from her position and knocks her head against the metal head of the alien holding her hostage, making it stumble back. She grabs its gun and starts firing. But with a single look from the queen, Rayen is back on the floor, trembling and shaking, her screams piercing our ears.

We're outnumbered. More aliens start crawling in through a side door, and there's no way that we can fight them off. Laser blasts zoom past us, and we try to avoid the blows. And standing at the middle of it all is Andy, frozen.

"There is only one way to end this!" The queen's voice echoes, and Andy hesitates. "Show it to me, how cruel you can be."

Andy doesn't move. She's been hiding something else from us, a power that lies deep inside her, and as her skin starts glowing again, I can tell that she's trying to repress it.

Violet looks up from the floor, where an alien is holding her down. "What is she talking about, Andy?" she asks, confused.

Andy doesn't move, and she doesn't answer the queen's nightmarish metal smile.

"End this," the queen says, daring her. Mocking her.

She doesn't believe that Andy is capable of doing anything. She will doom us all.

But the queen is growing tired of her playthings. She turns to us and lashes our brains with another scream, but I breathe deeply, tuning it out. What I can't cut out completely are my friends' shrieks, which fill the room. I can feel the blood inside my head. Even Violet seems shaken, and blood runs from her nose as she looks around, trying to find a way out.

I look at her and mouth silently, "I have the gun."

She nods her head slightly, letting me know that she understands.

We turn our attention back to Andy, whose whole body is trembling as black holes explode all over her torso.

"No," Andy says, stepping back. "Please, let them go!"

"Finish it, Andy," Violet murmurs.

Andy turns around, and the whole room seems to stop in time, as if waiting for whatever is about to happen, holding its breath for this one instant in the universe that seems to be the most important of all.

"I can't," she says, a tear running down her cheek.

"She can't," the queen repeats, sneering. "She's just like all the others."

Suddenly, an alien reaches for Brooklyn, and I hear the crack of a gun slamming against her ribs, breaking them. Brooklyn screams. The queen concentrates her gaze, as if telling the aliens exactly where we are, ordering them to finish us, not a single ounce of pity in her.

Violet lunges forward, escaping the alien that was restraining her and grabbing on to the queen. And as if my feet are weightless, as if I can't feel every crack inside my body, I follow her.

I slam my fists against the alien that's holding me and grab its gun. And then I'm rushing forward, pointing the alien gun at the queen, aiming straight between her eyes.

I take a deep breath. There's only the length of my arm between us, between the end of all of this. I grip the gun tighter.

"Are you going to shoot me, little ant?" she asks, amused. "I'm impenetrable. I am the queen."

"Even queens have to die."

I can taste blood in my mouth. One of my teeth hangs loosely inside it. It's painful. It reminds me that I need to stay alive. She watches me, delighted, as if I'm nothing but a toy.

The watch on my wrist counts down, taking time away from us with every tick.

"Then do it."

Deep down, I know that I'm doing this wrong. I know that I can't win this one. I've never wanted to be a hero, and now I might die for nothing.

Violet catches my attention. She gestures toward my back.

The queen thrusts herself forward, reaching for my neck,

screaming inside my brain as everything blazes into a hundred different colors. But I understand what Violet wants to do.

We know a way.

Andy won't fight back. She won't watch us be killed. She is the last of a pacifist species, and only the deepest grief will bring her powers to the surface. It's the ultimate self-defense—a weapon to be used only when all hope is lost.

There is only one way to wake her powers.

I look at Violet standing in a light of her own, like an angel in the darkness. She understands.

I reach behind me, pull out Abuelo's gun, and throw it. It flies through the air and lands perfectly in Violet's hands, as if it were meant to be there all along.

She nods once. I bite my lip, because I know what's about to happen. Because Violet is ready to make the biggest sacrifice of all.

"What are you doing?" snaps the queen.

Violet raises the gun to her own head.

"What…" Andy starts to say.

"I'm sorry," Violet mouths.

There are no tears in her eyes.

Andy lunges for her, but it's too late. Violet presses the gun to her temple, and, closing her eyes, she pulls the trigger. The bullet goes straight through, splattering blood on the wall. Violet falls, still gripping the gun, her dead eyes staring emptily.

Andy screams.

And the whole universe bursts.

CHAPTER 51

I watch the universe being born. A single, tiny particle explodes into a million stars and comets and asteroids and planets, and I'm sent flying through space along with them, watching the universe grow and expand as it shapes itself. Black holes suck up stars and constellations and planets, and galaxies form around dust clouds and particles of light. The particles settle into planets and revolve around themselves like an orchestrated symphony, brilliant and bright. The universe moves in a perfectly choreographed dance, with itself as its only partner.

I watch as the first sentient beings appear in the Universe, as their species grows together in knowledge. I watch as wars erupt and structures get built and species travel across space. I watch human beings evolve, just a tiny sliver in this gigantic, cosmic universe, having been forgotten long ago by everyone else. I watch as planets are created and destroyed, as the universe renews itself in different forms, as it expands and expands and expands until my eyes burn.

And I finally understand what is happening—at the center of the universe, a single being is grieving for a lost friend. For a girl who sacrificed herself and her entire species so she could save everyone else. So she could save the entire universe.

The universe is chanting her name, and the stars spell out her face, creating her features as they explode into light. At the culmination of everything, the last of the Universals has used her forbidden weapon, exterminating everything else around her. I watch as the alien parasites burst into light and vanish into potential energy.

There's something else, too. I see Andy glowing, like the nucleus of a star. She opens her mouth and starts to sing, a forgotten melody that rips the universe apart and then builds it up again. The language of the universe itself is changing. Time is winding back, and with the fabric of a thousand different lights, I see Violet's body being patched up. It's too bright for me to look. Andy holds her in her arms, and with every tear a new galaxy is born.

As I watch, everything gets created and destroyed, the universe is remade, light razes through space and time, and everything burns and aches, all at once. The Hostemn get wiped out in the wave, the enemies forgotten. Andy's power burns through all of them, cracking their beings. As I watch the history of the universe unfurl, I'm suddenly thrown back, and my body slams against the floor.

My bones scream for mercy as I try to comprehend what just happened. I open my eyes, and there's just emptiness. In the middle of the spaceship, Andy is kneeling on the floor, glowing, her eyes full of tears.

I stare at her in utter awe, my mouth hanging open as the whole of the universe seems to dim, and the only thing left standing is Andy.

It's a new Andy, though—taller, stronger. Her eyes burst with knowledge in a hundred different colors, and her skin reflects the universe beneath her. Her hair is fuller, all dark blue and black. Her body is made of nebulas and stardust, of dark matter and supernovas.

I try to get up, stumbling, and see that everything else around us is gone. Completely vanished. Except for my friends. They still lie on the floor, but they are here.

In the moment that Violet sacrificed herself, Andy had understood the universe. She had forged a connection, a strong emotional bond, and that had allowed her to finally become a Universal.

I approach her carefully, my knees trembling.

The aliens are all gone, ripped to pieces by Andy's powers. There's not a single one in sight.

In the end, Violet was the hero that she never thought she could be. Violet did not die a coward.

I kneel next to Andy, and when she sees me, she throws

her arms around me and sobs. I hold her carefully, for fear of breaking this being that could break the entire universe. I hug her back, awkwardly at first, and then easily, because I know what it feels like.

Slowly, everything comes into focus. Rayen, Brooklyn, and Avani sit around us, and lastly, Flint. We stay quiet. We don't want words to break apart what we're feeling. We've won, but we've also lost.

Violet lies on the floor. There's no wound in her head anymore, but her eyes are closed.

My throat is raw. Andy holds Violet's shoulders, bringing her into a hug. And when she does, it's like Violet is absorbed once again into the light.

I hear a small gasp.

The room, the spaceship, the whole universe holds its breath.

Violet coughs. "Ouch. You're hurting me."

Andy pushes her away, her eyes wide. Then she starts crying again. Then she's laughing, and soon, her laughter is contagious.

Andy pulls Violet into a tight hug. "How did you know that I was going to save you?"

Violet blinks and shakes her head. "I didn't."

Andy pulls her into another hug. After a moment, Violet pulls away from the embrace, squeezing Andy's hands. Then she looks at me and nods.

"Thanks," she says.

"I'm glad you're okay."

The watch on my wrist beeps, and we're all brought back to reality.

"The bomb!" Avani shouts.

"The ship!" Brooklyn yells.

We all get up and scramble, tearing through the empty corridors. I feel like a piece of me still lies here with this ship, something that I'll leave here forever. But even though we're running and there's no time to lose, we're filled with a feeling of wholeness, something between happiness and inner peace.

The ramp to the Arc is down, and we climb inside.

I sit in the command chair, sliding into it like it's a second skin. I start the engines, and I feel no anxiety. I've accomplished everything that I wanted to here.

As I exit the bay, I have a new feeling of hope. A feeling that maybe the world isn't over. As we hit outer space again, Earth stares back at me, and it's like my own planet is telling me that my mission there is finished. Everything I had to do, I've done.

I'm free.

Flint lets out Sputnik, who comes bounding toward the control room, trying to jam her head against the controls and lick my face. I let her, keeping my grip on the wheel.

And then the impact of the spaceship blowing apart hits us full force, like a storm blowing us forward, as millions of pieces go flying. Everyone straps themselves in, and I speed up, cruising past the moon and turning around the other side. Behind us, the last remains of the parasite species have exploded, and nothing is left.

We hover in space, watching the explosion finish itself. Earth, impassive, turns slowly. It's peaceful, almost blissful. And as I watch it turn, I know that my future doesn't lie there.

I know that we can't go back.

We all seem to share the same thought as we sit there in the spaceship, hovering. The realization dawns on us—going back to Area 51 seems unthinkable now. I look at Earth, waiting for it to call me back. But it doesn't. It stays there, spinning slowly, and I watch it with renewed strength.

We have a spaceship, and we could go anywhere we wanted. But where? We have no plans. Our old lives got left behind.

But we still have each other. We're each other's family now. We're all that's left.

I turn my chair around. "Where to?"

We all exchange looks. Avani and Brooklyn hold hands. Flint is relaxed in his chair, and Rayen looks lost but ready to take on anything. Violet peers at Earth, her gaze distant. Sputnik is being Sputnik, running around the ship and trying to knock down the computer screen.

And then there's Andromeda.

She looks up at me, and ever so slightly, she shrugs. "Anywhere, I guess."

"The final frontier!" Brooklyn says with conviction, a wild grin spreading across her face.

Turning the ship around, I refrain from making a similarly nerdy comment. I touch the controls, and they're all mine, just buzzing to be taken anywhere. To be taken everywhere. To just go, without a destination. To seek a new objective, and to see things that no other human has seen before. To belong with me up here, in the sky, in outer space, in my place. Just like every Martinez who has come before me.

There's a whole future ahead of us.

We just need to boldly go.

At random, I pick a direction. I watch the stars blinking in the distance. Two for my grandparents. One for Noah. One for Adam. One for each and every person who lived on the planet below us.

I've spent my whole life running toward this.

Running toward the sky so it will engulf me whole.

AUTHOR'S NOTE

Clover struggles with suicidal thoughts and depression throughout the novel. It was important for me to portray it in a way that showed how this illness could affect a person and that living with depression did not make her weak. I know how terrible struggling to find a reason to live is, how often everything seems hopeless, but *The Last 8* is a story of hope. It's a story of surviving when the worst happens—it's a story about learning how to live.

Clover survives. So can you.

If you're struggling with depression and suicidal thoughts, please seek help. You're not alone, and you never have to be.

National Suicide Prevention Lifeline
1-800-273-8255
suicidepreventionlifeline.org

Crisis Text Line
crisistextline.org

Society for the Prevention of Teen Suicide
sptsusa.org/teens

Trevor Project
For LGBTQ+ teens
1-866-488-7386
thetrevorproject.org

IN BRAZIL:
Centro de Valorização da Vida
188
cvv.org.br

ACKNOWLEDGMENTS

When I first started writing this book, it was the journey of a girl who crashed into spaceships. If I haven't crashed into any spaceships while working on this book, I owe my thanks to the people below.

Mom and Dad—thanks for encouraging me, for reading Harry Potter in bed, and for not getting too mad when I was on road trips screaming "I can't leave! I haven't finished my word count!" during NaNoWriMo. Clara, my sister, who has read all my words and has never said anything mean about them (greatest achievement for sisters). For all my aunts, uncles, cousins, nieces, and nephews, who are far too many to name—eu te amo. We don't choose family, but I'm lucky as hell to have been born in this one.

To Sarah LaPolla, my agent, who read the story first and fell in love with this ragtag group of weirdos and for not getting too creeped out by aliens and whatever else was going on inside my head. Thank you for being my number one champion.

To Annie Berger, my editor, who picked this book and decided that it deserved to be out in the world. To Sarah Kasman, Cassie Gutman, Michelle Lecuyer, and everyone who helped to get this book into its best possible version, thank you. I'm so grateful that this book found a home at Sourcebooks Fire. Thank you to everyone who worked relentlessly, I couldn't ask for a better team.

Thank you to Vanessa, Anna Luiza, Fernanda, and Priscila—I would be nothing without you guys. You're my best friends. If I write friendships well, it's because of you. Thanks for reading my crappy fan fiction since we were fifteen and actually believing something would come out of it. Thank you to Emily, Samia, and Rafael, for also believing in me, this book, and for forgiving all my tardiness literally every single time we met. Here's to many more years of friendship, sharing the creepiest videos and probably talking a lot about Naruto. To AFB, who has long been my support. Bia, Lis, Lari, Paulo, Trix, Thais, Adria, Mayumi, Bex, Panda, and Mamá—you're the best of the best. Thanks for all the BuzzFeed quizzes and the procrastination. This book would probably have been finished months earlier without you.

Solaine, achou que não ganharia seu próprio parágrafo? ACHOU ERRADO, OTÁRIO! Thanks for reading all my rambling, thanks for never letting me forget the mermaids (ever), thank you from the bottom of my heart for all the audios, the emails, and the long notes on all of my manuscripts. You've been my number one fan, and I would not be here without your support. I can't believe I get to call you my friend. (This is cheesy, so I know you'll like it.)

Dana Nuenighoff and Deeba Zargarpur, you guys are the best CPs a girl could ask for. I'm so glad to have found you both in my life. To Lindsey Hodder and Lyla Lawless, who both also have killed all my darlings only to bring better darlings to all my writing. To everyone who has ever read a piece of this book or my other writing and helped me get here. Thank you, thank you, thank you.

There are friendships that change the world. Iris Figueiredo, Bárbara Morais, and Mareska Cruz: you're it. Thank you for always being there to hear my complaining and to talk me through all panic attacks and remind me why I love writing. Also, sorry for that time where I only talked about Star Wars. Love you!

To Olivia, Tassi, Mayra, Vitor Martins, Lucas, Vito, and everyone from Página 7: thanks for being here. Bruna and Ruan, for encouraging all my megalomaniac writing habits and being here for the villains. To Sylvia, Gabriel, Victoria, and all my friends from Tumblr: thanks for sticking with me. To my friends from school, who read my earliest writing ventures and copied down my homework so I could spend my time writing more (don't do this at home, kids). Shout-out to Bruna Buher, who typed all my fan fiction so I could focus on drafting the next chapter.

Beth Phelan and DvPit—thanks for connecting me and Sarah! Thank you to my #DvSquad, for being the squad of dreams and the best support I could ask for. To the Fight Club. The first rule of Fight Club is not to talk about Fight Club, but thanks for being there in desperate times, for guiding me with wisdom, for having enlightened conversations, and for literally all the tea. I have cherished every moment. To KidLit AOC, for providing a safe space and for being awesome. Special thanks to Heidi Heilig, who is an amazing human being. I learned so much from you. Thank you for including me, always.

To my debut group, the Novel Nineteens. Special shout-out to Kosoko Jackson, Emily Duncan, Joan He, Claribel Ortega, Kat Cho, Karen Strong, Swati Teerdhala, Nina Moreno, Tehlor Mejia, Hanna Alkaf, Rory Powers, Molly Owen, and Christine Lynn. It's an honor to begin this journey with you, and I hope we get to sit together on the shelves for a long time.

Thanks to all my readers, old, new, or those who read the acknowledgments first (I do that, too!). Thanks for giving a chance to my girl pilot and the rest of the gang. Things can be tough, but they always get better. Just don't let anything crash.

And lastly, thanks to the people who inspired this book in the first place. To all the science fiction writers who came before me and told me of amazing stories and amazing places and taught me what it's like to be human. Thanks to Steven Spielberg, who introduced me to sci-fi. And to Will Smith. I want to be you when I grow up.

READ ON FOR A PREVIEW
OF THE SEQUEL,

THE FIRST 7

CHAPTER 1

The sky out here is never the same shade of blue as home.

The levels of oxygen, nitrogen, and ozone don't match in the atmosphere, reflecting directly into the darkness of space, or some strange psychedelic color that makes me feel like I'm inside a video game. Sometimes, on one planet or another, I look up, and there's a shade in it that reminds me of the cloudless summer sky. A second later, I blink, and it's gone.

I really shouldn't be thinking of anything other than the Arc as home.

"You ready?" Rayen's voice sparks behind me, and I turn around from the Arc's command. "Everyone's already waiting."

I nod. I turn around to check Sputnik, who is wearing a

glass helmet and trying to lick the surface to no avail. I pat the helmet, and the Bernese mountain dog barks.

"Come on," I say to her, and we leave the Arc together, Rayen by her other side. The Arc's ramp closes behind me.

The sky, of course, is nowhere near blue.

It's a pinkish glow of stars and lights, and there is no visible sun. The atmosphere is thin, and for the first couple of seconds, my lungs shrink, and the air seems empty. But then it settles, and I breathe normally again. A beach stretches from the edge of the cliff, the Arc sitting in sparkling silver above it.

The beach looks like a collection of small universes put together, a quilt woven into the fabric of the planet. Colors and noises pop out of different tents, easily standing because of the low gravity center of this planet. There are aliens floating in pools of clouds, and a transparent walkway marks the path for those who can't fly. A hundred different species of aliens wait on the beach, where the ocean is made of something that looks like shining butterfly wings, coming and going with the moon that glistens above us like a giant pearl.

It's a spectacle that never ceases to take my breath away.

I follow Rayen to the beach along with Sputnik, weaving between the species of aliens that are beyond any human's imagination. There are insect-like aliens with ten arms or tentacles, furry aliens with huge, glass-like eyes, aliens as tall as houses, aliens that look like houses. No one pays attention to us as we cross the beach looking for the others.

Out of the beings that circulate the universe in these parts, humans don't call attention. We don't have extravagant colors, and we aren't especially tall. We don't have more than one set of arms or legs. If anything, others note that we're ugly and scrawny, which I'm fine with. I'd rather look like this than like the 1 percent of the Hostemn alien genes that run inside my cells. I spot our blanket, lodged between two magnificent tents, small compared to the others. But that's exactly what we want—to go unnoticed.

I see Flint sitting on the blanket, and I wave over to him. Sputnik pads over to Flint, wagging her tail. I let go of her leash, and she runs to him.

"Don't let that dog go anywhere," Flint calls out. "I'm not ready for another God-Sputnik mission."

"You gotta admit it was funny," I tell him.

Flint shakes his head. "I'm done with aliens worshipping dogs and then trying to kill us for wanting to take Sputnik back. Once was enough for me."

I pat his shoulder, sitting down on the blanket beside him.

"Where are the others?" I ask.

As soon as I say it, I see Brooklyn and Avani weaving through the crowd, hand in hand. Brooklyn is wearing her usual black, her dark-brown hair now reaching her shoulders. Avani wears her hair pinned up, her pastel-pink skirt blending in perfectly with the beautiful colors of the beach. They wave to us, and Sputnik barks again, belly up for scratches. Avani kneels down on the ground next to her, rubbing the dog's belly through the special suit.

"Good parking spot," Brooklyn says by way of greeting me. She sits next to us on the blanket and looks up at the sky.

"So what are we doing next?" Rayen asks. "After this."

"There are a couple of options," Brooklyn says. "Diving on the Klurian Sea. There's this weird space coffee that I'm dying to try out. This alien over at space Hot Topic recommended it to me." We all sigh collectively. "Oooh, I know. There's a space race in the rings of Ndonya. It's very Mad Max."

"Damn, that shit sounds wild," Flint says, taking a sip of his drink. "Y'all be safe."

Brooklyn glares at him. "You don't have an option. You're coming with."

Flint sighs. "That's the worst thing about the end of the world. I can never tell people 'my mum won't let me' and stay home instead."

I laugh. "I'll take you."

"As long as you're not driving," Brooklyn says.

"I have a clean record in space."

"No, you don't. You crashed the Tesla."

"You said it'd be just like driving a spaceship."

"Clover, you crashed the *only* car in space. The only one. Ever. Congratulations."

While some things had changed since we had been in outer space, some definitely hadn't.

More than a year ago, spaceships arrived on Earth. One week later, the invading species had easily decimated more than a third of the population on Earth. I'd survived because

I was invisible to them, and I spent six months wandering around traveling, and that's when I'd found Sputnik. After six months, I heard a message on the radio calling out for other survivors.

I'd run as fast as I could to Area 51. There'd been tension at first—I wanted to fight back, and the other survivors didn't. We set up a trap and caught one of the aliens, but things went wrong, and Adam, one of our own, was killed because of it. Area 51 hid a lot of secrets, too, including a whole spaceship in the basement. With the captured alien, I started putting two and two together only to find out that the last surviving members of our species were hybrids. Our friend Andy was a Universal, an alien capable of changing the windings of the universe, and the Hostemn were after her power. Putting the lies aside, we'd decided that there was only one thing we could do: fight for Earth.

After Andy used her power to destroy the Hostemn fleet, we'd been wandering space for the last seven months. We'd been to the edges of the Milky Way, visited black holes and red dwarves, seen nebulae eight times the size of Earth, surfed along the stars, and seen things I hadn't even imagined were out here.

The Arc took us anywhere we wanted to go. Anywhere but the place we'd left behind.

This stop on the edge of the Shrofina complex was just another one of our destinations. Brooklyn had managed to find a file in the Arc with the most amazing phenomena to be seen in the universe, and we were crossing out each stop, one by one. This time, there was a giant supernova that scientists had predicted was going to burst in only a couple of human hours. All the aliens gathering at the beach had been waiting for weeks—or maybe seconds according to their own time—for the single moment when the energy would dissipate.

"I think it's about to start," Avani says. "Should we call the others?"

I frown. "Yeah, where are Violet and Andy?"

Brooklyn shrugs. "I don't know. Getting drinks or something."

"Brooklyn," I say in a warning tone. "You know you're not supposed to leave the two of them alone."

Brooklyn rolls her eyes. "They're not children. They can take care of themselves."

Rayen and I exchange a look. It's not a problem, usually, but both of them together call more attention to themselves than is warranted. Andy tries to pass as human, but Violet's another thing entirely—she doesn't survive out here like we do since she's not a hybrid. She has to wear a full-on space suit, and though we've found one as discreet as possible for her, which wraps around like silk over her skin, she still has to wear a helmet to breathe.

"I'm gonna go find them," I announce, getting up and brushing my pants. Sputnik barks, following me, and I get her leash.

I move through the tents and blankets that crowd the beach. Most of the aliens are looking up to the sky, waiting for the supernova to burst. It's worse than the year my grandparents decided to go to LA to see the New Year's Eve fireworks, where there wasn't breathing room for bodies as we waited for the spectacle to start. Some things don't seem to change, no matter where you are in the universe.

I finally spot Andy and Violet almost opposite from where we're sitting, and I make my way through to them.

"Hey," I say when I arrive. "We're all back at the blanket already."

"Okay." Andy nods. "I was just getting myself a drink."

I look at her drink, and it looks good enough to try out. Behind her, there's some kind of improvised bar, and I see all types of aliens ordering something.

Maybe it's going to bite me in the ass, but maybe it won't. Andy says we're supposed to survive everything, so space food and drink are definitely on the list. I lean against the improvised bar, waving to the bartender. Some things definitely don't change when you leave your planet.

"Get me one of those bubbly drinks," I say, gesturing. I'm not exactly terrible at speaking in the common alien language, but Brooklyn is the best of us. She picks up languages as easily as I drive a spaceship, and for all I know, I could be telling the alien to go fuck himself.

"Where are you from?" the alien asks, looking at my weird, gangly limbs. I've heard arms described that way more times than I can count.

"Earth," I say.

"I've not heard of it."

"It's mostly harmless," I reply. "Thanks for the drink."

"Enjoy the supernova!" the alien says. Or maybe the alien says something else entirely. I'm assuming the best.

I grab the drink in my hands and move over to Andy and Violet, who looks at it wistfully.

When we turn around to go, our path is blocked by another alien. Kreytian's smile stretches big when they spot Sputnik.

"Oh, there's the most beautiful creature in the entire universe!" they exclaim, looking up to me. "Oh, there's your pet, too. When are you giving this magnificent being to me?"

"My dog is not for sale," I tell them flatly.

Kreytian shakes their head. "A marvelous thing, a dog. So few of them up in space. Evolution has not graced many planets with this gift."

Their skin is a tanned brown, their robes a polished gold, and they wear a blue eyeliner over their eyes. Their hair is combed back, and if not for their four eyes, they would almost look human.

They finally turn to see Violet and Andy standing next to me.

"Andromeda."

Andy nods back in acknowledgment. "Kreytian. Come to see the supernova, too?"

"Well, I've seen hundreds, but I grow bored," they reply. "We all have to entertain ourselves in some way, don't we?"

Kreytian stretches their mouth into a smile, but it's tense.

They're a fixture at the Blssian market, one of Brooklyn's favorite spots. They gather as much information as possible, and that means that seven newcomers in a ship of Universal making don't go unnoticed by them.

"Yes," Violet replies. "We all do. If you'll excuse us—"

"Just a moment," they say, stretching out their arm.

Nobody dares to move. I exchange one look with Violet, and the light reflects on the glass surface of her helmet. We've been through similar situations. That's always been our number one rule—we don't call attention to ourselves. If there's trouble, we run as far away from it as possible. Don't let anyone spend more than a second thinking about these tiny humans and what they're doing here.

"I haven't had the opportunity to speak to a lot of humans," they say. "And I value dearly all the opportunities for learning. It's not every day you encounter survivors of the Hostemn massacre."

Every single one of my muscles snap in place, tense. I tighten my grip on Sputnik's leash, and she feels the tension, too.

"You know the Hostemn came to Earth," I say. It's not a question.

"I also know they were destroyed there," they reply. "If your friend is the only survivor of the Universals and she now walks among humans, there's not that much to guess. The Burst is not something that goes unnoticed. Especially when it's not only used to destroy."

Kreytian gives one look at Violet, and her shoulder tenses.

Andy steps forward, shielding her.

Kreytian doesn't seem threatened by it. Instead, they're almost amused. They turn to me.

"Has Andromeda told you about the origins of the Universals?"

I don't look at Andy.

"We know about the war," I say, my lips dry.

"The Hostemn were dangerous," they say. "Planet wreckers. But not the most dangerous thing in this universe by far. Wouldn't you say so, Andromeda?"

"I don't know what you're talking about," she replies.

Kreytian keeps smiling.

"No one likes their species being villains. The Universals loved peace, and they loved knowing everything. I can tell you this because I remember the war, and I remember the day the Hostemn took over."

No one dares to move.

I've seen this conversation play out many times already. We arrive someplace, and then someone recognizes Andy for what she is—it's almost inevitable. The change in her eyes, her skin, her hair. She tries to look human, but there is no hiding what she is. There's nothing that can cover up that kind of power.

"I have seen many wars," Kreytian says casually. "I'm seven thousand years old by the human standard. Young for my species. Young for the universe. And yet I can remember every single battle and war that's wrecked it. I've seen planets blown to dust, vanished into nothing." They glance at

Violet. "Your Earth is just another in the cycle. Not important. Universals never tried stopping a war. We wouldn't help them stop theirs."

"We had rules," Andy hisses, unable to contain herself. "We never interfered. Free will above all."

Kreytian's smile widens. Their teeth shine like mother-of-pearl.

"Benevolent like gods," they say. "That's what you called them on your planet, correct? Gods. Able to mold the universe yet refusing to do anything significant. And oh, how we would plead. We would go to Universali and beg for intervention. Beg for them to descend from their mighty chairs and save us."

They continue without hesitation.

"They never intervened. I watched my planet burn while they did nothing, even though they could have. Your species had the power to change everything, and yet they refused."

Andy's soul is a burning fury, and the temperature around us grows cold, chills climbing my spine. There's a burst of energy around her, the same energy I saw back at the Hostemn ship. I hadn't seen it since that day, and her power flutters to the surface, rippling across the galaxies.

It grows and expands all around us, echoing, until Violet pulls Andy back, grounding her. Around us, some of the other aliens have stopped talking, eyeing Andy.

I feel the energy still, though, like it has expanded throughout the universe, a burst of light that has gone from inside Andy and been let out freely.

Kreytian ignores Andy's outburst.

"There won't be a people who miss the Universals," Kreytian says, "but there will always be those of us who remember what they did not do."

"Enough," Violet snaps. "That's enough. Let's go."

"You feel it, too, don't you?" They turn to her. "You don't forget what happened to your planet. What happened to you. You should be careful, human. You may not be the same as you were before."

There's a flash of something in Violet's eyes, almost like she's ready to break. Like she's ready to come undone. I think back to that one moment, seven months ago, when Violet did the unthinkable to stop the rest of the universe from ending. When she sacrificed herself so Andy was free to use her power, to rewind the universe and kill the Hostemn.

It burns a hole in my stomach.

"Not everyone will welcome Andromeda," Kreytian says.

"Is that a threat?" Violet asks, her voice calm.

"No. It's a warning." They look again at Andromeda, and there's pity in their eyes. "There's not a single place in the universe you're going to be safe. We don't forget that easily. She's not welcome here."

Andy steps back.

"Let's go," Violet says again, and this time, we listen.

I turn my back.

I know Kreytian's right.

Andy is never going to be safe, no matter where we go.

ABOUT THE AUTHOR

© Ana Beatriz Omuro

Laura Pohl is a Brazilian writer who lives in São Paulo. She likes writing messages in caps lock, quoting *Hamilton*, and obsessing about Star Wars. When not taking pictures of her dog, she can be found discussing alien conspiracy theories. She has not crashed any cars or spaceships yet.

You can find out more about her on her website at onlybylaura.com.

FIREreads

— #getbooklit —

Your hub for the hottest young adult books!

Visit us online and sign up for our
newsletter at FIREreads.com

 @sourcebooksfire

 sourcebooksfire

 firereads.tumblr.com